Hard Return

Hard Return

Book 5 in The Amy Lane Mysteries series

by

Rosie Claverton

HARD RETURN © Rosie Claverton
ISBN 978-1-912563-03-6
eISBN 978-1-912563-04-3

Published in 2018 by Crime Scene Books

Cover design by blacksheep-uk.com
Printed and bound in Great Britain by Marston Book Services Ltd, Oxfordshire

For Faith – by the time you're old enough to read this,
you'll be too cool for Mummy's books.

Acknowledgements

Thank you to Sarah Williams and everyone at Crime Scene Books for producing a fifth (fifth!) book in the Amy Lane Mysteries, in the same year that saw the whole series in paperback. You are tireless and unceasingly supportive.

Thank you to Deb Nemeth, my excellent editor, who pointed out that this mystery book was a little too mysterious! You saved us all from suffering through an impenetrable enigma.

My biggest thank you to my ever-patient husband, who entertained the baby for days and nights and weeks while I actually sat down to write this thing a whole year after I intended to start.

And thank you to Faith, for the best squeezy hugs and trying to add her own contribution every time she saw Mummy with her laptop. All typos are hers, honest.

Chapter 1: Behind Bars

The cell door opened, the thin beam of the torchlight hitting his open eyes. 'It's time.'

Lewis Jones stopped nervously twisting the old analogue watch on his wrist and picked up the anonymous black holdall that contained all his belongings. He stepped into the corridor and obediently followed the single guard down the hallway, the rest of the prison silent and somnolent.

It felt like his last night on earth.

Lewis was not going to miss Swansea Prison, but it had become familiar territory. Nothing like home, not comfortable, but somewhere he felt safe to sleep at night. It had been almost four years since he was sent down, a very different man to now – a child, really. A bloke who solved his problems with his fists and his boys around him.

Yet when his little brother had been murdered, everything had changed. He hadn't wanted to be that man anymore, didn't want anything in common with the scum who had done for Damage. When this chance had come up, he'd grabbed at it with both hands. This was the reprieve he had been waiting for, the opportunity to remake his life like his best mate had.

The same, single guard opened the doors in turn, all other faces in shadow. No goodbyes, no friendly smiles of encouragement. No one wanted to be involved in what was happening that night. No one wanted to know, to be culpable.

As the door opened onto the outside world, Lewis felt the bite of cold air on his face, the last nights of winter making their presence felt. The waiting prison van stood open and he entered without prompting, knowing this was part of the plan. He hadn't received a letter confirming the details, but he hadn't expected one. You didn't get nicely typed letters for shady operations.

Lewis felt like he was in video game, like he was either lucky or losing his mind. He'd been headed to an appointment with the chaplain, but he was greeted by an unsmiling man in a suit instead. *'Do you want the opportunity to start again?'*

After that, he'd barely cared about the details, knowing that any 'opportunity' with that kind of reward would take its toll. After he'd signed on the dotted line, the unsmiling man had delivered his verdict: *'You're in. Midnight, February 29th – the van will be waiting. Be ready.'*

A lucky day for new beginnings? Or a damned day that would send him down a damned path? Lewis had never been one for superstition, but his mam was a chapel-going, God-fearing woman who refused to believe her one remaining son was beyond salvation. He would do this for her. He would prove himself worthy of her faith in him.

If Jason Carr could go from ex-con to assistant to some fancy hacker for the National Crime Agency, Lewis could turn his life around too. He and his best friend were alike in so many other ways, from their shaved heads and hard muscle to the Welsh dragons curled up on their right shoulders. To the days of their youth that had forged them into men brave enough to rob the gold exchange shop, and set their lives on the course that had landed them in Her Majesty's finest hotel for crooks.

The door to the van closed, plunging him into darkness. They hadn't bothered to shackle him. He was outside the rules of the prison now, outside the system altogether. His mam would be informed he was on a 'special rehabilitation programme', but no more than that. If he was successful, he would have a place in the world again. If he wasn't...

Lewis hadn't asked about failure. He hadn't wanted to know, to consider the possibility. Anything had to be better than his dull, grey existence in Swansea Prison. The chance at a new beginning was worth any price.

He sat alone in the dark with only his breath for company, the van swaying gently, the sounds of the motorway surrounding him before fading to nothingness. The occasional low of a cow disturbed the air, but it was otherwise silent beyond the walls of the van. He was travelling into the country, or to the coast. Somewhere out of the way.

After almost two hours, the van came to a stop. The door opened, floodlights blinding him as he stepped out into the night. Lewis tried to hold his head up, not wanting to squint, to cower. First impressions were important, in prison and entering whatever place this was. He didn't want to show anyone he was afraid.

His first impression, beyond the dazzling light, was of a sizeable single-storey concrete building, ugly and grey. From somewhere close-by, he heard sheep calling to each other and he could smell the sharp stench of manure. The area felt enclosed somehow, though he couldn't see much because of the light. It was deliberate – to intimidate him, to keep him off-balance.

The next thing he registered were uniformed men around him, the light bleaching their skin whiter than white. One man appeared to be an officer, with two men flanking him in dark, nondescript uniform. Their features were obscured by deep shadows, but they stood like men who could break you without a moment's hesitation. Lewis knew that kind of man intimately. For a brief period of his life, he had been one of them.

The prison escort left without a word, shutting up the van and driving away down a gravel track. Lewis thought he caught the edges of trees in the headlights. Where the fuck was he? What was this place?

'Name?'

The officer scrutinised him, his face giving nothing away, his lean frame still imposing despite Lewis' build.

'Lewis Jones.'

He stared back, fighting the urge to draw himself up to his full height and square up to the bloke. He just needed to watch and wait, understand the rules before he started to play.

Abruptly, two black men came out the door dressed in the same uniform, with a third, ghost-pale man between them. Lewis' eyes, adjusting to the glare, thought it looked like a dark forest camouflage – but his attention was quickly diverted to the third member of their party. He was naked except for a pair of boxer shorts, soaking wet and shivering.

Lewis knew him.

Alby Collins. One of the boys he had run with as a kid, one of the men in his gang when he'd been sent down for armed robbery. In his desperation to distance himself from that past, Lewis had cut all ties with Alby in prison, avoiding him until the man took the hint and left him alone. He hadn't even noticed he was missing from the crowd at dinner or on the football field.

The two men shoved Alby down on the ground in front of the officer. He didn't move, didn't speak, didn't even look at Alby.

One of the new uniforms broke the silence. 'He's a thief.'

The other nodded, the movement of his dreadlocked head casting strange shadows on the ground. 'Second offence, sir.'

The officer nodded.

They dragged Alby to his feet again and gave him a push. 'Round the block with you then!'

Alby's breath was misting in front of him and he was covered in goosepimples, like a turkey ready for the oven. He stood stock still, as if holding his body rigidly might somehow protect him from the wind stinging his dripping, naked flesh.

Alby looked up then, eyes searching for someone to help him. Lewis resisted the urge to duck his head, waiting for Alby to meet his eye. He wouldn't play the coward and deny his friend. Yet a small part of him didn't want to fuck this up after only a couple of minutes, especially not for Alby Bloody Collins.

Alby probably had nicked something. Lewis was the one who had trained him to thieve after all, and he was bloody good at it. What he wasn't good at was discretion. If he'd stolen something of value, he wouldn't have been able to keep himself from flaunting it. He deserved whatever punishment was coming to him.

Even death?

It was hard to judge the temperature when Lewis was just out of a metal box, cocooned in sensible layers against the chill. It wasn't freezing, but it wasn't a balmy summer's evening either. Would Alby get hypothermia from jogging round the block? Was Lewis leaving him to die out here?

Were these men prepared to take that chance? What rules were there in this place anyway? What happened if a man died out here? Would anyone care?

Alby saw him. 'Lewis! Lewis, you wouldn't let them do this, would you?'

All eyes were suddenly on him. He felt the officer watching him particularly, as Alby took one staggering step towards him. The man who'd shoved Alby hauled him back and tried again to propel him away from them, away from the bright light and into the darkness.

'Wait!'

He hadn't meant to speak. Yet the focus was back on him, as Lewis stumbled forward and unzipped his fleece jacket. He chucked it at Alby's chest, furious with his friend, and at himself for losing front so quickly. But his fucking conscience wouldn't let them send Alby out into the night like that.

'Run fucking fast,' he said, voice harsh even to his ears.

Years of instinctive obedience kicked in and Alby ran, not even stopping to put on the jacket, swiftly disappearing into the inky blackness beyond the floodlights.

Someone grabbed at his T-shirt, but Lewis stuck his palm flat against the man's chest, holding him away. The dreadlocked man held him fast.

'You ain't been here five minutes and you're already interfering. It won't go well for you.'

Lewis didn't move, didn't speak, just stared down the bloke until he released his shirt.

'I don't make the rules here.' The officer spoke with an accent from deep within the heart of England. 'You make them, you play by them.'

He fixed Lewis with his dark eyes, the rest of his face completely in shadow.

'You live by them. You die by them.'

Chapter 2: Three's Company

Jason was sick of the sight of Owain Jenkins.

'Cup of tea?' he ground out through his teeth.

Owain didn't even look up from his laptop, just shaking his head and continuing to type. The man might've once been Jason's friend, but now he was a thorn in his side whose niggling presence was driving Jason closer and closer to losing his cool.

'I'll just make breakfast then,' he said, retreating to the kitchenette at the back of the living area of the flat.

It was bad enough that he had to share space with Owain, day in and day out. That he'd been forced to give up his bedroom to the snooping bastard as part of their deal. No, worse than that was Owain's systematic destruction of his relationship with Amy.

When Jason had signed on as assistant to altruistic hacker Amy Lane, he had felt sorry for her. He'd seen a skinny nerd who never left the house and lived through her computer, and he'd thought she needed someone to take care of her. He'd never imagined that he'd find someone with a quietly dark sense of humour, a creative and curious mind, and a ruthless dedication to seeking justice. A person who didn't care about his past in a prison cell, and honestly believed he could make something of himself.

He'd never imagined he would fall in love with her.

Jason scowled to himself as he threw some eggs in the pan, with onions, mushrooms and chorizo. Protein and vegetables, first thing in the morning, was the appropriate start to the day. He would do his job to the best of ability – what was left of it, anyway.

They'd come close to being something more than friends. Amy had finished her mental health treatment programme, at the insistence of the Ministry of Justice, and then moved into their new flat, ready to start her job as a white hat hacker for the National Crime Agency. They had been full of enthusiasm, ready to embrace this new life together, whatever it might bring.

Except Frieda Haas had to ruin it. The manipulative bitch had diverted Amy from prison to work for her and she had one caveat to her generosity: Owain Jenkins would be Amy's 24/7 minder.

The same Owain Jenkins who'd betrayed them all to Frieda in the first place, as a lowly detective sergeant with South Wales Police. Now living in their fucking flat all the fucking time. They'd both thought it was a temporary measure, just until Frieda learned to trust them. Over a year later, Owain was still haunting them like a ghost who just couldn't be exorcised.

Amy was effectively under house arrest. When Owain disappeared on the weekend, a man in a dark suit sat in a dark car across the street and watched the block of flats. Amy was certain the flat had been bugged and, without the equipment to check, they continued their lives in the same stilted, awkward way, as if Owain was still sitting in their living room.

Jason set the kettle boiling for their morning caffeine and poked his head into the corridor to listen for sounds of Amy. The shower was running, which meant she'd only snoozed her alarm twice. He didn't miss the days of dragging her out of bed and trying to keep her nourished despite her apathy, but he did feel increasingly like a spare part. He'd even started working part-time at Dylan's garage, since his mate had decided to go 100% legit.

As he poured out the water, Amy entered the room and perched at the breakfast bar. He served up her omelette with fresh toast and her morning coffee, acknowledging her grunt with a small smile. She was always non-verbal before breakfast.

Owain sat next to her at the breakfast bar, where Jason grudgingly served him toast.

'Frieda has a new assignment for you.'

Jason took his own breakfast to the futon, his bed restored to its day state, and watched the news on mute. Owain talked at her for a few minutes, something about an auction site for stolen goods and stolen people. He wanted her to create a plausible way in, and then hand it over to a specialist agent to utilise.

It always boiled down to the same thing – 'make an agent's life easier', as if she was a tech-savvy PA who only existed to provide evidence or a password or a cover identity. No detective work of her own, no role for Jason in a wider investigation. Only ever pieces of the puzzle and never the bigger picture.

When Owain had given his briefing, he moved away from the breakfast bar and retreated to his place on the sofa. Jason stuffed the last piece of toast in his mouth and pointedly returned to the kitchen, unable to bear being near Owain for even a few seconds.

Amy had finished her omelette and drained her coffee. She looked up at Jason, the bleached streak in her newly-bobbed hair still holding a faint hint of lilac. He remembered the greasy mess of her mousy hair when they'd first met, the faded T-shirts, the fragility of her frame. Now she was slightly curved where she had been slight, her nerd finery giving way to loose tops in neutral colours. Her hair styled with a blowdryer and straighteners and regular trips to the hairdresser.

Jason was exactly the same, from his scuffed work boots to his worn leather jacket, his vintage Harley Davidson to his twice-weekly suppers round his mam's. While everything was shifting and changing around him, he was desperately trying to hold on to what remained of the familiar past. When Amy had felt close to him. When she had needed him.

It was selfish to wish for that. When he had first met Amy, she had been ill. Withdrawn and depressed and unable to open the door. He couldn't wish for a return to that, no matter how much he wanted to feel useful again. Wanted to feel wanted.

Something nudged at his hand. 'I'm done.'

Her coffee cup was pressed against his skin, still-warm china denting his calloused fingers. And beneath the pad of his thumb, something strange – a thin edge, a slight curl up into the whorls of his fingerprint. *A scrap of paper.*

Jason picked up the mug, careful to trap the paper against the side, and took it over to the sink. He passed the mug deftly into his left hand and shoved the paper into his jeans pocket, resisting the urge to look at it. Methodically washing up from breakfast, he muttered something about bread and milk, before grabbing a carrier bag and heading for the door.

It was only in the relative security of the corner shop, between the tinned veg and the plastic cheese, that he dared to unfold the tiny note. The writing was hurried scratches of thin black ink, a list of unfamiliar words, letters and numbers. What the hell was '16GB DDR4', or 'AX 860'?

Something stirred in the depths of his memory. Amy waving memory sticks at him, pointing at the printed letters on their shiny cases: 'GB is for gigabyte. I said *terabyte* – that big, black shiny thing over there. You never learn.'

But he did learn. He would never operate at the same level as Amy, but he could work out the meaning of this list even if he had no clue what it was about. These were bits of tech, maybe even bits of a computer. She was defying Frieda. She was going to resurrect AEON from scraps, restoring her beloved homemade computer, and fuck the NCA.

He turned over the paper, to see if she'd left further instructions, but there was only one phrase printed there:

Don't give up on me.

Jason would never make the mistake of underestimating Amy again.

Chapter 3: A Really Useful Engine

'Enter.'

Mole swung open the door to the little cupboard that the Governor used as office and bedroom, secluded from his elites and the common prisoners. The man himself was behind his desk, going over a sheaf of papers – the latest register of inmates, the rough map of the complex, the list of questions that needed answering if they were ever to get out of there.

'You finished, guv?'

'Mm.'

The Governor didn't look up, just waved at his clean dinner tray and mug, the cutlery neatly arranged. Everything about him was neat and together, despite his thinning hair growing longer with every week they spent cooped up inside the compound.

'Will there be anything else tonight, guv?'

'How is the vote looking for tomorrow?'

'Oh, it'll be Alby, guv. No one liked him much anyway and then he went and nicked Joe's watch right off his wrist. Who could trust him after that?'

'Who indeed? Thank you, Mole.'

Mole piled the dinner things on his tray and turned to leave, tongue poking out between his lips as he manoeuvred around the filing cabinet on his way out.

'Mole? Tell Nikolai that I won't oversee curfew tonight. He can, if he wants.'

'Right you are, guv.'

Shutting the office door with his elbow, Mole made his way to the kitchen. Some of the men would be playing cards, gambling away their duties, and one of the newer boys would rummage through the shitty board games and puzzles, half the pieces missing and rotting with the damp. In the summer, the Governor had sometimes let them sit out of an evening, but no one wanted to be out in the frozen countryside in early March.

The kitchen was a good size, but poorly lit and poorly equipped. At first, they'd survived just on the dull canned rations they'd been handed. Then the Governor had asked for fruit and veg, and from there, they'd planted and reaped the rewards of a decent harvest. Their meat still came out of a can, but at least their potatoes came out of the ground. Mole had never realised how satisfying it could be to grow peppers and tomatoes, under sheets of cracked glass they'd found discarded in a corner of the yard.

Some liked to talk shit about the Governor, but in Mole's book, he was all right. Without him, they would be far more miserable, and they would never have made such good progress on the Project. Of course, Mole wasn't smart enough to work on the Project but he knew there was progress. Everyone said so. And everyone couldn't be wrong, could they?

Mole filled the stainless steel sink and sighed over the pile of trays on the surface. He'd been stupid early on in his time here, playing poker for chores when he'd had no idea how good the others were at cards. Or at cheating. They'd landed him with washing up 'in perpetuity'. Once he'd asked the Governor what that meant, he'd realised how badly he'd been screwed over. But he'd got his revenge, voting out each one of those smug twats in turn. The Governor looked after his own.

Still, he didn't mind his time alone in the kitchen, not really. He didn't fit in with the others, couldn't keep up with their jokes and mocking remarks. He kept himself to himself, busied himself with the kitchen and his chores, and did whatever the Governor needed him to do.

It was a role he was used to. He'd been the lackey for his big brother when he was on the outside, helping with little odds and ends. Unloading stolen TVs, watching over some poor kidnapped sod, disposing of the evidence in the Taff.

Then his brother's little empire had fallen, and they'd all been running scared from the new boys in town. Mole had been frightened for his life, for his brother. So, he'd turned snitch, laying out everything he knew for the cops, and getting a reduced sentence. His brother would never forgive him, but he was safer in some jail in Scotland than hiding in their nan's basement.

Scrubbing at the trays, he carefully set them out to dry one by one. Twelve trays for twelve men, then twelve mugs, then twelve knives and forks – well, only ten knives, because Lewis only used a fork and Alby had a spoon. Mole knew these men, their habits and quirks, from the very first day they arrived.

A shadow obscured the light from the doorway. Mole glanced up, then returned to washing his mugs. 'What do you want then?'

'Got anything for me?'

Mole shifted from foot to foot, his hands stilling in the murky dishwater.

'Not really, no.'

He could feel him moving closer, a casual swagger that told of power, confidence.

'That isn't what we agreed.'

'I'm not sure—'

'You need to get sure, and fast.'

Mole bit the inside of his cheek. The problem was that he was pretty damn sure but he didn't have the guts to come out and say it.

'I need more time.'

'Come on now, Mole. Are you my friend or not?'

He should be brave. Turning snitch had been brave. Offering to help the Governor had been brave. But both of those things had also been driven by fear, and he was still afraid, terribly afraid. Trapped in this place with eleven men who could tear him apart without breaking a sweat. His brother had called him Mole because he'd rather go to ground than stick his head up out of the hole.

'I'm your friend,' he mumbled.

'Yet you're not acting very friendly-like, are you?'

He squeezed Mole's shoulder tight. He felt his arm shift in its socket with the force of the squeeze but he gritted his teeth against the pain.

'I don't want no trouble.'

'I think trouble's already found you, don't you?'

His hand shifted, and suddenly it was on the back of Mole's neck. He tried to cry out, but his face was already flying forward into the scummy water of the sink.

He tried to scream, to free himself, but the water rushed into his mouth and nose. Something sharp caught his cheek and the water filled with red, iron in his lungs, choking on his own blood.

He couldn't see.

He couldn't breathe.

He couldn't get out.

Chapter 4: Girls and Boys, Come Out to Play

Dressed in her best jeans and a faux leather jacket, her bleached streak newly-dyed bubblegum pink, Amy waited for Frieda to grace them with her presence.

A car had showed up that morning and demanded her attendance at the National Crime Agency regional headquarters in Bristol. Jason had decanted her morning coffee into a travel mug, gleefully told Owain he'd lost his, and waved them off with ill-concealed jealousy. Amy could've done without the latest round of their pissing contest this morning.

Does she know? That was the only question twisting through her mind. She couldn't think of any way Frieda would've found out. She'd written the note alone in her room, from memory, and Jason had taken it away. He wouldn't have brought it back into the house – Jason knew the value of secrets, and Amy trusted he wouldn't betray her. He would die first.

She felt Owain's uneasiness as he sat across from her in the small waiting area. They'd been escorted through the ostentatious lobby without a word spoken, before being dumped in this anonymous corridor to wait. Frieda liked to play games. Amy remembered that well enough.

If she could see past how much Frieda controlled her life, she could almost admire her. A smart, powerful woman at the top of her profession, an expert manipulator of both people and information, and a nose for the right talent to get the job done. Amy had to admit that, without Frieda, she might still be stuck in her heavily-fortified flat, barely able to visit the outside world. She would've been free of Frieda's influence, but it was a poor sort of freedom.

Then again, congratulating Frieda for Amy's improved mental health felt like praising The Joker for transforming Barbara Gordon from Batgirl into Oracle, after he broke her in two. The strength came from within Barbara, as the strength came from within Amy. She remembered patiently explaining this analogy to her bewildered therapist, who had nonetheless seemed pleased with her progress. There were worse idols for a tormented hacker than a superhero computer whiz, defiant in her wheelchair and surrounded by those who danced to her tune.

The door to Frieda's office suddenly opened and the woman herself beckoned them inside. Amy always forgot how tall she was, her pinstriped tailored suit and high-heeled boots only emphasising her stature. Her ice-blond hair was swept back in a bun, not a strand out of place, but Amy refused to feel self-conscious in her presence. She had already changed so much, affecting to please her, biding her time while Frieda was lured into a false sense of security.

The office was barely furnished, devoid of personal touches, and her desk held only a closed laptop. The room was as unreadable as its owner's face.

'Coffee?' she asked.

'No, thank you.' Amy wasn't going to risk being drugged on NCA territory.

Frieda crossed to a small stand in the corner, where she poured herself and Owain mugs of filter coffee, black. He mumbled his thanks, and they sat in the bare metal chairs opposite Frieda's plain black office chair.

'What do you have for me?'

Owain handed over a small pen drive, all in black with a subtle white crown on the end. Frieda opened her laptop, the small window behind her not reflecting anything within the room, including its screen, and inserted the drive. They waited in silence while Frieda perused its contents.

'This is sufficient.'

Amy suppressed a smile. That was her standard line when she couldn't find anything to fault with the work. As close as Amy could get to job satisfaction was hearing Frieda say those words, even if the task she'd been given only commanded a fraction of her talents.

'I have a new assignment for Agent Jenkins.'

Amy said nothing, glancing over at Owain. He was also trying to master his expression, but it was clear he was equally surprised by the news. Was Frieda finally going to trust them to live their own lives? Just her and Jason, alone together in the flat.

Would she be able to find out if that kiss, over a year ago, still meant something to him?

Amy felt her hand drifting up to her lips and clasped her hands together in her lap. She couldn't afford a moment's lapse in Frieda's presence. She turned her attention to the agent, who was watching Owain's reaction. She had called him by his title – her favoured manner of address when issuing orders. She only turned to first names when she was trying to exploit them, make them feel vulnerable, persuade them. Amy thought she must expect Owain to just roll over like a good dog if she was dealing in orders instead of persuasion.

'Agent Jenkins will leave his post on Friday. His replacement will arrive on Monday and will require the same...hospitality.'

Frieda's focus switched to Amy. She didn't bother to hide her scowl of displeasure. A stranger in their flat was an imposition even worse than Owain. At least he didn't ask questions or try to make conversation. They tolerated each other, only interacting when necessary for the job. Her brief fantasy of actually being able to talk to Jason vanished in a puff of smoke.

'Man or woman?'

'Agent Appleby is very discreet. I picked her for this post myself.'

A woman. Amy curled her lip in disgust. As if her relationship with Jason could get more complicated. Perhaps Frieda had planned it that way. After all, she knew first-hand how susceptible Jason was to feminine wiles. But her face was a mask of professionalism, giving away nothing at all. Amy envied her inscrutable expression.

'I trust you will make Agent Appleby welcome.'

'I trust you will ensure she's housetrained.'

They exchanged calculated looks, before Frieda returned her icy gaze to Owain.

'I will brief you on the particulars. Agent Lane, wait outside.'

Amy left without question, smiling slightly at the correct use of her name. One of the advantages of living in the light once again was the ability to officially change her name and identity, rid herself of her father's influence once and for all. Her sister Lizzie still had some hope for reconciliation, but Amy knew he would never change into a person she wanted in her family. She had Lizzie and she had Jason – they would always be enough.

Jason would not take the news well. As much as he disliked Owain, she knew he would be more annoyed that a total stranger was living with them – even if she was beautiful. Even after all they'd been through together, Amy still dreaded that he would leave her behind. Wasn't this just another thing to drive him away? He'd already started working with Dylan again, spending more and more time at the garage in Canton.

That was what had spurred her to rebuild AEON. For herself, she could live like this. Confined, constrained, but still able to work with a computer, find some purpose. Yet Jason could not be so restricted, not without suffering for it. Amy wanted a piece of their former partnership back, even if it was only a fraction of what they'd had.

She wanted to set him free, so that he wouldn't fly away.

Chapter 5: Reappearing Act

Jason had never thought he'd regret seeing Owain leave the flat. Yet he felt strangely sorry for him as he packed up his little case, movements heavy and slow, literally dragging his feet about leaving.

He made an effort to shake Owain's hand even though he couldn't bring himself to wish him well. Amy only vaguely grunted as Jason reminded her that he was off to Swansea Prison, his regular visit to check up on Lewis and find out the gossip on the inside.

It would be good to see Lewis again. He tried to get down every week, but his bike had been playing up recently. It had been a good month since he'd last made it down to Swansea, and he felt guilty for being away from his friend for so long. He was sure Lewis would needle him for it.

He gave the duty guard his visiting order and ID, and waited patiently for the old computer system to check his details.

'Sorry, we got no one of that name here.'

Jason frowned at him. 'What? Has he been transferred?'

Surely Lewis would've let him know if he was being moved, or his mam Elin would've sent word to him, despite their past differences.

'Record doesn't say. He was here up until the 29th February – and then nothing. Someone's forgot to file the paperwork, that's all.'

Jason set aside his irritation and wondered what to do next. If it had been sudden, Lewis would've struggled to get the word out – but why hadn't he contacted them from the new prison? Something was up here and Jason didn't like it at all.

'That's all it says.'

Jason could see the guard wanted rid of him now.

'Thanks.' *Thanks for nothing.*

He returned to his bike, mind turning and twisting faster than he could keep up. Maybe Lewis had decided that Jason reminded him of an old life he no longer wanted any part of. Maybe he'd been nursing a grudge over what happened to his little brother Damage. Maybe his best friend had abandoned him.

Jason shook his head. Even if all that were true, Lewis wasn't the type to slink off into the darkness. He would've told Jason straight what was wrong between them and then told him to fuck off. Nothing about this situation made any sense, least of all the missing prison records. Jason wished Amy was at her full hacking power, so she could find out what had gone wrong with it. No way someone forgets to file the whereabouts of an armed robber, even one as rehabilitated as Lewis.

His mobile buzzed in his pocket and he fished it out. 'Yeah?'

'Jason, it's Bryn here. I've got a mate of yours at Cardiff Central Police Station, says he won't talk to me unless you come over. Says it's something about your mate Lewis.'

Jason's mouth went dry and he swallowed past the bile rising in his throat.

'Who—Who is it?'

'Says his name's Alby Collins.'

'I'll be half an hour.'

Jason stashed his phone and brought the bike to life, tearing out of the prison as if the devil was on his heels. Alby Collins was meant to be in prison for another six years, serving the same sentence as Lewis. What the fuck was he doing with Bryn?

The desk sergeant showed him through with minimal fuss, and he spotted Detective Chief Inspector Bryn Hesketh easily enough. He was standing in front of a monitor, running a hand through his greying hair while drinking from a polystyrene cup. His suit was slightly better than when Jason had last seen him at work, but that had been before the promotion. A year and a lifetime ago.

'He looks like shit.'

Bryn jumped, and Jason was quietly pleased. For a big man, he could move like a shadow.

'You took your time.'

'I was in Swansea. Trying to figure out why Lewis wasn't in prison anymore.'

Bryn stared at him. 'Your mate Lewis? The armed robber?'

Jason jabbed towards the CCTV feed showing Alby pacing the small holding cell.

'The one who's meant to be in prison with him.'

Bryn turned to the nearest computer terminal and pointed at the screen. 'This is Alby Collins' criminal record.'

It was completely empty.

'That can't be right…'

'He marched right in here, off his head on speed, and asked to speak to you. If it hadn't been for the desk sergeant swearing up and down and blind that he knew him, I would've thought it was a prank.'

Bryn called up Lewis Jones' criminal record. Or, at least, what should've been Lewis' record. Like Alby Collins, all his past sins had been forgiven and forgotten. What the hell was going on here?

'Try mine,' Jason said.

He called up Jason's record – but no, all his convictions, including his prison sentence, were dutifully noted and catalogued. Even the arrest warrant from Frieda's spiteful phase was there.

'Something's wrong.' Jason watched Alby pace – back and forth, back and forth. 'I can't see either of them making a deal. Lewis is on the side of the light now, but he's no snitch. Neither is Alby. Who would offer that kind of pardon anyway?'

Bryn hesitated a moment, before speaking. 'Amy—'

'No chance.' Jason didn't even look away from the screen. 'Not with Frieda owning all her tech, and Owain looking over her shoulder.'

He knew he sounded bitter, but he relied on Bryn not to push. He likely didn't want to talk about his former colleague either, especially given how he'd betrayed them all to get into bed with Frieda and the National Crime Agency.

'Can I talk to him?'

'With me.'

'He'll never talk to you.' Jason wasn't judging. It was just facts. 'Stand outside the door – he won't even know you're there. Alby isn't the brightest, especially not when he's high.'

Bryn nodded slowly. Jason could see him calculating the time it would take for them to intervene if Alby tried anything, but Jason could handle him.

'Don't offer him anything.'

Jason laughed. 'Alby and I aren't exactly tight. What could I give him anyway? Nothing better than what he's already got.'

Without waiting for Bryn, Jason started down the corridor. He knew this place as well as any copper, finding his way to the cell, and waiting for the uniform to let him in. Bryn was trusting him to fly this one solo, even though he knew the perp. He wouldn't break that trust.

'Y'alright, Alby?'

Alby Collins looked far from all right. He had always been a small man, but now he was gaunt, as if he'd been stuck in la-la land for days, weeks even. He had stopped pacing and was staring at Jason with a mixture of hatred and disgust. The last time they'd seen each other was in Swansea Prison, where they'd briefly shared a cell, and Alby had let Jason know exactly how much he despised him.

'Coppers must have you on a tight leash to get here so fast.'

Jason stilled his body, fighting not to react, to lash out. What was on that tape that Amy listened to? *I am a stone resting on the bed of the river.*

'You want to talk or not?'

'I'm doing you a favour, I am. Least you could do is act polite.'

Jason resisted the urge to roll his eyes, to shove Alby with his shoulder, remind him who was a leader and who was a follower. But it wasn't like that anymore, was it? Alby didn't need him anymore, didn't respect him.

Or did he? Jason could see the tautness of his frame, waiting for the blow, waiting for things to fall back into place again. To be led. To be part of something.

Jason slammed his shoulder into Alby's, nudging him into the wall hard enough for a startled 'oof' to escape his mouth. He heard stirring from outside the door, but hoped Bryn had the sense not to intervene. To trust him to handle this.

'Come on, Alby. We both know Lewis sent you. Tell what you know or get out.'

Alby avoided his gaze, squirming to get away, like a rat in a trap.

'You don't own me.'

'Maybe.' Jason released the pressure on him, just a little, before bringing him close once more. 'But up here?' He tapped on Alby's temple. 'I still got you.'

He released him fast, watching him stumble, before turning his back. Giving him time to control himself, regain respect. They had always pretended not to see him cry, to let him prove himself a man. They were bastards back then.

'He didn't send me – not like that. But he needs you, Jay Bird. He needs help.'

Jay Bird. The old nickname brought it all back, the role he'd been playing suddenly real again. Running with Lewis at the head of the pack, owning these boys and knowing they were responsible for them all. Bleeding from the nick of a Swiss Army knife on the banks of the Taff and becoming brothers beneath the moon.

'Where've you been, Alby?'

He was jittering again, the shock of Jason's shove mixing in with the last gasps of the speed. He paced the cell, over and over, making it feel smaller with every step he took. Constantly moving, running his palm over his face, again and again.

'I don't know. Some place in the country. An army place.'

'With Lewis?'

'Him, and the others. All cons. It's an experiment.'

Jason couldn't make any sense out of Alby's words. What was this drug-fuelled nightmare Alby had conjured up? What was its relationship with the truth?

'What do they do there?'

'It's the Project. I can't say nothing else. I was there weeks before they voted me out.'

It sounded like some bizarre version of *Big Brother*, but the wildness in Alby's eyes conveyed fear as well as intoxication. He believed this shit, even if it was total fantasy. For now, Jason had to play along, if he was to have any hope of getting useful information out of him.

'Can't Lewis just get voted out then?'

'They need him. But it's worse than that. It's not just a test anymore. Somebody *died.*'

His eyes were wide now, dark pupils erasing his pale irises, pleading with Jason to believe him and do something, anything.

'They killed Mole, and they'll kill Lewis next.'

Chapter 6: Ice Cream Friday

It was time for Owain to leave.

He stood awkwardly in the centre of the living room, seemingly waiting for Amy to say something. She got up from her desk, closing her NSA-issue laptop, and moving closer to him – yet still a world away. That gap would never be bridged now. It hurt too much.

'I guess you're going then.'

'Yeah.'

'Is it somewhere exciting?'

'You know I can't tell you that.'

She knew, but she was grasping for something to say. She wasn't sorry to see him leave. She didn't want to thank him for his service or tell him he'd be missed. What did you say to someone who had essentially been your prison guard for over a year? Who had once been your friend, and then betrayed you?

'Good luck with it then.'

His closed face softened a little and she could almost see the old Owain, who wore floppy brown hair and bounced with excitement. The man who'd been replaced by this hard, bitter creature with a military-style haircut and a military-style attitude.

'You know I never wanted this.'

'You did it anyway.'

'I thought I could...' He glanced up at the lampshade for a fleeting moment. 'I thought I was protecting you.'

Amy laughed, surprising herself with the ugly sound. Owain wasn't the only one who was chock-full of bitterness. She wanted to rail against him, call him naïve and a fool. Tell him that she knew the truth – that he had done this for himself, for his career and his reputation, to better his life at the expense of all of theirs.

But she didn't say any of those things. She didn't want to be cruel.

'Goodbye, Owain.'

He looked like he would say something else, try to justify himself, convince her that he really cared. But his face closed off again, and the old Owain was gone.

She turned her back on him, returning to her laptop and pretending to work. She ignored his mumbled goodbyes, the closing of the door, the ending of it all. She ignored the pricking of her eyes and the slight tremble in her hand. She didn't want to feel anything. She didn't want him leaving to matter to her.

It was dark when Jason returned, carrying with him the smell of Indian takeaway and the faint salt air of Cardiff Bay. She mechanically left the laptop and fetched spoons and plates, as Jason laid the greasy containers on woven mats. Almost domestic. Familiar, yet not comfortable.

She could feel that he had something to say, something that couldn't be said. They knew they were being watched, monitored. Amy knew why Owain had looked up at the lampshade – he knew where Frieda's eyes were in the flat, knew she was listening in.

'How's Lewis?' she asked.

'He's...he's been transferred.'

She tried to read his expression, but he was intent on arranging his plate, not meeting her eyes over the lamb samosas.

'Where is he now?'

'A special programme of some kind. Good behaviour, something like that.'

Something was very, very wrong. Amy wanted to seize hold of him and make him talk, find out every inch of the problem. Then, they could solve it, together. As they had always done before. Before Frieda and Owain and stilted, meaningless conversations.

They ate in front of the television, in silence, neither watching what was on the box or tasting the food they placed in their mouths. Longing to speak and to hear but trapped in a place where to be known was to be targeted. She could only see one chance to learn what Jason knew, and it meant confronting the darkness, reliving old fears, surviving under the stars.

Amy finished her food – and lied. 'I fancy a walk.'

'Me too,' he said, too quickly, reading her mind.

They abandoned their plates and pulled on coats as they opened the door, every second counting. How far could they get before Frieda mobilised? What were her limits without Owain?

They reached the ground floor. Amy barely had time to take a breath before they were through the doors and out into the night. She knew she could survive outside, but the night brought its own demons.

The familiar black sedan had its engine on, ready to move. But they were on foot and, for now, that gave them an advantage. Jason took her arm, as they walked briskly, as if driven by the cold and not dodging potential spies.

'Ice cream?' Jason asked.

'Yes, please.'

Cadwaladers had a place over the water. If Frieda's people wanted to get close, they would need to send in an operative. And they still had the walk.

They crossed the road and headed for Roald Dahl Plass, where a car could not follow them. The light from the windows of the Wales Millennium Centre made Jason's face seem stark, haunted, the brass armadillo watching over them but only keeping away the worst of the darkness that surrounded them among the tall pillars of the plaza.

'Bryn picked up Alby Collins,' Jason murmured. 'He said Lewis has been taken to some weird military place.'

Alby Collins. One of old Jason's gang contacts, last seen in Swansea Prison. From what she recalled, he was a shit-stirrer destined to always be someone's lackey. She had never understood why Jason had been friends with them, but charismatic leaders always needed followers.

'What kind of military place?'

She heard the fear in her voice, and knew she was reacting to the look in Jason's eyes more than the words he was speaking.

'Alby was pretty off his face. He could only say it was a compound, locked down, and run by some bloke called the Governor. Men come in, men go out – voted out by each other.'

'Why?'

'Don't know. Alby said it was a secret – something called "the Project".'

'That's not sinister at all.'

'You're telling me. Bonus – someone's been murdered. My best mate is trapped in some fucked-up military game with a murderer.'

Amy stopped, but Jason marched her on. They didn't have time for shock, for curiosity, for anything but action. Frieda wouldn't allow them to be unmonitored for long.

'Do you have a plan?'

'I have to go.'

'I'll come with you.'

The words were out before she'd thought them through. It was ridiculous, absurd. She was in recovery, not bulletproof. How would she infiltrate a men's prison compound?

It was Jason's turn to freeze in surprise, but she carried them forward half a step before his bulk stopped her.

'Are you sure?' His voice was urgent, filled with a meaning she couldn't quite discern, as he cupped her shoulders in his hands.

'Yes. We'll find a way. I know…how much Lewis means to you.'

He drew back, nodded once, and then propelled them on again. The moment was broken, and she'd been the one to break it. They couldn't afford moments.

'We need to find a way in.'

'Can Bryn help?'

'Will he want to?'

'I don't know.'

Their words snapped back and forth between the gusts of wind coming off the way, brief but more significant that anything they'd said to each other for a year. Amy knew she had to focus on the task in hand, but she wanted to savour this feeling of closeness, of returning to their old ways – being a team again.

'What about Cerys?'

'I don't know if she has the access.'

'I can help.'

'What about...*her*?'

Frieda's eyes were everywhere and Amy didn't have any device that was currently unmonitored. She and Jason both carried NCA-issued phones as part of their deal with Frieda, for this poor imitation of freedom, and they had to assume all their calls and messages were under surveillance. The NCA were probably attempting to listen in right now, but the Friday night crowds were in their favour, so much so that they could barely hear each other.

'I don't know,' Amy admitted, finally.

'Then, we do this the old-fashioned way.'

'We need Bryn.'

Amy hated relying on anything outside of the technological but operating off the grid was the only way they would be able to this safely. When Jason had shown her *The Wire*, she had been disappointed at the lack of promised technology, but she now understood the significance of anonymous telephone boxes, 'burner' phones, and conversations out in the open air.

Cadwaladers was in front of them, alluringly bright and warm after the chill night, with a few couples and friends enjoying sundaes and waffles after dinner or before the bar. However, a pair of uniformed police officers were currently heading towards them on the walkway.

'Miss Lane? It's after curfew.'

Amy checked the digital watch on her wrist – 20:33.

'I have half an hour,' she said.

The officers exchanged glances.

'That's not the information we were given,' one said hesitantly.

The other made a move to grab Amy's arm, but Jason stepped between them.

'Curfew is 9pm. Check again.'

They were drawing attention now. Usually, Amy would balk at the gathering crowd, the proximity to the water, the feelings of being too small and too trapped all at once. But her blood was already up, simmering in anger at Frieda's casual manipulation of the truth. Her curfew was 21:00 to 06:00, but Frieda knew that. She was just showing her authority, her ability to check anything they did if she so wished. Just in case they were plotting, considering taking advantage of Owain's absence for, well, anything at all.

'We have our instructions,' the cop said, like an automaton. 'Stand aside.'

'We're getting our ice cream first,' Amy said.

'Ice cream?'

The police officer was clearly confused. Had they thought she was making a run for it? She almost burst out laughing at the thought of her jumping into a speedboat and racing off into the night, to the Côte d'Azur, or Monaco, or wherever exiles went.

Amy pointed at Cadwaladers.

'We're going for ice cream. Would you like some?'

Chapter 7: Overheard Heddlu

The cake in the canteen was very bad. At least it gave Cerys an excuse to eat it very slowly.

She saw Bryn first, awkwardly nodding to his former colleagues, painfully aware he was the most senior officer in the room. He sank into the chair opposite her and tried to make himself disappear, shoulders hunched up and head down.

'Cerys.'

'Bryn.'

'It's, uh, good to see you.'

'You too. Oh look, there's Catriona!'

The red-headed detective sergeant wove her way through the tables at speed, also trying to be inconspicuous. Cerys wasn't sure if this was their normal canteen routine or if they were both acting weirdly because she'd texted them about helping her on their day off, and they'd put two and two together to make a conspiracy.

Catriona Aitken had never been Amy and Jason's biggest fan, but after Owain abandoned them for Frieda's empty promises, she'd finally seen them all for the law-bending but genuine people they were. Which is why Cerys had asked her to come in on this.

Catriona sat down next to Bryn and nodded to them both.

'Fancy seeing you here,' she said, and it sounded almost genuine.

Cerys opened the plastic container that had once held her peanut butter sandwiches and offered it to them. Inside, her phone sat on top of a sheet of tin foil, with a short note:

PHONES BUGGED. NEED HELP. JASON SAYS HI.

Catriona withdrew her phone from her pocket and placed it in the box. Then, they both looked to Bryn.

Bryn took a deep breath. 'I'm not sure I've got time for this.'

Cerys shut the box.

'Caffeine's on me,' she said lightly. 'You've got time for a cuppa, right?'

Bryn hesitated, but she'd already stood up, heading to the counter to collect three disposable cups of bad tea. While she was waiting, she stole a glance back at the table. Bryn and Catriona were sitting in silence, with Catriona still staring at him and him staring down at the table.

She guessed Bryn had more to lose than the rest of them. He had his promotion now, had lost some of the disgrace that had clung to him after Amy's fall from grace and Owain's defection. Maybe he didn't want to sully his reputation once more, give Frieda the opportunity to pull the rug from under him. He didn't have that long until his retirement.

Part of her still blamed him for what had happened with Owain. If only he'd supported him, dealt with the fears that had driven him away… But she wasn't on Owain's side anymore. Whatever there had been between them was dead, even if she hadn't quite managed to cut him loose. What remained was meaningless. She kept telling herself that.

She returned to the table, the hot tea burning her fingers through the cups as she carried them in a taut triangle. Catriona nodded her thanks. Bryn just stared at her.

'Strange business with Alby, wasn't it?' Cerys said. 'Funny what speed will do to you.'

'We sent him away with a slap on the wrist,' Bryn said, finally taking his cup. 'No mileage in a charge of "wasting police time".'

Cerys wasn't sure if that meant he had dismissed it as a fantasy, or if he had labelled it that to avoid further scrutiny. She didn't know Bryn well, couldn't tell what he was thinking. Owain would've been so much better at this, or Jason – even Amy would've had a good shot at the truth. Except none of them were here.

She had wanted to handle this without help. Maybe bringing in Catriona. But it made sense to go to Bryn – he had the connections, the rank, the reputation for decency. If anyone could get away with doing something shady, it was him. Cerys' position in the police force was precarious at best. She had never quite shaken that association with her ex-con brother.

She was just the messenger and the lackey. She had grown used to the role since joining the police. It reminded her of running errands for Jason and his gang when they were kids. It felt like a different life entirely, but it hadn't even been ten years. She wanted to hold on to this new way of existing, but she couldn't leave Jason behind. She had to make this right for him.

'Amy and Jason want to go on holiday,' she said, carefully. 'If they get…permission.'

'I don't work for the NCA,' Bryn said, hiding behind his cup.

'You could put in a good word,' Catriona interjected, before turning to Cerys with a significant look. 'What are their plans?'

Cerys seized the lifeline with both hands. 'They'd like to leave Sunday evening. Any week, really – but sooner rather than later.'

'Where are they going?'

'Somewhere local. Jason said they'd probably start in Penarth, and then head north – through The Valleys, I think. Not more than two hours or so. Amy's not keen on cars.'

Bryn huffed, took out his notebook, and jotted a couple of things down. Cerys squeezed her fist tight, trying to keep a lid on her optimism.

'Travelling will be difficult,' Bryn said.

'I thought they might break it up, a couple of different car trips. Get a van for the rest of the journey. If they leave about midnight, the roads won't be so bad. Do you know a place?'

He wrote: *Midnight to collect, need a van.* He turned the notebook slightly, so Cerys could check the details.

'I might.'

He was in.

Chapter 8: Last Night of Our Lives

They were as ready as it was possible to be while knowing nothing about where they were going or what they would do when they got there.

Cerys had popped round to drop off some DVDs of Jason's – and leave her laptop in the bathtub. Amy was 90% sure there was only sound surveillance in the bathroom and they didn't have time for more stealthy methods. Time was precious, and Jason wouldn't delay while there was a chance Lewis was in danger.

Amy felt almost jealous of their relationship, the way Jason would drop everything to be at Lewis' side. She had never had a best friend, preferring her own company or friends across the web. Controlling how she was seen, wanting to be admired and never pitied.

Yet she did know that feeling of loyalty, because she was knee-deep in it now. She was voluntarily placing herself in a situation where she could not plan and wasn't even sure what she would do when she got out there. Hang about in the woods sending coded messages? Break into the compound to graffiti on the walls? Bang on the window in Morse Code?

She only knew that Jason couldn't go alone. Nothing ever went well when he went places alone – whether it was investigating dealers in Cardiff or jumping on a motorbike with a sociopath, the boy's judgement could not be trusted.

What she didn't know was whether her judgement was worth anything at all. She had ended up in pressurised, anxiety-provoking situations before – but that was in the heat of the moment, not walking into the fire with her eyes open. How would she react? What would she do or say? Was her brain strong enough for what she had to throw at it?

She heard the door close, and shut down her NCA-issued laptop, which had been idle for an hour or more. Jason entered the living room, rucksack over his shoulder.

'I'd left a few things at Dylan's,' he said, loud enough for anyone who might be listening.

Dylan was one of Jason's oldest friends and could get hold of anything and everything. He also had a garage full of loud machinery, perfect for drowning out conversations that could be monitored. If Dylan had come through, that bag contained everything they needed for their trip. She'd tried to make discreet choices, items that any gang boy might want rather than a collection of items that screamed 'hacker on a spending spree'. Frieda hadn't knocked on her door yet.

'I'll look later,' she said. 'The pizza's on its way.'

It would be a normal night. Pizza, beer and a movie was their Sunday night tradition. With Owain lurking in the corner, silently watching. But not anymore.

Amy felt strangely on edge. It wasn't the thought of going outside, putting herself in an unknown place with unfamiliar people intent on doing cruel and unusual things. That breed of anxiety was an old friend.

No, it was being here, with Jason. Alone.

The apartment suddenly seemed vast with just the two of them, but the sofa seemed small. She let Jason pick the film because her mind was buzzing, distracted, and they got half an hour through *True Grit* before she realised what it was. She'd hardly tasted the pizza, her whole being focused on Jason. On how close he was, how far away he'd felt this past year, and now that they were alone…

Amy dropped her pizza slice and kissed him.

It was inelegant at best, her limbs misbehaving as she launched herself at him, his 'oof' of surprise as she toppled him – but then he held her, and kissed her back.

She pressed herself against him, drinking him in with her whole body, wanting to know and be known all at once. She'd thought about this moment for a year, maybe two – most days – most hours – planned it and dreamed it and angsted over it. But now she didn't think at all..

He pulled back for a moment, spreading his broad hand over her chest, her heart leaping up to meet it joyously, wildly. 'Are you sure?'

'Yes.'

He looked up towards the camera's eye, but she was kissing him again before he could think or second-guess himself and her. They had danced around this for a year, waiting for Owain to leave, really *leave* – and not to care anymore what Frieda thought, what she could do to retaliate, to hurt them. They were going to blow everything up in Frieda's face. What was one more sin?

Jason's fingers were working open the buttons of her blouse. Expertly, with a practiced hand – but she wouldn't dwell on that. That he was treading a well-worn path and she was decidedly…not. She wouldn't make it awkward. She wouldn't cast that shadow. Tonight was not for the shadows, but the incredible, all-consuming light.

She somehow hauled up his T-shirt, and he eased it off, flung it on the floor. *He'll have to clear that up before Owain gets back*, she thought. But Owain wasn't coming back. They were leaving, and he wasn't coming back.

Jason sat forward, bringing her with him, and forced her to take her own weight on the floor. He stood and lifted her by her waist, even though she was heavier than the last time, even though she didn't need to be carried. She wrapped her jean-clad legs around his waist and he laughed, walking her backwards out of the room, down the long dark corridor, and into the room where she had wanted him to take her for days, months, years.

No more waiting.

Chapter 9: Frieda's Midnight Runners

It was just after twelve when Amy tapped him on the shoulder and said, 'It's time.'

Jason wanted to stop, to say something, but she was throwing on her clothes at speed and he was in danger of being left behind.

'How long?' he asked.

'There's a two-hour skip on the surveillance,' she said. 'It was the best I could do tonight.'

'What about the corridors?'

'The program affects all the recording devices in this building. I don't know how many they've got.'

She sounded tense, preoccupied. Was it the anxiety of what they were about to do, or the many unspoken questions in their relationship? Like, was that a we-who-are-about-to-die, one-time deal? Or was it a promise to continue when they got back?

'Jason! Please pay attention.'

He turned to her, trying to look contrite. 'Sorry.'

'When did you leave the gift?'

'When I got in. They'll be well on their way by now.'

The plan was simple, but it was his plan. Jason was used to living like this – with more luck than judgement to get him out of a scrape. Amy hated it, but they were low on options. He had a good feeling about it, so she'd rolled her eyes and reluctantly agreed.

Was she having second thoughts? About the plan, about them, about him? Jason smacked his own arm. Now was not the time for an attack of sentimentality. What the fuck was wrong with him?

They picked up their bags and headed to the door in silence, leaving their phones on the bedside table. Amy opened the front door, and almost tripped over a drunk women about to knock.

Their neighbour, Virginia 'Ginny' Walters. The one who *liked* him.

'Thank you for the champers,' Ginny slurred, before giving a high-pitched laugh that could've been heard in Swansea.

'You're welcome,' Jason said, shutting the door behind him and locking it.

Leaving the gift had seemed like such a good idea at the time. Ginny had helped him out when his shopping bags had split outside her front door, and he'd thought—

'You coming to join us?'

She was falling out of her dress, and her blonde hair was framing her cleavage just-so, but Jason couldn't give a flying fuck. They had work to do.

'Can't, sorry. We're going, um, backpacking. Easier to travel when the roads are quiet.'

'Oh. But I was hoping you would share a glass with me?'

Jason saw two glasses in her hand, both half-full of Champagne, and realised she was ignoring Amy entirely. *Time to go.*

'Next time,' he said, escorting Ginny down the hallway to the lift, hoping that Amy was following and not sulking.

The lift was still on their floor and the three of them squeezed in, before Jason sent it down to the ground floor.

'Where are you…backpacking?' Ginny asked, before downing one of the glasses.

'Brecon Beacons.'

The lies came easier now, tripping off his tongue.

'Your sister doesn't say much, does she?'

Jason didn't chance a look at Amy.

'Amy's not my sister. She's…my girlfriend.'

It felt simultaneously too much and not enough. How could you describe someone who your whole life was dedicated to, with a side of kissing?

Ginny huffed and drained the other glass, as the lift doors opened.

'Happy backpacking,' she said bitterly, and staggered back to her flat.

Jason looked towards Amy, but she was already heading for the back door to their small private garden, which was locked.

'Shit.'

Jason had been relying on the door being wedged open, for the smokers at Ginny's party to indulge without bothering with the hostess to let them back in. That has been his plan – the entirety of his stupid plan.

If they used their key fob to get out, Frieda would know. Amy was certain their entry and exit times were closely monitored and leaving at this hour would definitely trigger an alert.

Amy looked up at him, the first flecks of panic in her eyes.

'What do we do?'

He had no answers for her, no backup plan. He could leave through the front door, maybe, draw the attention of their monitors. But the door was heavy and would be difficult to keep open, and Jason also needed to make their rendezvous tonight.

What the hell do I do?

The back door opened, and Ginny's flatmate Dahlia stumbled in, with a boy on one arm and a girl on the other.

Jason held the door for her, as Amy made a pretence of checking their mailbox. Dahlia didn't even acknowledge their existence, and her friends were equally stoned.

They were out before Dahlia tripped over the threshold.

Chapter 10: Take Him Away, Boys

Bryn's nearly-new Mercedes Benz stuck out like a sore thumb in the Grangetown car park. Amy grabbed for the back door handle with a sweat-slicked hand, and almost wrenched her arm off as she flung it open.

She slid across the seat, as Jason's hooded shape followed her in. As soon as the door was shut, Bryn switched on the engine and moved off, driving like an angel out of Grangetown and towards Penarth – out of the city. Far away from surveillance and as many of Frieda's spies as possible. Amy thought she must have better things to do than keep tabs on them, but then the incident at the ice cream parlour told her different.

Amy was aware of the unnatural distance between her and Jason. Of course, they were separated by the empty middle seat, but Jason would usually be leaning into her, peering at whatever she held in her lap. Touching her arm, her shoulder. The casual touches had lessened since Owain had been around, but she felt he was holding himself away from her.

That suited her just fine. She didn't have the spoons to process what had happened, to deal with the emotional fallout of what they had done. What she had longed to do. She couldn't think about it when he was about to be separated from her again for who knew how long.

Catriona twisted in her seat and passed a small bundle back to Amy, who pushed back her hood – but only so far. She knew exactly how many of Cardiff's streets were monitored, after all.

'As requested. I'm not sure how well it will function in the Valleys, mind – the hills play havoc with the signal.'

Amy unwrapped it and found a touchscreen device about the size of a smartphone, but considerably lighter. It came with two small silver discs, barely as big as her thumbnail. Amy handed one disc to Jason, who placed it in one of the secret compartments of his bag. She held up the other one and hesitated. She needed to insert it into the hem of his hoodie, but now the thought of touching him, of lifting his clothes, felt too much and too close.

'I'll do it,' he muttered and held out his hand for the disc.

She dropped it into his palm without touching him, cheeks starting to burn, before stuffing the handheld device into her own bag.

'What's this now?' Bryn asked, straining to see in the rear view mirror.

'Do you really want to know?' Jason asked.

'In for a penny, in for a pound,' Bryn said lightly, but Amy could hear the hesitation, the fear that Frieda would switch her attention to him, his career, his family.

'GPS tracker. We need to be able to follow his movements – unless your friends have told you where he's going tonight.'

Amy caught the clench of his jaw in the brief flicker of a streetlight.

'No. They haven't.'

'How'd you do it then?' Jason asked.

Bryn paused, caught between taking the credit and deniability.

'It took a big favour,' he said, cryptically. 'And a lot of whisky for the Governor.'

Amy had thought she was in favour of keeping things need-to-know, but when it was Jason's wellbeing at stake, she needed to know everything.

'What happens now?' she asked, hearing the tremor in her voice. 'Can we rely on these people?'

'Do you trust me?' Bryn asked.

'Will you tell me?' Amy countered. It wasn't about trust. It was about feeling in control tonight, even though it was only an illusion.

'You're a very special prisoner, Jason,' Catriona said, sounding glee-ful about the whole thing. 'You're a prisoner of interest to Prevent, and your location and movements have to be hidden from your neo-Nazi comrades.'

After a prison transport van had been hijacked in the Welsh val-leys, the police had been very keen on precautions – and they might take more still if the cops involved knew they were conveying the same prisoner.

'The next prisoner for "the Project" has food poisoning,' Bryn said, finally. 'It's lucky we had a replacement ready to go.'

'Lucky,' Jason echoed.

'The uniforms we're meeting will convey Jason on to where the official prison van is waiting, but only those guards know exactly where they're going. I couldn't get any information about the location out of anyone. I don't think they know very much about this whole business.'

'It's dodgy as fuck,' Catriona said. 'It can't be legal, can it? Experimenting on prisoners...'

'We'll need the GPS sooner than we thought then,' Amy said.

'We're almost at the first meeting,' Bryn said. 'Time to start the show.'

'Put these on,' Catriona said, tossing a pair of cuffs to Jason.

He caught them with one hand, handling them with reluctance, before silently requesting Amy's help. He murmured guidance to her, but still that stilted formality and distance remained. She fumbled with them a couple of times, unable to focus, driven to distraction by trying to work out what was happening in his head.

The cuffs slid into place as they approached the deserted seaside car park Bryn had chosen for the handover. A patrol car was already waiting, engine and lights off, but the area was pretty much deserted. Across the water, the Barrage tried to hold back the sea. Amy knew how it felt.

As the car stopped, Catriona got out and opened the back door. Jason shuffled out, hood still up, and Catriona closed the door smartly behind him. Amy and Bryn watched in silence as she escorted him the few steps to the car, opened the back door, and guided him inside. Within a minute, she was back in the car, and the patrol car had already moved away.

As planned, Cerys met them at a secluded caravan site. She wordlessly shouldered Jason's backpack, as Amy clutched her own bag close, barely paying attention to her surroundings, consumed by an all-encompassing sense of dread.

'We don't know where they're taking Jason,' Bryn told Cerys. 'It could be around here, it could be fifty miles away. Amy put a tracker on him.'

'She's got the monitor,' Catriona added. 'You just need to follow the map.'

'Don't engage anyone unless you have to. Find his location, and then get out before you're seen.' He turned to Amy. 'Be careful.'

Amy was so far beyond caring about 'careful' that she almost laughed in his face. 'Careful' was staying at home, eating pizza, and talking your assistant out of rescuing his best friend from the twisted military experiment he was caught up in. 'Careful' was paying attention to the details of your probation contract, the written and unwritten rules of Frieda's employment offer, and doing exactly what you were told.

'Careful' was not climbing on the back of a motorcycle with a 20-year-old adrenaline junkie when you had just sent her only brother into certain danger.

Amy passed Cerys the monitor, which she mounted on her bike where her phone usually sat. They turned it on and waited for the trace to appear on the map.

'He's not far,' Cerys said, relieved. 'That's about fifteen minutes away – and still moving.'

She got on the bike and motioned impatiently for Amy to join her.

'Hold on,' Cerys said, pulling down her visor.

In her dreams, Amy had ridden on the back of a very different motorcycle with a very different Carr. Unlike Jason's vintage Harley Davidson, this bike was petite and sleek and dark – yet still capable of breaking the speed limit before Amy had taken her first full breath. She clung on to Cerys and tried to lean with her instinctual movements, even though she felt like she would fall off at any moment. But she didn't have enough fear left for this. It was all tied up with Jason.

She finally let her thoughts and feelings about last night come to the fore. She had wanted him but the longing wasn't enough. He had known exactly what he was doing and she had felt childish, awkward, for having to be guided. It was rushed and messy, and yet she wanted more. To start over, to repeat, to take all the time in the world in just the kissing alone.

But she couldn't. Because of Frieda and Lewis and Owain, and all these people who kept getting in between them. Who made her feel afraid of endings, instead of hopeful for beginnings. She hated all of them, but she hated Jason most of all. For doing the right thing, the selfless thing, and leaving her feeling both bereft and ashamed.

The bike suddenly slowed and Cerys pulled over, tapping impatiently at the mounted tracking monitor.

'Signal's gone.'

'We can wait.'

'We fucking can't.'

Amy had almost forgotten that the legendary Carr impatience was magnified in Cerys.

'Once he's at his destination, he will stay there. We have time.'

'Until they see he's a fraud and shiv him.'

Cerys' fearful anger was unfortunately contagious and Amy found herself feeling both irritable and terrified within seconds. She felt too hot inside the helmet, but she resisted the urge to throw it off.

'Fine,' she said shortly. 'We head for his last known location.'

Cerys opened her mouth to protest but shut it again.

'Fine,' she echoed.

They surged forward, perhaps even faster than before – or was that the adrenaline making her dizzy? She could not afford to panic now. She reached down to brush the strip of little blue pills nestled inside her jeans pocket. Just in case.

'Hold the fuck on,' Cerys yelled.

Amy did as she was told, as they rounded a corner and came up to a large security gate. A sign said: DANGER HIGH VOLTAGE.

This was the place. Amy was sure of it. *Shit.*

Cerys started backing up. They were too close. Bryn had told them to keep their distance. They didn't want to charge down the front door, draw attention—

A swarm of black-clad figures emerged around them, seemingly formed from the darkness of the shadowy trees. They were barely visible, only the sheen of their guns giving them away.

Amy felt the tension in Cerys' body, recognised the coiling of a fight-or-flight spring, and placed her hand in the centre of her back.

'Engine off!' A voice barked out, coming from everywhere and nowhere. 'Step away from the bike!'

It seemed they were going in the front door after all.

Chapter 11: Know Thy Enemy

Jason had been inside the prison van for what seemed like forever before it finally halted.

A wave of relief washed over him. He thought he'd be fine but being inside the van again had brought it all back. Hearing the sounds of men dying outside, knowing he was next, and barely able to run. Just like back then, he had to keep his head together. One wrong move could end him up in worse trouble than a midnight country stroll.

The doors opened and he stepped out as fast as he could, eager to move, to take control and stop feeling so helpless. Three men were waiting for him, as Alby said they would be – all in shadow. Playing silly games.

'We were…expecting someone different.'

The voice was slightly posh and very English. Some kind of prison guard? No, wait – what had Alby called him? 'The Governor.'

'They brought my time forward,' Jason said, not too fast, not too slow.

'Food poisoning or something,' his escort piped up.

'You may go.'

Jason caught sight of the transport guards' rolling eyes, but their faces closed off as soon as they knew they'd been seen. They weren't going to mock anyone openly, not tonight in the deep, dark wood.

The two other men were looking at the central figure, expectantly. 'Elites,' Alby said. Was Jason due the newbie's speech? Was this guy trying to intimidate him by making him wait?

Jason resisted the urge to square off to him. His job was to keep his head down, find Lewis, and get out. Preferably without breaking heads. There was also the issue of the dead guy, but Lewis could tell them all about it once they were gone.

The Governor eventually spoke.

'You obey the rules or you will be punished. Dreadlock will make sure you know them.'

Something about this was wrong. The words sounded strange in the guy's mouth, as if he wasn't used to them, or as if Jason had expected him to say something else.

The Governor turned and, for a split second, the light fell on his face.

'You!' Jason said, all caution gone. 'Fuck me, it's really you.'

The Governor turned fully into the light but said nothing. What did you say to the man who had put you in jail for life?

Jason realised the others were staring.

'You're a murderer,' he said. 'All those girls…'

Kate. Melody. Laurie. And Carla.

'You're The Cardiff Ripper.'

Amy traipsed through the woods, Cerys a few steps in front of her, flanked on either side by silent armed men. They had taken her backpack but neither of them had been searched. Amy was almost afraid of what Jason's sister might be carrying.

Cerys had tried to introduce herself, to show her badge, but she was silenced with a gun against her chest. These men weren't interested in explanations. Amy had watched Cerys barely control her temper, her panic. It made her deeply afraid to see that Cerys was as helpless as she was.

The sliver of moon had disappeared behind a cloud, and the woods were eerily quiet. Had the wildlife all fled before them or had there never been any? Had this bizarre experiment wiped them out somehow? Was Amy growing more hysterical with every step deeper into darkness?

A mist was rising, coiling around her body like a sinister snake. With mounting horror, Amy watched the fog swallow Cerys whole, the guards' torches useless within this shroud.

It could've been ten minutes or it could've been a decade before Amy ran into the back of Cerys, almost sending them both to the ground.

'Sorry!'

Her voice was too loud, almost a shout. *Idiot.*

'Don't panic on me,' Cerys hissed.

A heavy hand fell on Amy's shoulder, pushing her forward, until her foot nudged at a raised edge. Something whistled past her face, before landing with a soft *thud* – somewhere below her.

'Climb down.'

Trembling, Amy lowered her body into a crouch and reached out. The metal was burning with cold as she leaned forward, noticing the presence of dim lights like cats' eyes on a midnight motorway. Leading her down a bare metal ladder into a hole in the ground.

She couldn't back down now. Jason was committed, probably already inside, and he needed her to be present. This hadn't been what they'd planned for, but if she could somehow get this team to accept her, she could keep him safe.

If she just climbed down into the bowels of the earth with a gun at her back.

She climbed in. The light gave everything a red-tinted glow, like the mouth to Hell, and she wanted to close her eyes against it. She counted thirty-nine steps before her foot hit solid ground, then the second.

Two men were waiting for her, in the same black uniforms, but the low lighting continued down the tunnel so she couldn't see their faces. A coincidence, or a deliberate strategy?

They were silent as they preceded her down the tunnel, their footsteps echoing in the close space. She suddenly looked behind her, but there was no one else there. No guards, no Cerys.

'Where is—'

'Your driver made her delivery, didn't she?'

The guards didn't stop walking and Amy trotted to keep up. She noticed that one of them seemed to be holding her backpack in his hand. Was that the object that had been dropped past her face before she'd entered the manhole? Is that what he thought Cerys' delivery was?

Had they mistaken Amy for someone else? If they had, how long could she maintain the charade? With preparation and the separation of a computer screen, she could lie like a pro, but here, like this? She wasn't sure she even knew how.

The familiar sick feeling was rolling in her stomach and her lungs felt compressed, unable to coexist with her frantically-beating heart. She wanted to run, to get out. She had to get out.

A vault door appeared before them, with no external markings. It opened outwards, towards them, and Amy was escorted inside.

The corridor beyond was as gloomy as the tunnel, but it was definitely a corridor. Light flooded out of the room ahead and she found herself walking faster, eager to get out of the darkness and into a place where she could see.

The room was bright with strip lighting and she squinted to see. A large screen took up one wall and was subdivided into nine CCTV streams, which rotated every thirty seconds. Six workers sat at two long desks, three on each side of a central aisle, all facing the screen. At the back of the room, in the centre, there was an empty desk with no chairs, much higher than the rest. It reminded her of the footage she had seen of NASA, but on a much smaller scale.

'Sir, the technician is here,' the guard said, then retreated into the darkness.

A technician! Yes, that was the perfect cover. Perhaps she could bluff her way through this after all.

'IN3, find her a bunk and a laptop. She'll join us on the day shift.'

Amy stopped and stared. In front of her was the man she had seen every weekday for an entire year. *Owain Fucking Jenkins.*

How the hell could he be here? What the fuck did it mean that he was?

Her brain, already running at full throttle, helpfully filled in the blanks. He was here because he was working for Frieda Haas, which meant the NCA were here. And Amy had run right back into their arms.

Owain knew she wasn't meant to be here, but it seemed he was going to pretend that she was. What game was he playing? When would she have a chance to find out?

'Questions tomorrow, Agent Lane,' Owain said, pre-empting her as he stood up from a terminal. 'We have a new prisoner to check in, so we'll be here all night.'

He was looking at her as if she was a complete stranger. As if he hadn't lived with her and the 'new prisoner' for over a year. But that was for the best, wasn't it? He was treating her like any other NCA agent, not some mad dog that had escaped the leash.

'Yes…' He kept staring. 'Sir…?'

He looked away.

'You may go.'

Dismissed, Amy followed the guards towards a door on the other side of the control room. She glanced back once, to see Owain staring at the screen – and Jason staring back.

Chapter 12: We're All In This Together

Walking into the compound felt like the start of a horror movie, the cheap kind that was filmed in some abandoned factory that was one loose screw away from falling in on the cameraman's head.

A drip from the ceiling fell beneath Jason's collar and oozed its way down his back, as he followed the Governor and his goons down the barely-lit, narrow corridor. 'The Governor', that would take some getting used to. Martin Marldon had been Jason's adviser at the job centre, just before Amy discovered he was the Cardiff Ripper. Back then, Martin had both held the power and been terrified of Jason. He wondered how it stood with them now.

What did it mean that he was here? A place to reform armed robbers and petty thieves he could understand, but lifers? He was the first Welsh serial killer for decades. He was dangerous and unrepentant. Jason remembered Lewis and Alby's blank criminal record. Is that what Martin's looked like now?

What the fuck were they doing here that made it worth releasing the Cardiff Ripper?

The corridor suddenly opened out to a T-junction, corridors stretching away from them on either side, about fifteen feet in each direction. Ahead of them was an open door and the welcoming committee.

The sparse room was fitted out like a particularly hard-up café, with cheap plastic tables surrounded by cheap plastic chairs. At a glance, Jason counted eight people in the room, making them twelve in total. Twelve angry men.

He picked out Lewis instantly, but forced himself to keep his gaze moving, landing on each man in turn, trying to meet his eyes. He was out of practice at this kind of thing – sizing up a man, showing his mettle, knowing his place in the scheme of things. He'd have to remember fast if he wanted to get to the bottom of this.

'This new boy is Jason,' the Governor said. 'He's picking up Mole's duties – for now.'

Jason watched the expressions of the men in the room. Some looked smug, so the duties must be pretty shit. Others looked uneasy, even frightened. If Alby was the last man voted out, then Mole must be the one who'd left in a body bag. He chanced another glance at Lewis, who subtly nodded. Jason could already feel their minds working together, travelling the same paths, ready to take on the world.

'Stoker, fill him in on the rules. Then show him to the kitchen.'

Again, some laughter, some uncomfortable. Was he being directed to both Mole's regular hangout, and where he met his death?

'We start at seven tomorrow.'

The Governor left the room without fanfare, leaving an uneasy silence in his wake. Everything was coming at Jason too fast – too much new information, new connections, and so many fucking questions. He didn't have time to think right now. He had to remember himself, the self he'd left behind in Swansea Prison.

'Jason, is it?'

One of the uniformed men ambled up to him, even bigger and broader than Jason. He wore a layer of short dark fuzz over his head and was maybe slightly younger than Jason, early twenties. The other elites were letting him take the lead, standing behind him – two black men and one white, all easily the tallest and broadest in the room. The Governor clearly had his ideas about strength.

'It's Jay Bird,' he said, without really thinking.

The man nodded, accepting it without question. 'I'm Stoker. We'll be going through your bag – standard, it is. Just like on the inside. Then I'll take you down to the kitchen.'

The bag search was brief and perfunctory. Amy's toys were well-concealed, and Stoker didn't come near them. His toiletries were removed and set to one side, as were his cigarettes. Just like prison, there was a tax on the lower orders to appease the higher-ups. He was going to need to get the hang of the rules if he wanted to survive here.

'Kitchen it is then. Follow me.'

As they walked out of the door, the noise picked up behind him, as if they'd been waiting for a chance to gossip about him. Stoker turned right down the corridor and Jason tried to pay attention to the layout. Three doors on the left, two on the right – but then the mess room was easily the biggest room in the place.

At the end of the corridor on the right, Stoker introduced him to the kitchen. He closed the door behind him and the sounds from the mess hall faded to nothing, leaving them alone with a utilitarian metal surfaces and piles of dirty plates. A nice place for a bit of murder, very quiet. Where he was currently standing with a stranger who was one of his suspects.

Stoker smiled at him. It was at such odds with the direction of his thoughts that it took Jason a moment or two to smile back, slightly awkward, keeping a tight grip on his bag just in case. Not that a few pairs of boxers would do him much good.

'Lewis says you're an idiot, but he's glad you're here.'

His heart rate sped up, but he felt something in him loosen and unwind. Lewis was pleased to see him. He'd already made friends here, people he could trust. That was going to make this thing a whole lot easier and get them all out of here faster.

'Tell him he's the idiot.'

Stoker nodded, the smile fading to a smirk.

'Oh, I know. I'll leave you to it then. The bunkroom's down the end of the corridor, last door on the right. Take care in the dark.'

He opened and closed the door before Jason could respond. To thank him? To shake his hand? All his instincts were gone, but he was glad he had allies here. Dropping his bag on the floor, he started scouting out his domain.

The kitchen hadn't been taken care of for a good long while, possibly since Mole's death. There had been some effort to clean plates, but nothing had been put away, the surfaces cluttered. Peering into the industrial-size fridge, Jason saw mainly vegetables and open cartons of UHT milk and orange juice. A further nose in the cupboards turned up tin after tin of meat, beans, and tomatoes. Pasta, rice, cereals, and potatoes came in generic bags, probably supplied by whoever was running the place. The only fresh food outside of the veg was bags of bread, poorly sealed and already growing an impressive amount of mould. Jason was disappointed not to find peanut butter – maybe someone was allergic?

He stopped himself. This wasn't the task he had been sent here to do. Alby hadn't said anything about how this man was supposed to have died, just said he'd been found in the garden. The only name he'd produced from his addled brain was 'Mole'. It hadn't been enough for Bryn to get a definite match, especially as his criminal record had likely gone the way of the others'.

If no one had been picking up the chores and this was the place Mole had died, Jason might still find some evidence here. Though what the hell he was to do with it, he had no idea. A splash of blood was perfect for the forensics lab, but pretty useless out in the middle of nowhere. He didn't even really know what he was looking for, this kind of thing more suited to the medical examiners.

He wished he had some kind of recording equipment on him, but Cerys had ruled it too suspicious and Amy had wished aloud for more time to run wires and camera leads through his hoodie to somehow make it work.

They hadn't had time and Cerys had been right. He was carrying only one piece of tech, which was a miniature mobile phone, beloved of criminals and prisoners, and something that wouldn't be out of place if it was discovered though he very much hoped it wasn't. He needed at least one connection to Amy. He hoped Cerys was taking good care of her out there in the dark.

He shook his head to clear it. He wasn't used to late nights anymore, to maintaining his focus. He had to get on and get down to the bunk, before anyone noticed he was taking a stupidly long time to wash some dishes.

He found a dustpan and brush under the sink and went round every inch of the floor, making a half-hearted effort to sweep while sniffing to pick up the scent of bleach and watching out for signs of blood between the old tiles. Nothing.

Which meant that Mole probably didn't bleed here. How did he die then? Poison? Bang to the head? There were 101 ways to kill a man and Jason was becoming grimly familiar with all of them. He could always ask around to find out how Mole died, if anyone knew, but that would raise suspicion, especially as he wasn't supposed to know about it at all.

He opened the sink cupboard to replace the dustpan and brush, when he noticed a thick strip of water damage on the edge of the cupboard floor. The wood was discoloured and warped, as if it had sat under water for days. The wood between the pipes and the damage was unmarked, so there hadn't been a leak there. He looked at the back of the cupboard door and spied an array of thick lines, the course of water running down, but very faint.

Peering closer at the cupboard floor, he saw little patches of white dotted along the warped wood, no one bigger than his littlest fingernail. It looked like the beginnings of mould, which meant this damage was very recent. As recent as last week?

Jason shut the cupboard door and filled the sink with water, checking the overflow and bringing the water level up to just below it. He sunk his arms in up to the wrist, and then the elbow. The water benignly trickled out of the overflow, not coming close to breaching the sides.

He glanced back at the door. It was behind him to the right, enough of a distance that it could open without disturbing whoever was at the sink. A person could take one or two steps, and—

Jason plunged his head beneath the water.

He felt it rise up, soaking his hoodie and slopping down the front of his chest, down the cabinet. Suddenly, a hand was yanking him back, pulling him away from the sink and shaking him at the same time.

'What the fuck do you think you're doing?'

It was the black guard with dreadlocks, an expression of anger and disbelief on his face. He got it together when he saw Jason's shocked expression and let go of him, awkwardly patting him on the back.

'It's, uh…it's not that bad here, mate. Better than the inside. You'll be all right.'

Jason spluttered, took a breath. 'I wasn't…that wasn't…'

What other explanation did he have? 'I was just trying to recreate a murder' wasn't the impression he wanted to give either.

'We'll keep an eye on you,' the man said, still patting. 'I'm Dreadlock, by the way. Everyone calls me that. Who are you then?'

'Jay—Jay Bird.'

'Jay, right. I'll take you down to the bunkroom to find a friend. Keep you close, right?'

Shit. His stupid experiment meant he was getting a nanny, rather than freedom to explore in his own time.

'What about the dishes?' he mumbled.

'Your new mate can help you out in the morning,' he said. 'Come on now.'

Reluctantly, Jason grabbed a teatowel, scrubbed the water from his skin and dabbed at his soaked hoodie, before taking his bag and his pride down the long corridor to the bunkroom, Dreadlock watching him all the way.

Chapter 13: Nanny State

Amy's 'bunk' was a folding bed in the locker room.

'Sorry. We're kinda short on space down here.'

'IN3' did look apologetic, but also anxious to get back to her station. She was young, maybe only Cerys' age, with long dark hair plaited away from her face. Amy thought she might be Japanese American, from her features and her accent. She wore the same white top, black bottoms as the others, like waiters at a restaurant. Her modicum of choice had been used on a white blouse and a black pencil skirt, with thick black tights.

'How many people are sleeping here?'

The agent glanced at the door again.

'Six agents, six guards. The other shift is in the Eye Room or in the Security Hide. Agent Jenkins has his own quarters, of course.'

'Of course,' Amy echoed flatly.

'I really need to—'

'Do you have a name?'

The agent blinked at her for a moment.

'We, uh, tend to go by our designations. I am IN3.'

'IN3?'

Amy could tell the agent was beginning to get suspicious. She needed information, allies – not enemies and informers. Her brain was struggling to remember details of the types of work she had provided support for, but they had all been solo or duo missions, never anything requiring this amount of infrastructure.

'I provide a remote supporting role to agents in the field,' Amy expanded. 'This is my first time in this kind of…setup.'

'Oh, you're NCA, aren't you? Yeah, all the NCA newbies struggle with this part. I is really Eye, as in 'I spy with my little' one. N for the night shift, and then I'm the third worker from the left. If I get transferred out or move position, then the designation shifts to the new person who occupies that spot. Little bit clearer?'

It wasn't clear at all. Did 'NCA newbies' mean that they put fresh recruits here, or did the emphasis on 'NCA' mean this was a joint operation with the military? International agencies? How big was this thing?

'That makes sense, yes,' she said.

'Only Agent Jenkins uses his name here. You'll probably get a designation too.'

'Are there other technicians here?'

'Nope, no technicians here.'

'That makes me TD1.'

IN3 beamed at her, as if grateful they were back in familiar territory.

'I guess it does. You'd better get some rest though. The day shift starts at eight.'

IN3 left her alone in the locker room with her folding bed and a head full of questions. The reason she couldn't recall NCA information about this kind of work is that, until now, she hadn't known this kind of work existed. Sure, her agents thought of themselves as Bond boys or Mata Haris, but they were mostly just liaising with police forces, trying some low-level infiltration, or bluffing their way into privileged circles. What the hell were they doing involved in this?

The questions threatened to overwhelm her, the lack of certainty pressing in on her from all sides. She took a breath, then another. She just had to focus on getting through tonight. One night at a time. One task at a time.

Amy found some instructions for the folding bed inside its canvas cover and, after a few false starts, managed to get it the right way up and with all the legs locked in place. She cast a quick glance over the laptop, but it asked for her NCA password on startup, so she closed it again. No need to alert Frieda right away that she had slipped her lead. She couldn't think about Frieda right now, her hands already moving on to the next mundane thing.

She laid out the sleeping bag on top of the folding bed, before checking her backpack. Cerys' laptop hadn't survived the fall down the shaft, the screen completely shattered. It wouldn't be much good down here anyway, not with an NCA network. Amy wrapped it in a plastic bag and shoved it in the bottom of her locker. She'd get her a new one if they got out of here. *When.*

Security hadn't troubled the secret compartments, which was good news. She partially withdrew her cheap mobile phone, but there was no signal. Of course – she was underground. She had to hope Cerys wouldn't do something stupid like try to mount a rescue, like her brother would under similar circumstances.

It had been hard to see Jason on the screen and walk away. To know that she could have access to his every moment, and yet be denied. It was going to be an exercise in self-control to not be in that room every moment she was awake. Which was probably going to be a lot of moments if she was stuck in this freezing-cold locker room on a flimsy bed.

She found the bathroom next door and brushed her teeth before returning to the locker room to change. She had a wind-up torch in her bag, which she set going before venturing to turn out the lights. Making her way back towards the light, she tripped over her shoes and her backpack before wrestling the sleeping bag over her body. She only just about fitted on the folding bed, so she had no idea how Owain managed it.

She couldn't believe Owain was here. They had waited a whole year for time away from him, and then here he was. He must be the only reason she hadn't been arrested or…worse. If the NCA was capable of running a place like this, then it was more than capable of disappearing people. Amy had underestimated both the Agency's power and their lack of moral code.

The door suddenly opened and the lights were flipped on.

'I know you're not asleep.'

Amy resisted the urge to snap back at him and sat up in her sleeping bag. Owain let the door close behind him and looked tiredly at her for a moment or two, before letting himself fall back against the wall.

'I thought I left you behind at my old job.'

'I didn't realise your new job was experimenting on prisoners in a murder box.'

'Neither did I,' he said.

She heard the bitterness, recognised how it had been growing in him, twisting him. She had sounded like that once, after Lizzie had left, before Jason. She recognised the poison, but she didn't know who was going to be the person who might untwist him. All those who had once cared about him had run far away. She couldn't blame them.

'What the hell is going on?' she asked.

Owain sighed and scrubbed a hand through his short, cropped hair. It made him look even older, wearier. Amy almost felt sorry for him.

'I don't know everything,' he began. 'Its origins go way above me, above Frieda. I'm not even sure who's involved, or—'

'Skip to the end.'

He looked up, but didn't comment on her abrupt tone and lack of patience. He'd seen enough of her to know when not to push. Amy knew she hadn't learned the same.

'There are twelve prisoners in one ex-military compound. Every week, one leaves and one arrives. How they choose them, I don't know, but there are lots of different skills in there. Violent men, clever men, liars, thieves, gangsters. Every stripe of criminal you can imagine.'

'I heard the prisoners vote out the rejects.'

Owain nodded. 'You heard right. Frieda wanted them to have as much control over the mix as possible. The idea was that the group would keep only the most useful people and get rid of the wasters. That way we would learn something about how criminal groups form, how they bond, how they go on to commit terrible acts together.'

Amy felt a chill go down her spine. 'This isn't about any ordinary criminal act though, is it? This is about…'

'Mass murder. Or terrorism, if you like.'

He was so calm, so matter-of-fact, that Amy thought she must've misheard him.

'Why?'

'Because we don't understand it. This way, we can observe how gangs and cells form, what keeps them ticking, what gets the job done. At least, that's the theory. In practice…'

'It's not working out so well.'

'This is the last centre still operating. The other two collapsed within the first six months – the inmates lost interest, or started a riot. Frieda is determined that our experiment will work.'

At her name, the fear returned full-strength. 'Are you going to tell Frieda I'm here?'

'Of course I am,' he said, as if it was obvious. 'She'll find out soon enough.'

'You can't—'

'I'll tell her I brought you in, you and Jason. To clean up the mess left by my predecessor. She won't like it, but she needs me here. I'm the only one she trusts now.'

'Does that make you feel special?' Amy said, unable to let that lie.

'It means I'm doing my job,' he said, face inscrutable. 'You never understood why I left.'

'I never wanted to, and I don't want to now. I want to get Jason and Lewis out of here as quickly as possible. That's all.'

'Who's Lewis?'

'Lewis is Jason's best friend. He visits him every other week, or hadn't you noticed?'

'I haven't had a chance to catch up with the files,' Owain said, rubbing a hand over his face. 'Of course it would be one of Jason's friends in here. Of course.'

'One of two,' Amy said, unable to resist scoring another point. 'Alby Collins just left, but history isn't important, right? We don't count former friends.'

She watched him take the hit, his jaw tightening. She watched and hated herself a little bit for scoring points when he was hurting. But he had hurt them too. She couldn't let herself forget that. There had been times, in their year together, when she had felt herself falling back into the old rhythms of their friendship. Then, she'd catch herself, see the look on Jason's face, and withdraw again. She would never let herself go back. Never.

'Amy, I'm having a shit weekend and it's about to get worse. I am doing you a fucking favour, so can you just knock it off for five minutes?'

She nodded, feeling the guilt grow inside her, before she shoved it back down.

'Yes. I can.'

'Your designation is TD1. You start at eight o'clock tomorrow morning. Your job is to find new ways of obtaining surveillance from the subjects. Under no circumstances are you to contact Jason. He is fine just where he is.'

'How is he fine when he's locked in that place with a murderer?'

Owain's eyes looked at her, dark and blank.

'It wouldn't be the first time, would it?'

Chapter 14: Me and My Shadow

Stoker was Jason's new best mate.

Jason had been given the bunk above his by Dreadlock, evicting a drowsy Lewis, who was sent to sleep in the other bunkroom. Each room had three bunk-beds, with two elites in each room. The bunk-rooms were either side of the corridor, at the opposite end of the complex to the kitchen, with a bathroom next door to each.

If Jason had expected some privacy for his morning shower, he was mistaken. As the new boy, he had to take the last shower, and the water was ice-cold. Stoker stood outside for the whole two minutes, humming some jaunty tune that Jason vaguely recognised but couldn't quite place.

At breakfast, he had a spot at a table with Stoker and Lewis, with cereal and toast on offer alongside a large mug of tea.

'The Governor's trying to bring in chickens,' Lewis said.

'He can do that?' Jason asked incredulously.

'He can ask,' Stoker said.

Jason wanted to ask about the Governor, but he had no idea where to begin. It seemed that Martin held a respected position here and Jason doubted he had come by it by default. How had he reached the position of 'Governor'? Did his elites keep him there, or was it reputation alone? How did this place work anyway?

'What's the plan for today then?' he asked.

'Lewis has to work on the Project,' Stoker said. 'I'm on gardening duty. You're welcome to come out, see how you like it. Though the kitchen is your main thing says the Governor – lunch, dinner, all that. Keeping it tidy too.'

'What's "the Project"?'

'Need-to-know,' Stoker said quickly, before Lewis could answer.

Lewis shot him a look of disbelief, but then just shook his head. Jason was stunned. Lewis Jones, not putting up a fight? Just accepting someone else's word without an argument? Jason had scrapped with him for every victory, physically more often than not. Then again, they had both changed, hadn't they? Older, if not wiser, and not best mates anymore.

People were starting to move, the clock coming up to seven. A dark South Asian man came up to their table, with a milk-white teenager hovering by his elbow.

'You ready, Lewis?'

'I am,' he said, getting up from the table. 'This is Jay Bird, by the way – meet Roshan and Pansy. My Project mates.'

They nodded their hellos before Lewis left the mess room with them, waving over his shoulder. Two elites followed him out, but Dreadlock stayed behind. Jason figured him for the Governor's right-hand, the one keeping everyone in line. There weren't any screws in here but the prisoners seemed to have taken on that role anyway. Perhaps the familiarity was comforting.

'Where's Joe now?'

'Reckons he's got flu,' laughed a man Jason vaguely recognised.

'I'll turf him out. Stoker, don't lose your shadow. Anchor, Gareth – get stuck into the laundry until it's light enough to see out.'

The grumbling from Anchor and Gareth was par for the course, but it seemed good-natured enough. Stoker, however, didn't seem down with the plan. His mouth formed an unhappy line and he followed Dreadlock down the corridor. Jason curiously followed them down the windowless corridor, taking note of the store rooms this time, one each side of the corridor to the exit. He'd spotted the laundry room next to the kitchen yesterday evening, and another room opposite. That must be where the Governor was lurking.

'Why are you coming?' Dreadlock asked without turning round.

'What are you going to do?'

'We're having a nice chat.'

'Oh, "nice", is it?'

The tension was high between them and Jason kept his distance. Did Dreadlock and Stoker resent being out here with the blokes not good enough for this mysterious "Project"? Maybe they had beef from somewhere in the past. Jason knew all about that.

Dreadlock barged in to the bunkroom on the left, the one Lewis had been moved to last night. The room was a mirror of the one on the opposite side, with bunk-beds against each wall except the one holding the door.

The bundle huddled in the sleeping bag was on the top bunk of the beds on the right side, the same bunk Jason occupied in the opposite room. He thought the person inside was shaking, the tremors increasing as Dreadlock marched up to him and yanked open the zip.

'Morning Joe. Not working today then?'

'Dread…Dread, I'm dying.'

'You are not dying. Get up.'

'I've been poisoned, Dread. Whoever did for Mole, he's done for me now.'

'Like fuck you've been poisoned. Get up, Joe.'

'Dreadlock, mate,' Stoker said, surprisingly softly-spoken. 'Do you think we should get him checked out? He looks a bit green.'

'It's fucking nothing, Stoker. He doesn't need your tender loving care.'

'Dread—'

'Get out or your number's up.'

Stoker held up his hands and turned his back on the scene, jaw clenched.

'Come on, Jay Bird – Dreadlock is going to be "nice".'

Jason wanted to stop – protest. What was this Dreadlock guy going to do to Joe? What information did Joe have about Mole's death? Had he been wrong about the drowning, and it was really poison? Was the murderer working on his second victim?

But his feet were already moving, carrying him away from the bunkroom. His instincts told him to get out of there, to follow the order, to stay in line. The old prison vice was starting to squeeze again, penning in any stray thought until it fitted inside the eat-sleep-work life that he'd been trained to embrace. If they'd pulled randomers off the street, this experiment would never have worked. But they picked prisoners, men accustomed to small spaces, tight routines, and mindless tasks. They picked them to be dangerous but docile.

He let the door fall closed on the first cry from Joe and tried not to feel like a coward.

Chapter 15: Just Jammin'

Cerys waited until dawn before deciding that Amy wasn't coming back.

She shook off the blanket and boiled water for coffee in the tiny kitchenette, skills honed by years of caravanning in Tenby with her mam and Jason. As the steam started to rise from the surface of the water, she tried to think through the sleep-deprived fog that had settled on her brain.

She had been sent away, as if she wasn't of any interest to them. She'd heard one of the armed men receive a radio message, but hadn't caught anything more than 'Let the blonde one go'. She had thought about fighting her way out, but they had guns and she had left her death wish in her teenage years. She wasn't sure she could get herself out, let alone Amy.

And then she'd realised what those words meant. It was a strange thing to say, wasn't it? Not 'Let the driver go', as if she was dropping off a delivery or acting as a taxi service. Also, it was dark – the guard had squinted at her to make sure she was indeed 'the blonde one'. What kind of camera system had full-colour night vision?

Unless the person behind the camera had recognised her. Who did they know who worked for a shady organisation that liked to fuck around with people?

Cerys should've seen this coming. If you fall back into your ex's bed, you should at least check out what horror-of-the-week they're committing. Owain said he was going away for a while, but she didn't think he meant into some creepy underground bunker to experiment on prisoners. That was a new low even for him. She couldn't believe she kept going back to him, kept hoping he was a decent person underneath all the shit.

The last time they'd been together, when he said he was going away on assignment, she'd told him that Jason would be delighted and that she definitely wouldn't miss him. He'd said nothing, and she'd left his bed and got dressed, leaving without either of them saying anything more than a muttered 'see you around'. It seemed she wouldn't have time to miss him anyway.

She'd still been reluctant to leave Amy, but there was nothing she could do. Returning to her caravan, she'd waited out the night, running through possible options. She'd tried Owain's phone, but it was out of service. Unsurprising if he was in that underground den. She'd fired off an email to his personal account – 'Call me sometime.' If he had access to his email, he would know she meant 'Call me right fucking now'. However, that was also unlikely in a work environment as tightly-controlled as the NCA's.

One option was to leave the whole thing alone. She had done her part, escorting Amy to a position from which she could monitor Jason. If Owain was in there with her, he would take care of them both, to the best of his ability. She honestly believed that of him, if nothing else. Her work here was done. She could go back to work, to the career she had worked so hard to grasp and keep.

Or she could keep sticking her nose in until she knew exactly where Jason and Amy and Owain were, and had made sure they were all playing nicely – and then she could go back to work.

It wasn't really a choice at all, put like that, so Cerys settled up at the caravan site and headed back towards Cardiff. On the drive back, she thought about who might know the local area well enough to give her some insights. The Ministry of Defence had a huge presence in Mid and South Wales and it made more sense for this to be one of their retired installations than a purpose-built torture chamber.

Bryn had a vast knowledge of local affairs, but his knowledge was mostly confined to Cardiff and the history of his lifetime. She needed someone outdoorsy, someone who felt at home outside the city, maybe even knew a bit of local history. She was suddenly reminded of traipsing across the Brecon Beacons, looking for a body dump and finding only deer – with Catriona Aitken's state-of-the-art equipment.

She pulled over and checked her messages. She'd never been to Catriona's place but Gwen, their mother, had insisted on sending every one of 'Jason's little friends' a Christmas card, and so Cerys had easily got hold of Catriona's address. She sent Catriona a quick text to let her know she was popping over before work, then headed for her place in Caerphilly.

The town was just north of Cardiff, separated from the city by a mere mountain. Cerys' trip through the one-way system took her past the impressive castle and out the other side of town, where she stopped in front of an unassuming house in a cul-de-sac. It had seen better days, but there was something pleasantly 1970s about it, and Cerys was reminded of her own home as she approached the door to knock.

'We don't have salesmen here!' a man's voice shouted through the door, gruff and irate.

'I'm here to see Catriona,' Cerys replied.

'What do you want with my Cat? Buzz off. You boys are all the same. I try to tell her.'

Cerys made a point of ruffling out her helmet hair.

'We work together, Mr...uh, Mr Aitken. Could you just call her?'

'Work together? What, down at the bakery? There are no young men down at the bakery. Have you been snooping around there? Hoping for the leavings?'

'Dad, get out of the way.'

The door finally opened, with Catriona half-in her uniform, leaning around an old man with grey hair and a suspicious expression on his face.

'Oh, you're one of those lesbians, are you? Didn't know we had them down the bakery neither.'

'Leave it, Dad. Cerys and I need to...well, we need to work on a project, before...before school. Mrs Thomas will be here soon.'

'I hate Mrs Thomas,' he grumbled. 'She doesn't clean like your mother.'

Cerys stepped inside and realised nothing had changed here since the 1970s. She followed Catriona down the hallway, as her father shuffled into the kitchen, still grumbling.

'You'll be in your room, will you?'

'Yes, Dad.'

Catriona went upstairs and Cerys followed her. There were photographs of Catriona through her school years, but nothing after. As if time had stopped when she was just fifteen. However, the top floor of the house was a completely different place. Fresh paint, photographs from university, from work parties, from the ramblers' society. Aside from the bathroom, there were three bedrooms and two of the doors were open.

Catriona led her into a den of sorts, with a widescreen TV, gaming consoles, and a desk housing pieces of a computer. She settled herself on the sofa and gestured for Cerys to do the same.

'I guess you didn't get my message.'

Cerys pulled out her phone to check, but Catriona just kept on talking.

'It just upsets him, that's all. New people, new things. He'll have forgotten all about it by this afternoon, but that's not the point. He'll be a nightmare for Mrs Thomas now.'

'I'm sorry,' Cerys said, unsure what else she was meant to say.

'You're not the first,' she said, matter-of-factly. 'Anyway, what's gone wrong?'

'We lost Jason's tracking device and Amy walked into an underground bunker surrounded by armed guards.' She paused for a second, before continuing: 'Owain's probably in there too. Jury's out on whether that's better or worse.'

Catriona pulled a face. She was one of the few people who had been more screwed over by Owain Jenkins than Cerys, losing her dream job in South Wales Police's Cyber Crime department when Owain defected to the National Crime Agency.

'They're probably using a jammer to block GPS signals. They'd probably also cover mobile phone communication. That's what I would do – if it were legal, which it's not.'

'I really doubt they care, Cat.'

'Don't.' The word was harsh, bitten out. 'It's Catriona, okay?'

'Okay. So, how do we get around it?'

Cerys could sense Catriona's relief that they were moving on, that she wasn't pushing it. She'd been an expert at rubbing raw spots, probing at them to find weaknesses, to bring people down. To protect her own closely-guarded wounds. Her instructors said it was a gift. It was now telling her to stay clear if she wanted to be Catriona's friend –and she did. She liked having friends she didn't have to beat down.

'We don't,' Catriona said. 'The only way to disrupt the jammer is at the source. Amy might be able to do it, if she knows what she's looking for and has access to the device. I doubt Owain's going to let her anywhere near it, though. He's a controlling bastard, that man. No offence.'

'None taken,' Cerys said, evenly.

Cerys had never considered Owain controlling, but then she'd never seen him at work. Part of what exasperated him about her was not being able to pin her down – to *rely on her*, as he put it. Cerys hadn't been looking to be reliable, to encourage dependence. She already had her mam in her life. That was enough smothering love.

'Cat! You'll be late for the bus!'

'I'm getting a lift, Dad,' Catriona shouted back.

'Not on that bike, you're not!'

Catriona stood up and irritably slammed the door, like the teenager she was pretending to be.

'What about if we didn't want to get around it?' Cerys said slowly. 'What if we just wanted to find it?'

Catriona's face changed from irritation to excitement in an instant. 'Yes! Follow the noise! If we can track the edges of the jamming signal, we can guess at its centre.'

Catriona picked up a box of what appeared to Cerys to be metallic junk and pulled out a piece of circuitry.

'I think I can put something together. Give me a day? After work. Is that all right? We can go tonight.'

Cerys grinned. She was so glad this smart woman was on their side.

'Tonight.'

Chapter 16: No One's Driving This Train

Amy was woken at 5am by six angry security guys all wanting access to their lockers, and again at 6am by six tetchy surveillance agents. She regretted her life choices.

Stuck at the back of the queue for the shower, she observed that there was an absence of casual chat, which suited her temperament entirely but was useless for finding anything out. She grabbed a couple of pieces of toast from the canteen at the opposite end of the bunker, before making her way to the Eye Room to start her shift bang on eight o'clock.

Owain was there already, wearing the same clothes, as if he hadn't gone to bed at all. Even she knew that was a bad look. Jason's policing of the wash basket stopped her wearing the same cardigan every day for a fortnight, but she hadn't truly understood his objections until now. The other agents were all subtly veering away from Owain, spending a little too long looking at his clothes, the slight slump of his shoulders.

The Eye Day shift took their places, while Amy hovered awkwardly near the door in her one off-white top and black jeans. Without turning round, Owain beckoned her forward to his standing desk at the back.

'Agent Haas has been informed,' he murmured. 'I need you to provide oversight of this room today.'

She opened her mouth to panic at him, to tell him she had literally no idea how to oversee a room – any room, really, but particularly this room full of smart people with superior technology and their very own Stanford experiment. Then, she took a deep breath and remembered she was an NCA agent, she oversaw intelligence gathering for a living, and she could adapt to working in a room like this.

A little thing like this didn't threaten to break her anymore. Not if she could just keep breathing. *Fake it 'til you make it.*

'Of course, Agent Jenkins,' she said, her voice taut but controlled.

'Your access has been extended.' He gestured at her laptop. 'I'll be in my office.'

He left the room without waiting for a response from her, leaving her in charge of the show. As she booted up her laptop, she heard someone on the right say, 'He'll be in bed, more like'.

She felt a tension fill her shoulders, but she said nothing. This was the part she really had no idea how to handle – the management of people. She had never operated as a handler in the NCA, only as their source of information and technological fixes. She was technically the boss of Jason, but he usually managed himself and he never made petty comments about his co-workers – at least, none she didn't agree with.

How was she meant to handle insubordination? How did Owain handle it? This part was new to him too. In the police, he had worked as Bryn's partner before heading the Cyber Crime division, but he'd only had Catriona working with him. In the NCA, he had been Amy's handler, nothing more. Wasn't he equally out of his depth in this environment?

Which posed the question, why had Frieda sent a relatively junior and inexperienced agent to manage this operation? Maybe Owain was here for a different reason altogether. One skillset he did have was solving murders. Frieda had accepted her presence here very readily. Was it because she shared those skills? Was Owain really here to find out who murdered Mole?

Not that he would tell her if he were. Owain now played his cards close to his chest. If he wanted her here, he must have a good reason, or he would've sent her back to the flat. That possibility was still on the table and they both knew it. He had always been reluctant to use the powers he'd been given over her, but she knew that he would if he felt it was necessary. Owain was a good soldier when it was Frieda giving the orders.

Was she also a good soldier? This place was already a horror story – a secret military experiment designed to study the formation of terrorist cells. She wondered what had happened to the other experiments, how they had ended. Had it been bloody? Had there been casualties? Deaths?

Amy was not Frieda's puppet. She had to tell someone about this, but who? What could Bryn do about it? Would he even believe her? If she couldn't persuade Bryn, then there was no point going to a journalist. What would the NCA do if they felt their secret was being threatened? Would they come after her? After Jason?

She knew how to do the right thing, even if it was the illegal thing, but she also knew how to survive. She had survived by taking Frieda's job and avoiding prison. She had to first survive this experiment on the opposite side to Jason, and then they could work on tearing it down, on running if they had to. She had played Frieda's games for too long.

For the time being, she had to focus on the here and now. Amy logged in to her laptop and connected to the local network inside the bunker. She seemed to have managerial level access, because she could view basic employee information for all the current and past agents in the bunker, as well as the anticipated surveillance feeds and logs.

From the notes, it appeared that each agent was assigned two prisoners and, with their partner on the night shift, they monitored their charges continuously. The prisoners, like the agents, were identified by their position rather than any defining feature – and just like the agents, when one left, another came in to take his place.

Jason was designated P8. He was being monitored by ID4 and IN4, and he had inherited his number from Mole. The files on the prisoners were empty of any identifiable information – the only reason Amy could place Mole was because his file contained the word 'DECEASED'. Instead, the files listed their criminal convictions and some strange bits of trivia, like the fact P9 had lost an expensive watch and P6 had an anchor tattoo.

Amy pulled up the logs for P8. She scrolled back through the record until she came to the first week of March. The entries were brief, mundane: 'AM: 5am rise, shower, breakfast, washing up, laundry. PM: lunch prep, lunch, washing up, cleaning, dinner prep, dinner, washing up.' Over and over, the same thing. Mole's final days had been filled with thankless tasks.

The log entries ended on 4th March. His last documented action was washing up on Wednesday night, then nothing. Was his death not considered notable? For an awful moment, Amy considered that this might not be the first death in the compound, that this was a mundane, everyday thing to them. To be swept under the carpet, but to be expected.

She checked the entries for other prisoners on the date. 5th March was blank for all of them. Had someone on-high shut down those entries as part of a cover-up? Had they been replaced in reports to the higher-ups with more laundry and dinner prep? Surely that was unthinkable – that a man could die in a place like this and no record of it survive.

No written record.

There it was, the missing link. These were reports on a screen, but they were made by people. People currently sitting in this room or sleeping the day away in their bunks. The people were still here. If she wanted to know what had happened on 5th March 2016, she had to question the people.

The thought of interrogating strangers made her queasy. She had done it once before, trapped in a building with people she needed to question, and it had gone badly wrong from the first attempt. She could feel herself starting to panic and took a deep breath, then another. She focused on the sensation of breathing, like she'd been taught, the connection of her shoes to the ground and her fingers to the keys, the low hum of technology all around her.

Setting aside the daunting prospect of interviewing agents, Amy returned to the familiar: the data. She couldn't find any link to the original video footage, so that would take some digging. However, the text entries for 6th March were freely available in all the records.

In an entry for P7, the agent had written: 'AM: 5am rise, shower, discovered body (P8), raised alarm (G), attended meeting (G), lunch prep.' The least absorbing way to write about a corpse in the history of crime.

Who was G? She double-checked the records and couldn't find any labelled G. She opened P1 and found it blank. The records started with P2, documenting every move of the other eleven prisoners, but completely omitting one.

Who was this prisoner and why was his record completely suppressed?

Her gaze drifted away from her computer screen to the position on the far left of the room: ID1. It must be ID1 and IN1 who monitored P1, but where did they record their findings? Was Owain privy to that information or did it get reported directly to someone further up the chain?

Amy shut her laptop irritably. She only had more questions, and no obvious answers. The information was there, but it was either locked away or contained only within people's heads. The first, at least, was hackable, but the second?

She would need a lifetime to crack it.

Chapter 17: Dig for Victory

The ground was surprisingly soft considering how bloody cold it was, and Jason started to enjoy the mindless task of turning over the earth.

He discovered that Stoker knew a lot about gardening. Prison rules said you didn't talk about another man's crimes, but Jason was beginning to wonder how this mild-mannered, green-thumbed giant had ended up inside. They were planting out potatoes and peas today, as March was the best time for them. Next week, they were going for carrots and turnips, but only under glass. This was really recycled old windows found in a pile of junk down the side of the building.

Jason had looked through the rubbish heap while collecting more glass but found nothing to write home about. It had obviously been picked clean of useful things by the inmates long before he arrived. The junk was mostly building materials, as if they'd stripped down the building but had forgotten to take anything away. The old windows were single-glazed in wooden frames, whereas the building now had double-glazed, vented windows more suited to its new purpose.

Gareth had laid out some crumbling bricks in a rough square, ready for Jason to set the glass on top. There were already half a dozen of these – what had Stoker called them? Cool frames, cold frames, something like that. They were building two more today, ready for the carrot planting. Beside them, there were two big plastic cylinders, one with a tap like a keg and the other with a hatch and the smell of rotting vegetables. If they were making their own compost, they were taking this thing seriously.

As Jason carefully laid down the old window, he looked for where Gareth had got to. He watched him bending over a frame, touching oddly at the glass. When he looked up, he swiped at his eyes, and then stared hard at his audience, as if daring Jason to question him.

'You miss him,' Jason said.

He was fishing more than anything. If Gareth was missing someone from in here, he might give something away; if it was about something else, he'd contradict him. People just loved to be right and making

91

statements about other people was the fastest way to find out the truth of them.

'So what if I do?' Gareth said. 'Doesn't make me gay or nothing. Just sad, isn't it? He loved those peppers. It's wrong that he ended out here.'

'Who did?' Jason asked, remembering that he was supposed to play dumb.

Gareth looked over towards where Stoker, Anchor, and Dreadlock were working on the planting, before taking a step closer.

'I don't like you, Jay Bird, but I reckon everyone here has the right to know. A man died here, just before you came. Went by the name of Mole, the one what loved the peppers – loved all the planting and cooking. Doing all the jobs you've got now, because he was a sucker who couldn't play poker. Sweet with it, though. Knew he was dumb as shit and just got on with it. The Governor was sweet on him, I think – not in a gay way. He was useful to him, kept his papers in order, though I don't think he could read too good. He was just tidy. Been here the longest too, right from the beginning.'

Jason tried to take in this burst of information quickly, but he was still stuck on the first sentence. What had he done to earn Gareth's dislike? He'd only been there five minutes! Suddenly, it clicked, where he'd recognised him from. He was one of Stuart Williams' boys, part of a gang that Jason and Lewis had opposed as soon as they were old enough to understand the word 'enemy'. Jason was surprised he hadn't already tried to punch his lights out. Then again, Stuart had been on the out ever since his big drug dreams had been doomed by the death of the mastermind behind them. Maybe Gareth figured it was better to be Jason's friend than his rival, especially in here where Stuart and his reputation couldn't protect him.

Having worked out why he knew Gareth, Jason belatedly thought to follow up on the real information. 'The Governor must be gutted to lose him.'

'He doesn't say much, really. Keeps himself to himself. But he'll need a new errand boy.'

That wasn't like the Martin that Jason had known – the stammering man who anxiously rambled his way through a meeting. It seemed prison had taught him to keep his mouth shut, that silent deadly men were the most intimidating kind. Coupled with his crimes, that might be enough to explain how he had managed to crown himself king of this place.

'You fancy the job?'

Gareth laughed, drawing the attention of Dreadlock. He saluted at him and continued.

'My writing's fucking awful – proper chicken scrawl. I was never into the accounts with Stuart. That was more the domain of your boy Damage.'

Jason felt the emotional punch to his gut as keenly as if it had been delivered by Gareth's fist. Damage was Lewis' little brother, murdered just to frame Jason for the deed. He would still lie awake at night, wondering what would've happened if he'd just stayed home that night. Damage would be alive, but the drug scene in Cardiff would've been a very different place, a more dangerous and cruel place. He just wasn't cut out to weigh lives, to judge if a thing was for the many or the few.

'I heard Lewis tried to end you after that.'

Jason couldn't read the tone of his voice. Was he pleased? Disappointed?

'You heard right.'

'You sorted it out, did you?'

'We did.'

'Good thing and all. Don't want no more deaths here. It's bad for the Project.'

'Jay Bird! You'd better start on lunch!' Dreadlock's voice boomed across the garden.

Before Jason could ask anything more, either about the murder or the Project, Gareth was back to contemplation of the frames and Stoker was bounding across to him, ushering him back round the front of the building and the only door in or out.

How was he supposed to find out information if he could barely spend any time alone with anyone? He hadn't even caught two minutes alone with Lewis! He just hoped Amy was having more luck, wherever she was, and that Cerys was keeping her out of trouble. Who was he kidding? Amy was probably fretting and Cerys was related to him, so trouble stuck to her like glue.

He had to make his own luck, right here. It was the only way out.

Chapter 18: Evidence of Absence

Owain relieved Amy of her post just before lunchtime.

He still didn't look like he'd slept, the circles beneath his eyes deep and dark, but he smelled of shower gel and he wore new clothes, so that was something. She shut her laptop before he could look over her shoulder, though she was sure all their browsing was logged for posterity. Frieda was nothing if not thorough.

'Stay out of trouble,' he told her.

How exactly she could find trouble in a sealed underground bunker, she didn't know, but if he thought she would hide in the locker room until bedtime, he was very much mistaken. Day and night were much the same here, the same strip lighting levels 24/7 making sneaking around theoretically impossible. However, at all times everyone was very much occupied either with sleeping or working or eating, leaving the corridors empty except for the fetching of coffee supplies or a trip to the toilet.

Returning to the locker room, she stored her new laptop in her locker and removed a small set of lockpicks from one of the hidden pockets in the rucksack. Jason had given her a lesson once in how to use them, but he was rusty and she had barely been paying attention. Still, some of it might've lodged in her brain and she hadn't much other choice.

Burying the tools in her jeans pocket, she headed back out into the corridor to take a look around. To her right, there were a pair of bathrooms and dormitories. The men's bathroom was directly opposite the women's, and she pushed open the door a few inches to peer inside. They were an exact mirror of each other, except for a standard row of urinals down one wall.

She hurried past the surveillance room and the exit door, to the next door on the left. It opened to reveal the laundry room, with one washing machine and one tumble dryer. There was the strong smell of detergent and a couple of mesh bags queued up on the floor, waiting their turn. It was a sad little room that reflected the sad little lives lived in this bunker.

The next door down had a small window with closed blinds, which she immediately pegged as Owain's office. Across the corridor was a closed door with no distinguishing features except that it was locked with a keypad. Of course it was. Who the hell used mechanical locks these days, especially in military-style bunkers?

It was a digital keypad and she inspected it for signs of wear. The 1 key looked a little scuffed, but otherwise she could find no distinguishing marks. She didn't know who had locked this door, so she couldn't begin to phish for information about them. Owain probably knew, but he wasn't going to hand over that intel to her. She looked around for any cameras trained on the corridor – who watches the watchers? – but she couldn't see anything obvious.

She scanned the wall for weaknesses where she might access the wires directly, though manual overrides were not her strength, and noticed that the floor was filthy. Whoever's responsibility it was to clean and empty the bins wasn't doing a very good job. How did you even provide security clearance for cleaners in a place like this?

She caught herself staring at a perfect boot print in the dust, a brownish tinge suggesting mud had been tracked in from outside – probably when they had brought her in last night. Had it only been last night? It already felt like an age.

So much had happened in the last forty-eight hours – their plan to leave, frantically finding equipment from all their sources, and then… yesterday evening.

Amy felt her face flush just thinking about it and forced the memory down. She was no good to Jason if she was daydreaming about his body instead of focusing on getting him out of there. Back to their flat, back to their bed…

Focus.

She was still staring at the boot print. Suddenly, seized with inspiration, she pulled down the sleeve of her cardigan, scooped up a pile of dust, and wiped it over the keypad. Gently blowing on it, she found that the most pieces were stuck to only four keys: 1, 2, 3, and 4.

Rolling her eyes at such poor security, she pressed the numbers in order and the light flashed red. Maybe not such terrible security after all. The numbers were unlikely to represent a birthday, but could be the date of a wedding anniversary or other recent event. Of course, it could be a random code that just happened to use those four numbers, and then she was stuffed.

Unless…

Amy entered the other obvious combination and the door flashed green. Opening it with a smirk, she allowed herself another little eye roll. Entering the numbers backwards did not a sound security system make.

The air inside was stale, as if the door hadn't been opened for days or weeks. It was also surprisingly loud, and she quickly shut the door behind her, so the noise didn't carry down the corridor. Fumbling for a light switch, she was greeted by a sleek, modern server coupled with its cooling system, plus a couple of filing cabinets, a compact desk, and a folding bed. A coaster on the desk had a pattern of 0s and 1s and, when Amy looked closer, it appeared to say GENIUS in binary.

This was the lair of an IT technician. So, where the hell were they?

IN3 had told her there were no other technicians here, but she hadn't said that she was first. She recalled now the security agent saying that 'the new technician' had arrived, again implying that she had a predecessor. Where had they gone – and when?

A couple of laptops were stashed next to the folding bed, this room a kind of all-purpose storage cupboard as well as the tech office and server room. One appeared to have been the victim of a coffee spillage, while the other had been cannibalised for parts. It was likely then that her laptop was the one belonging to the former technician.

Deciding that this was going to be her base from now on, Amy returned to the locker room, retrieved her NCA laptop and backpack, and returned to the office. If she could work out the programming code for the keypad, she could reset the passcode and be guaranteed some privacy. Owain wouldn't like it, but she was done trying to please Owain.

Logging back in to the laptop, Amy tried to locate any maintenance logs. She found the reporting mechanism easily enough, but couldn't see the previously submitted logs. The former TD1 must've had some way of accessing them and of being informed when there was a new request. Amy checked the secure messaging system to see if there was an additional tab and found all her messages were gone. In their place, she had four unread maintenance requests and hundreds more archived.

She was now TD1. Agent Lane had been put to rest, and she had inherited an identity.

Scrolling through the previous maintenance requests, Amy started to get a feel for the previous technician's abilities. The basic IT support skills were evident, including familiarity with NCA software, as well as a reasonably high degree of practical technological know-how. Most of the requests concerned the surveillance of the inmates, as Owain had told her – fixing and replacing broken cameras, finding better angles, increasing the gain on microphones, improving the night vision, and a list of a hundred impossible things. She was sure that the agents wanted an accurate heat map of the building, but they weren't getting one any time soon.

If she was to maintain the surveillance systems, there had to be a map of the system somewhere. She had a list of camera feeds, but no sense of the shape of the compound or where the surveillance devices were located. She could probably get a sense of it by watching the feeds for an hour or two, following inmates as they moved through the building, but that wouldn't help her locate the blind spots or the positions of the broken cameras.

It made sense that the map might not be available to all the agents, as there might be feeds that the supervisor kept privileged or that ID1 and IN1 used to follow their top-secret inmate. It might even be the case that there wasn't supposed to be a map, but the technician had to keep track of their assets. In a situation like that, they might even have to resort to paper.

She started hunting around the room for a large marked piece of paper but came up empty. She did locate cleaning supplies – yet another function of this multi-purpose room – and briefly panicked that it might be her job to tidy up. Jason would break himself laughing if he found out.

Yet something was wrong here. Would any decent IT technician allow bleach near their precious server? The smell was strong in that corner, so it seemed that some had already spilled, but the bottle appeared sealed. As she bent closer, she realised the mop was sitting in a bucket half-filled with murky water – and the stench of barely-diluted bleach.

She experimentally moved the mop, and it caught on something floating in the water. Lifting it a couple of inches clear of the bucket, she found greyish clumps sticking to the fronds of the mop. She knew better than to try to touch them, but they looked a lot like soggy bits of paper. The aftermath of an attempt to destroy a paper record, perhaps even the map she was looking for.

She put the mop back, leaving it all exactly where she'd found it. Until she could reset the lock, she wanted whoever had tried to destroy the papers to believe they were undetected. Returning to her laptop, she double-checked the maintenance request. The last read message was from 2nd March. The first unread message was from 6th March, listing several broken cameras. Deliberately broken cameras? Cameras that TD1 hadn't repaired on purpose?

This couldn't be a coincidence. The person responsible for maintaining surveillance disappears at the time when the need for surveillance was at its peak. Where was the former TD1? Had they disappeared, or had they been disappeared?

And now that Amy wore that identity, was she in danger of disappearing too?

Chapter 19: A Cold Front

Jason had thrown together a passable vegetable pasta for lunch. He was rooting out the ingredients for a corned beef hash for dinner, when Lewis knocked on the door.

'He's all right with me,' Lewis said to Stoker.

Stoker hesitated for a moment, before nodding slowly. With his departure, Jason lost his shadow for the first time since he'd arrived. He grinned at Lewis and pulled him into a hug, nearly squeezing the life out of him and receiving a bone-crusher in return.

'Y'alright, butt?'

'What the fuck are you doing here?'

Jason hadn't expected that level of disbelief, or the edge of anger that sat beneath it.

'I've come to rescue you, haven't I?'

'Rescue me? From what? The best deal I've been offered since I went inside?'

Jason blinked at him for a moment, before shaking his head slowly. 'What deal?'

'Early release, no more record, free as a fucking bird. What are you sticking your nose in for? How did you even find out about…'

Lewis trailed off, and then his expression turned stormy.

'I will murder that little fucker.'

'Don't fuck Alby up,' Jason said, holding up his hands as if to defend them both. 'He genuinely seemed worried about you.'

'Like hell he did. He was just pissed off that he didn't get to finish the Project, because he can't stop thieving for five fucking minutes. What's there to worry about anyway? This place is safer than inside – their people must watch us twenty-four hours a day. What could go wrong?'

'It's fucked up, Lewis! You're talking about twenty-four hour watchers as if that's a *good* thing? That's before you even consider that a man was fucking murdered.'

It was Lewis' turn to stare.

'Is that what Alby told you?' he said slowly. 'That Mole was murdered?'

Jason was thrown again. 'Wasn't he?'

Lewis leaned against the countertop, seeming to give the question serious thought. Jason picked up the bottle of Worcestershire sauce and threw it hand to hand, watching Lewis' face for any signs of where this was going.

'I found him out in the garden,' Lewis said, eventually. 'It was cold out and he…well, he was blue and stiff. There was frost all over him. He was lying in one of the furrows we'd dug for potatoes – maybe he'd been trying to keep warm.'

'In the garden? What would he have been doing out there?'

'He'd put the compost out after dinner. Maybe the wind caught the door—'

"Maybe the wind caught it'? Are they growing weed in that garden, Lulu? Open your fucking eyes!'

Lewis shifted awkwardly against the countertop. 'Maybe he took too long—'

'Maybe someone murdered him and stuck the body out in the elements.'

'Murdered him how? There wasn't a mark on him, Jay. I saw that much.'

'Drowning,' Jason said.

'Where? In the shower?'

'Right here, in the sink.'

Lewis pushed away from the counter, throwing his arms up in despair.

'You are fucking raving.'

'You don't think it's a possibility? We're not exactly surrounded by angels here.'

'Mole was all right, though. Nothing about him that any man could object to. Not enough to off him and dump him.'

'Alby was convinced he was murdered.'

'Alby has always been a scared kid, Jay. You know that. If they hadn't voted him out, he would've been wailing to take the other bastard's place.'

'You think there's nothing to it then? That Mole just died of cold out there, because the door closed on him?'

Lewis turned back to face him, and sighed, bone-deep and weary. 'Well, now I don't.'

Jason flashed him a smile. 'So, you'll help me find who killed him?'

Lewis still wasn't smiling. 'If you fuck this up for me, Jay…'

'The record's gone, Lulu – I've seen it myself. You're already walking free as soon as this thing's done.'

'You gonna cover my 10K too?'

Jason gave a low whistle. 'Alby got 10K out of this?'

'Not Alby, no. It's for the Project – and don't even fucking ask me about it. Stoker's warned you once.'

He sighed in exasperation, briefly sounding exactly like his mother.

'Fine. I'll be your better half again. Though what've you done with your girl?'

Jason was about to protest that Amy wasn't *his girl*, but that wasn't really true anymore, was it? The hesitation was enough to bring a wicked grin to Lewis' face.

'That took you fucking long enough. What you done with her then? I thought she was the NCA's bitch now?'

'She's out there somewhere.' Jason gestured towards the walls. 'Keeping an eye on things.'

'She's probably not, y'know. They've got some kind of signal blocking in this place – a couple of the lads smuggled in tech, but it's useless.'

'She'll find a way,' Jason said. 'It's what she does. Or she'll be beating down the door.'

'That's proper terrifying that is. What do you need me to do then?'

'Is there anyone we can rely on in here, to help me out even if they don't have the whole picture? What about that Stoker bloke?'

'Ben? Yeah, I guess Ben is trustworthy enough. He'll want to know why though.'

'Ben's one of the upper class though, isn't he?'

'Only because no one else has got the size for it. He's fair, so the norms like him, and he's hard, so the elites don't mess with him. And don't call him Ben. He won't like that I told you.'

Jason looked at him strangely. 'Private name, is it?'

'Something about reputation,' Lewis said quickly. 'What you doing for dinner then?'

'Corned beef hash. What reputation?'

'Wind your neck in, Jay.'

'All right, all right.'

Jason threw the bottle of sauce and Lewis caught it in his right hand, flipping it over in the air and into his left.

'What's your first move then?' Lewis asked.

'Oh, easy,' Jason said. 'I need to speak to the Governor.'

Chapter 21: 2πr

With Catriona's dad safely tucked up at his sister's, they were free to test out her new toys.

Cerys hadn't been able to follow half of what Catriona was saying, but it was something about a raspberry and a dongle, which sounded more like a sex game than a piece of tech. Whatever it was, it made Catriona act like she'd stuffed her face with cotton candy and was riding the buzz until she crashed out in the car on the way home.

It was already dark when they arrived at roughly the position where Jason's GPS signal had disappeared. Cerys parked the bike up on the verge, and Catriona waved her box of wires around.

'I'm detecting a jamming signal,' she said. 'It's working on multiple frequencies, as we suspected. How far along do you think the entrance was, where you were ambushed?'

'About two hundred yards, maybe three hundred. It's a dead end up ahead.'

Catriona juggled her tablet with the box, struggling to hold both in one hand and mark the spot, while sporting a pair of bright pink gloves that clashed with everything else she was wearing.

'Give it here,' Cerys said, taking the tablet and removing her leather glove with her teeth.

She walked a few paces back down the road, until the tablet found a signal again. Dropping a pin on the map, she then followed the road ahead with her finger and dropped another pin where the gate was. The map Catriona was using had it down as a 'private road', but Cerys hadn't seen any signs.

'What do we do now?' she called to Catriona.

She walked down the road to join her, her hiking boots shedding dried mud on the road. 'How far were you escorted before you got to the tunnel?'

'I don't know distances. We were walking maybe twenty minutes, but slow.'

'Let's call it a mile. In a straight line?'

'Hard to tell in the dark, but not too twisty.'

Catriona retrieved her tablet, exchanging it for her box of bits, and dropped a translucent circle about a mile distant from the gate in the same direction.

'Some of the jamming fields are unidirectional and some are full circles, or half-circles. It makes sense they'd have a jammer pointed at their gate, but they might not have one covering their arse. If we drive around to the other side, we can get a better idea of where the middle is.'

Catriona sent directions to Cerys' phone and they returned to the bike. Catriona was a good pillion passenger, leaning with the twists and turns of the Welsh country roads, and not anxious like Amy or complaining like Jason. She'd only pouted a little when Cerys had pointed out how badly her flame red hair clashed with Cerys' pink passenger helmet.

They drove as close as they could get to the spot Catriona had marked, which was in the middle of some farmer's field. They climbed over a gate with a sign that read 'PRIVATE KEEP OUT', because Catriona liked to ramble and Cerys had never paid much attention to warnings. It was white paint on wood, which made it unlikely to be a Ministry of Defence warning, but then they hadn't advertised their presence anywhere else in the area.

Holding her weird little tracking box in front of her like a divining rod, Catriona marched across the field, with Cerys in her wake, shining a torch to light their way and carrying the tablet with the map. They had overshot Catriona's estimate by about five hundred yards by the time the little box started beeping, right on the edge of the woodland bordering the field.

'If the woods are where they're lurking, it makes sense that their field covers only their lands,' Catriona said. 'They probably have the ability to customise the borders to a certain extent and it's better to overshoot on their private road than on some farmer's land.'

Suddenly, out of nowhere, a border collie lunged at them from the darkness, barking and snarling as it leapt at them. Catriona yelped and dived behind Cerys, who found herself squaring off against the dog with nothing but a torch.

She swung the high-intensity beam into the dog's face and the creature leapt away, yelping.

'Oi! Haven't you ramblers done enough damage? I've got a gun, you know.'

'South Wales Police.' Catriona shouted into the darkness. 'Call off your dog!'

A sharp whistle, and the collie was off like a shot. After a couple of minutes, a middle-aged farmer in a bodywarmer and a tweed flatcap entered their circle of light.

'What are you doing out here then?' he said, suspiciously. 'You're a bit far from home.'

Catriona held up her badge for him to inspect.

'Detective Constable Catriona Aitken. We're investigating your complaints of trespass. It's, uh, part of a national operation.'

The man's suspicion melted away to be replaced by a triumphant smirk.

'I knew there was something fishy about the whole business. I thought that young copper was having me on when he told me to report all the goings-on, but maybe he had the right of it.'

'Just to clarify the information we have,' Cerys said, knowing they possessed precisely no information, 'when did you first see the trespassers?'

'That was about two full years ago, that was. Thought they could come use my gate to move things into the council's woods by there. I told them to get gone, but they just moved it all in the night. Back and forth they were, for two or three weeks. Since then, it's just been a few odd blokes – all wearing black, like they're in a spy movie or something. Meg likes to go for them, but the last lot sprayed her with something. Affected her eyes real bad, it did.'

'Can you remember what things they were moving?'

'Fence posts and rolls of that chainlink stuff, like they were going to enclose the woods. However, I've never seen any sign of it from my fields, and I've got land on two sides of them. When your lot didn't do much, I called up the Council, and they said the land had been quarantined. Quarantine! Wouldn't tell me why though. We've had no trouble here with disease or the like, and we're Farm Assured, so we'd know about it. It's probably the military acting up again.'

'What makes you say that?' Catriona asked.

'It's always them round here, coming in where they're not wanted. Mind you, the pubs haven't seen any squaddies and there's no noise or nothing. It's all a strange business, if you ask me. As is sending you two young girls out here at night with your fancy gadgets.'

'We're just checking for radon,' Catriona said brightly, then noted the look of horror on his face. 'Nothing to suggest we'll find any, but as you say, the Council was a little vague on the particulars. Private contractors. You know how it is.'

'Bloody Tories get everywhere,' the farmer said sagely. 'I'll leave you to it then. Don't suppose you'll take a whisky after?'

'We'll be fine,' Cerys said, amused.

'Suit yourselves. Don't get lost in those woods now. There's trouble in there.'

Chapter 21: Taking Stock

Securing an audience with the Governor turned out to be surprisingly easy.

Lewis had a word with Stoker, who had a word with Dreadlock, who told Jason the Governor would expect him at nine o'clock with an up-to-date requisition list. Jason spent the next hour trying to make sense of dear departed Mole's system, before he discovered a dusty clipboard of lists in the storage cupboard out in the hallway.

The spelling left a lot to be desired, but there was a tattered printed list of the standard provisions and then notes about the type of things they were permitted to order as specials. Stoker, back at his side, explained that the garden's produce was almost at an end, so onions and potatoes would need to go back on the list.

Jason bumped up the requests for tinned tomatoes, baked beans, and frozen peas, before taking a chance on red wine vinegar and Marmite. He didn't ask for peanut butter. However, his mind was so cluttered with images of tins and calculations about mince that he had almost forgotten the real reason he was seeing the Governor in the first place.

Nikolai, one of the elites, came to fetch him just after nine. He was a tall Eastern European man with a permanent snarl like a ravenous wolf. He escorted Jason to the Governor's office, across the corridor and to the left of the 'Project Room'. As they entered, the Governor had his back to the door, staring at the bare window. Jason and Nikolai remained standing, waiting on the Great Man. Maybe he thought it was a power play, but Jason just thought he looked ridiculous.

He'd changed since they'd last properly seen each other, on that balcony at Amy's old place. He was thinner now, leaner, and he sat with his shoulders set. Unlike that cringing, stammering creature Jason had once known. A whole-life order would do that to a man.

'Nikolai, you can go.'

'I will stay.'

The Governor turned then, twisting on a chair that did not swivel though Jason could see he wished that it did. The awkward plastic thing ruined the effect he was going for, and he looked uncomfortable with the charade.

'There's no need for that.'

'There is a need, sir. We must take care.'

'Fine. The requisition, Jason.'

Jason handed over the clipboard, his mind trying to find a way to fix this. If he couldn't get rid of Nikolai, he'd have to find a way to talk to the Governor without their conversation being clear to the watching man. He'd already given away that he'd recognised Martin, but surely everyone here knew the Cardiff Ripper. There hadn't been another serial killer in Wales for over twenty years – at least, not one who was caught.

'This all seems to be in order.'

'Thanks,' Jason said, quickly, before he could be dismissed. 'I know my style's not quite the same as Mole's, but I'll do my best.'

'He did his job,' Nikolai said bluntly, stepping forward as if to haul Jason out of there.

'Can I just check these figures?' the Governor asked. 'Jason, is that a nine or a seven?'

Jason stepped towards the desk, where the Governor held on to the clipboard. He peered at the number the Governor was pointing to, which was very clearly a seven.

'Uh…seven, I think. I can run and check?'

'No need. I'm sure we won't run out.'

Jason felt a nudge at his side, moved his hand towards the pressure, and felt a scrap of paper catch on his fingers. He grasped it and pulled it up into his palm.

'Anything else?'

'Sir,' Nikolai growled. 'Didn't they teach you manners in Swansea?'

'Anything else, *sir*?'

'Jason and I go back, Kolya. He's having difficulty adjusting, but I'm confident he'll get the hang of things here.'

'I'm sure I will. Sir.'

Keeping the paper in his palm, Jason headed back towards the kitchen.

'No, you go where I can see you. I have cards to play. Come.'

Nikolai herded him down the corridor and into the mess, where some of the others were playing cards. Stoker and Lewis were missing, and Jason hadn't seen Joe since this morning, when Dreadlock had confronted him. Roshan came into the room briefly, but only to pick up a mug of tea before heading back towards the bunkroom.

'Do you play?' Nikolai asked Jason.

Jason looked at the table. They appeared to be playing Texas hold'em, a game he'd never been very good at, and the cards were so worried and torn that every man there probably knew the card just by looking at its back.

'I'll pass,' he said.

'Deal him in,' said Nikolai.

Jason resigned himself to losing what few possessions he had and reluctantly took a seat. He looked at each player in turn, knowing very little about any of them and certainly nothing that would be useful in a poker game.

Gareth looked very intent on his cards, as did Anchor. Bo, the other black elite, was trying to sneak a look at Anchor's cards. Dreadlock was leaning back in his chair, heavy-lidded eyes and loose limbs suggesting he was well on his way to drunk. Pansy wore a similar look, and Jason noticed that the mugs on the table had a clear liquid in them. As he had just thoroughly inventoried the stock cupboard, he was pretty sure there was no alcohol in it.

'It's vodka. Stoker doesn't count his potatoes.' Nikolai pushed a mug in front of Jason, and everyone waited expectantly for him to drink.

Jason drank, careful to control his reaction and swallow it without coughing. It was strong, strong enough to bring tears to his eyes, but he drained the triple-measure without flinching. Nikolai grunted what might have been approval and topped up the mug from an old squash bottle.

'Vodka in your belly, cards in your hand – what could be better, eh? Perhaps you might even win something tonight.'

'Kolya is a hustler,' Dreadlock intoned from his stupor. 'Don't bet anything you'll miss.'

'I am no hustler. I make no secret of the fact I am very, very good.'

Two rounds later, the vodka had gone straight to Jason's head, and the cards in his hand had blurred beyond recognition. They were mostly betting with clothes and portions of meat, as cigarettes were strictly rationed by the Governor and doled out daily. Jason had already given over the first helpings at dinner for a week to Nikolai, and a red T-shirt to Pansy.

Dreadlock had fallen asleep, snoring softly in the corner. Nikolai topped up everyone's mugs and lapsed into a language Jason couldn't understand. Bo and Gareth said nothing at all, but Pansy would not shut up, trying to get people to increase their bets.

'Hey, Jay—Jay Bird, is it? What did you bring with you? Have you got a watch? I like a watch. What about any contraband? A nice little phone, maybe? I'll even take a USB stick!'

Jason flicked up his sweater to show his boring analogue watch, and watched Pansy give an exaggerated eye roll.

'You blokes are all the damn same. Barely a functional piece of tech between you. All right, all right – what else you got to play with? How about a shag with your boy, yeah?'

Jason felt his body tense, heard the room inhale, and carefully laid his pair of cards face-down on the table. How he dealt with this would affect his whole time here. He had to play it right. Except he was swimming in high-proof, homemade vodka and he didn't have the best control of his temper on his better days.

'What did you say?' he ground out.

'Come on – everyone knows you know Lulu. Was this something you cooked up together, yeah? Send him in, get Stoker hooked good, and then bring a little rearguard action to claim your cash? Tell me you're at least pimping that beta.'

Jason knew they were all waiting on the answer. Seeing where Jason – and, by extension, Lewis – would settle in the hierarchy. Lewis had only been here a couple of weeks and it didn't seem like he'd made a lot of friends. Except this Stoker bloke, and that was drawing the wrong kind of attention. Jason was already fucking done with these prison games.

'Yeah, I know Lewis,' he said, finally. 'We ran together as kids.'

'Since you were kids, yeah? Were you his first then, Jay Bird? Did you pop that little cocksucker's cherry?'

Jason saw red.

'He's under my protection, Pansy. That clear for you? Or you need it written out in blood?'

He knew he had fucked up as soon as the words were out, the mood in the room hot and thick, like a volcano about to erupt. He had to fix it and fast.

'I fuck women,' he said, and then belched. 'Which is more than can be said for little boys like you. You even seen a real one, Pansy?'

A couple of laughs from around the table broke the tension. Jason noted they came from Gareth and Anchor. It was always good to know who was on your side, who enjoyed seeing the kid squirm. They might not be Jason's friends yet, but at least they weren't Pansy's.

'I've fucked lots of women.' The kid blushed to his ears, which didn't exactly work for his credibility. 'I'm a PUA, I am. Bet you don't even know The Rules.'

'I never needed rules to get laid. That's for your tiny painted men to go to war.'

Jason was comfortable now. He knew how to target nerd kids like this. He remembered how to be a bully, how he looked down on the kids who liked computers, science fiction, and tabletop roleplay. All the kind of things Amy embraced. If he'd known Amy when he was at school, he would've ignored her or shoved her in the corridor. What a dick he had been. How easy it was to slip right back into it.

'Pansy's got those playing cards with topless girls on them,' Gareth chimed in. 'Like a dirty old sailor.'

'Nothing wrong with a dirty old sailor.' Anchor hauled up his sleeve to show a pin-up girl flashing her assets on his bicep.

Everyone laughed, Jason picked up his cards, and the game moved on.

Chapter 22: Fly-by

At 7am on Tuesday morning, Catriona knocked on the door of the Carr house, looking for Cerys.

'Want to bunk off work?' she asked.

While Gwen made them bacon butties, Catriona explained her plan two or three times before Cerys' morning head really got the message.

'You want to fly a drone over the woodland to get aerial photos of the site. Will we be able to see anything?'

'Maybe.' Catriona pushed her tablet across the table. 'Take a look at that.'

Cerys peered at the screen, rubbing at her eyes to dislodge the sleep. It appeared to be a zoomed-in map application in satellite mode.

'I see…trees?'

'Mostly trees, yes. But look here. This could be a clearing. Big enough for a decent-sized building anyway. Definitely big enough if it's below the tree canopy. It might all be underground and then we wouldn't see much of anything, but we don't have anything else to go on.'

'Do you have a drone just lying around?'

Catriona lifted her backpack from under the table and pulled out a small cross-shaped device in black, with little propellers and a mount for a small digital camera.

'You'll have to move your robot just a little bit, *bach*.'

Catriona moved it onto one of the chairs, as Gwen served them breakfast before taking her own toast into the living room. Since Jason had started working with Amy and Cerys had joined the police, she had given up trying to understand the conversations they had with their friends.

Cerys took a bite of the butty, washed it down with a swig of tea, and then gave Catriona her full attention, the caffeine starting to do its work.

'Won't the drone have problems with the jammer?'

'I've thought of that. If I pre-programme a flight path in metres rather than relying on GPS coordinates, it shouldn't need a GPS signal to fly. We just wait for it to come back to us, like a boomerang.'

'What if the men in black shoot it down?'

Catriona looked aghast, as if she hadn't considered that a possibility. 'Shoot it down?'

'They won't,' Cerys said, hurriedly. 'I mean, probably not. It would draw too much attention, especially in the morning.'

'It needs to come back for us to get the footage. I can't rely on an upload, because of the jamming signal.'

'Are we going out this morning then?'

'As soon as you're ready. We might even make it into the office before midday.'

They finished up breakfast in companionable silence and polished off a second cup of tea each, before Cerys brought round the bike. Cerys was starting to feel comfortable in Catriona's presence, as if they were friends rather than people flung together. She hadn't spent much time with her, thinking of her as 'Owain's former colleague' rather than as an entity in her own right, but she liked Catriona's quiet determination, her bursts of excitement, and her quick thinking.

They returned to the farmer's field – after stopping by the farmhouse and refusing half a madeira cake – and sat down by the gate to launch their flight. It was a beautifully clear day, the storms of last night having washed away the last of the clouds, and Cerys was glad of her leathers to protect her from the soggy grass.

'The area covered by the jammer is about two kilometres in diameter,' Catriona said, consulting her tablet.

'That's ridiculous.'

'The area controlled by this group is probably much smaller than that, but they're cutting off all approaches. No one's really checking signal strengths out here.'

Catriona set up the drone and then fiddled with something inside a different box of bits from yesterday. 'The flight path will go to the centre of the circle, then loop out in ever-increasing circles to cover the whole area, before flying out. It should have enough juice, but it will bail if it detects less than twenty-percent power.'

'Like my phone battery,' Cerys complained.

'Ready for launch.'

Cerys observed a minute of solemn silence as the drone took to the air and headed towards the area of woodland, before becoming but a speck in the sky.

'How long will it take?'

'About half an hour, if the battery holds out. I brought a flask.'

'Unidentified flying object detected, ma'am.'

The security agent in the doorway looked unimpressed with the message he had to deliver, and Amy did her best not to laugh in his face. She was covering for Owain after his late night, not that he'd asked, and she had the attention of the entire Eye Room on her.

'Where is it?' she asked.

'It's flying in circles above our heads, ma'am. It will fly by the surface compound in about two minutes.'

Surface compound. This was the first time she'd had confirmation that their bunker and the place where Jason was being held were close.

'Have we dealt with anything like this before?'

'Not from above, ma'am. Only the odd rambler or farm hand.'

On the screen before her, she could see movement in the Project Room and the corridors, people heading outside to see what was going on. They had to limit the damage, take out the drone before the prisoners saw it and formed ideas, find the people responsible—

Wait. Think.

She was acting like an agent, not a woman looking out for her personal interests, working independently from the NCA. She wanted Jason and the others to see this drone, remember that there were other people out here. She didn't want the people behind it to be found, especially if those people happened to be enterprising young women whose names began with C.

'Let's wait for the drone to finish its flight,' she said. 'It's probably just some children messing around out there. Losing their drone would alarm them.'

'What about lockdown, ma'am?'

Amy fought against the panic that word instantly brought to mind. They could lock down the prisoners, remotely? Seal them inside the compound, or individual rooms? Confine them and cage them like animals? This really was just an extension of prison, and they were only enjoying the illusion of freedom.

'We don't have the external cameras to confirm, but I suspect the prisoners are already outside. It's a little late for anything else.'

'Yes, ma'am. It is.'

She felt the burn of his words, knew that he was telling her off, that her leadership was being questioned. She tried not to care about it, but she felt any retort stick in her throat. The agent turned on his heel and left.

On the monitors, every room was empty except one dormitory, where a man was sleeping away the morning and hadn't heard a thing.

Chapter 23: Somebody that I Used to Know

'Oi, Sleeping Beauty! The natives are restless for lunch and there was a fucking drone in the sky!'

Jason threw an arm over his head and tried to roll away from the voice shouting at him, but he was caught up in his sleeping bag and his sluggish body wouldn't move.

'Oh no you don't.'

Someone grabbed at his sleeping bag and dragged it off the bed, sliding him off the bed and onto the cold, hard floor. Jason groaned and batted feebly at the insistent hands, his head threatening to split open with the force of his hangover.

'I've been poisoned,' he whined.

'Not you too. It's just Nikolai's vodka – you're the idiot, you drank it. Most of us just nurse it for the night.'

Jason crawled pathetically out of his sleeping bag and then squinted up at Lewis. Everything about last night flooded back to him. Between losing rounds of poker, he remembered Lewis' name and Lewis' reputation being dragged – and how he had blushed to hear it.

'Where were you and Stoker then?' he asked.

The grin on Lewis' face faded. 'Me and Stoker? Who said we were together?'

Jason supported himself on the bunk as he rose unsteadily, ignoring the hand Lewis was offering him. He suddenly felt awkward about taking it.

'No one said anything. Neither of you were around, and you've been pretty inseparable since I got here.'

'It helps to be mates with the elites,' Lewis said, slowly, suspiciously. 'You know that – basic prison shit. Stoker's the least worst option.'

'I guess he is,' Jason said. 'What time is it?'

'What happened to your watch?' Lewis asked.

'I think Nikolai has it. Or Pansy.'

Lewis checked his. 'Coming up twelve. You've got time for a shower if you're quick.'

'Yeah, ta.'

Jason fell silent and they both waited awkwardly for a long moment.

'I don't need a nanny for my shower, Lulu.'

Lewis frowned. 'You keep calling me that, in here. You haven't done that for years.'

Jason shifted, offering half a shrug. 'You know, it's using my old name again, being in here. It's bringing it all back.'

'It's not like that now, Jay. It's just a temporary thing. We're different men now.'

'Different, yeah. It's just this place. I know it's not like the nick, but it's bloody weird.'

Lewis shrugged. 'You get used it. It's got its perks.'

Jason picked up his towel, as Lewis awkwardly nodded at him and left the room. Exactly how different was this Lewis from the man he had known? He was definitely hiding something from him. Maybe he and Stoker were cooking up some escape plan of their own, and Lewis didn't know how to tell Jason that he didn't need rescuing after all. Maybe Lewis had just caught an early night and Stoker went to report in with the Governor.

Jason sluiced off the sweat in two minutes, towelled off, and struggled to find clean clothes that he hadn't gambled away the night before. He was never drinking Nikolai's homemade vodka again. He was lucky he hadn't gone blind. He was grateful when Bo had called curfew at midnight, the only elite sober enough to do it. Well, the only one present.

Jason shook his head, trying to get Stoker out of it. He didn't want to think about what kind of guy he was if everyone in here thought Lewis was gay for him. He didn't want to think about any of that. He had to focus on the mission, the part of it that wasn't to do with Lewis.

He arrived in the kitchen and threw together a quick tomato pasta with some mushrooms, carrots, and tinned frankfurters. It was all out by twelve-thirty, with the minimal amount of ribbing by the men about his hangover. Jason took the last portion and looked for a seat. Lewis was sitting at a full table, apart from Stoker, who had taken up with Pansy. Jason avoided both of them and sat with Anchor, Gareth, and Bo.

'You slept through the drone,' Gareth said.

120

'What drone?' Jason said, just as his brain reminded him that Lewis had mentioned something about it when he'd been waking him up.

'It flew right overhead for a couple of minutes, spinning in circles or something. Probably just some kids – and they wouldn't have seen much of anything, really. It's not like we painted SOS on the roof or anything.'

'That wouldn't be the smartest way of getting out of here,' Anchor said.

Gareth looked at him, shocked. He whispered, 'How the fuck do you know about that?'

Jason looked between all of them at the table. 'Know about what?' he said, equally quiet.

'The question is,' Anchor said, staring at Gareth, 'how do you know?'

'Because I've been here for months and people talk.'

'Talk about what?' Jason said, patience thin with his still-throbbing head and no access to paracetamol.

'It's need-to-know,' Bo said, one of the rare times he deigned to speak.

'Well, everyone seems to know except me.' Jason could feel himself losing control of his temper, and almost punched Anchor when he laid a hand on his arm.

'The Project,' Anchor said. 'It's to get everyone out of here.'

'Out…as in, escape?' Jason was baffled. 'Back to the real world? Won't they just round us up again?'

Anchor slowly shook his head.

'No, see, because that's the whole point of us being here,' Gareth said, excitedly. 'We've been put in here to plot our escape!'

'This place is so fucked up,' Jason muttered.

'You get used to it,' Gareth said.

Jason waved his fork at him. 'See, you're the second person to say that to me today, and I don't get it. It's nothing like prison and yet everyone just gets on with things, as if we're still inside. Including working on a project that makes no bloody sense.'

'We've always been at war with Eurasia,' Anchor said with a cryptic smile.

They all stared at him. He shook his head, and ate another mouthful without comment.

'Well, maybe we'd understand the Project if we were all in on it,' Gareth said, pointedly. 'Except Mr G-is-for-God reckons some of us aren't good enough to be on the team.'

'Watch it,' Bo said, his low voice full of threat.

Gareth held up his hands. 'I'm watching, I'm watching. I'm just saying I might have a lot to offer, if I was given a chance.'

'Do you know the phrase 'too many cooks spoil the broth'?' Anchor clapped Gareth on the shoulder. 'You're the cook who dumps half a bottle of chilli sauce in it.'

'Everyone likes spicy broth,' Gareth said, squirming out of Anchor's hold, but looking less angry than he had.

They moved on to talking about chillies and the hottest they'd had, but Jason's mind was still stuck on the Project. Had the rumour mill got it wrong? How could the point of this place be getting a bunch of blokes to escape? It was a compound in the woods, not a prison, so they wouldn't learn anything about *The Great Escape*. Why would anyone want to study them plotting and growing vegetables and playing poker?

And how did this fit in with Mole's death? Had that been part of the plan from The Powers That Be? Did a little murder shake things up in the box? Maybe they were all getting too comfortable and the random death of their compatriot might get their arses moving.

The idea alone made Jason feel sick, or maybe that was the last of the vodka rolling around in his stomach. Why had he agreed to come into this place and be part of this experiment? Who knew how they were fucking with their minds in here. *We've always been at war with Eurasia.*

He had to get out, and fast. He needed to get a message to Amy.

Chapter 24: My First Is in Code

Someone was knocking on her office door. Amy reluctantly got up to open it and was unsurprised to see Owain.

'You changed the code,' he said, disbelievingly.

'Please come in,' she said, with a mock bow.

He strode in and grabbed for her laptop, where she had been reviewing the report about the earlier drone flight. A spiral of flight over them before disappearing from view. The security agents hadn't been fast enough to see who had been flying it, but it had come from local farmland. They'd put it down to 'boys and their toys'. Amy hoped they were wrong.

Owain pulled up the current feed from the mess, which was deserted. On one of the tables, the playing cards and chips had been left out, but there was something odd about them. They seemed to be in a pattern.

Amy's eyes flicked over it, recognised the pattern, translated it in her head, played a simple word game, and came up with an answer. She knew what she had to do. However, she suspected Owain wasn't going to let it go that easily.

'Jason left the cards and chips like this.'

'Okay.'

'You know why.'

'I can guess.'

'Explain it to me.'

'Would saying 'please' kill you?'

Owain thumped his fist down on the desk. 'I do not have time for this. Everyone in the Surveillance Room saw him do it. They're agents, Amy – they recognise a cipher pattern when they see it. They just can't understand why P8 is sending messages when he isn't an agent.'

Amy pointed at him in triumphant accusation. 'There are agents on the inside! I knew it!'

Owain glowered at her. 'I told you, I don't have time—'

'Is it the mysterious P1?'

'I'm the one asking the questions. Explain this cipher to me or I will throw you out.'

She could hear that he meant it and snatched up a piece of cardboard box that was one of the many bits of junk cluttering up her office.

'It's simply positional,' she said. 'Look, here's what Jason's done with the cards.'

She drew a grid of six by six boxes and shaded in the locations of the cards on the tables.

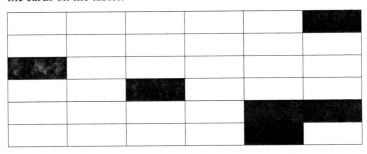

'What about the chips?'

'They're a distraction. It's only the cards that are important – six decks, in this pattern. Then we fill in the code.'

A	B	C	D	E	F
G	H	I	J	K	L
M	N	O	P	Q	R
S	T	U	V	W	X
Y	Z	0	1	2	3
4	5	6	7	8	9

Owain took the pen from her hand, and jotted down the results:

F M U 2 3 8

'What the hell does that mean?'

'It might not be in order. The code's too simple for that. I'm not sure what the numbers mean – I guess they don't know their prisoner numbers?'

Owain shook his head.

'No idea. This message is presumably meant for you?'

'This is a code we mess around with at home,' she said. 'It can only be for me.'

'Tell me what the letters mean then. I know you know something.'

Amy scratched at her head, trying to buy time.

'I am fucking warning you.'

She had never heard Owain sound so cold, so much like the agent Frieda wanted to make him. He was truly lost to them and he was never coming back. How had she ever trusted him?

She stared straight into his eyes, hoping she could be equally icy. 'FM is for 'Find Me'. The code doesn't allow for an SOS signal. The U is…well, it's for a nickname, between us.'

'What nickname? He's never called you—'

'Ursula,' she said, quickly. 'The sea witch from *The Little Mermaid*.'

'Why would he call you Ursula?'

'It's the song,' she mumbled. 'My work is for the 'poor unfortunate souls'.'

Owain slowly shook his head. 'You two are really weird, you know that?'

'I know.'

He picked up the piece of cardboard to take with him, heading for the door.

'Will you tell me, if he sends more messages?' Amy said.

'I hope for both your sakes that he doesn't,' he said, and closed the door behind him.

Amy sat down hard in her chair, and smiled to herself. 'Ursula…'

She picked up another bit of cardboard and wrote a new grid, double-checking her working:

T	H	E	Q	U	I
C	K	B	R	O	W
N	F	O	X	J	U
M	P	S	O	V	E
R	T	H	E	L	A
Z	Y	D	O	G	

This was the first cipher Amy had taught Jason, when they were messing around with the idea. She recalled the conversation vividly, curled up on the sofa in the old house, the end credits of some action movie paused on the TV screen.

'What if you're being held hostage somewhere and you need to send me a message?'

'I'll write HELP.'

'What if it's a secret message that you need to leave in a bottle, or tucked into a crack in the wall? What about that?'

'I'm still going to go for HELP. Or, better – AVENGE ME.'

She had whacked him with her slipper then.

'What about on camera?' she said. 'If I can see you, but you can't speak to me.'

That's when he'd agreed to learn one purely for the cameras, because he realised that happened pretty regularly and he needed a way to get out a message when his phone got inevitably smashed or stolen. They'd spent the night working through ciphers, sending each other messages, and he'd left tins on the counter or squares of toast on a plate to send her random things until they'd burned it into their brains, but never used it for real.

Shaking off her reverie, Amy wrote out the letters Jason had sent her:

I N S L A G

Rearranging the letters, she dismissed 'aligns' and came up with the only order that made sense in their situation:

S I G N A L

Jason had noticed the lack of phone signal from his miniature mobile phone, and he was asking her to do something about it. What the hell was she going to do about it?

From Amy's limited knowledge of signal jammers, they were a pain in the arse to keep running. Like computer servers, they needed reliable power and a good cooling system to work. She only had a passing familiarity with the civilian systems, many of which were portable for all your car-stealing needs, but she imagined any military-grade system would be beyond her technical knowledge – unless it had a large red button marked 'OFF'.

The first problem was finding it. Logic dictated that it was somewhere above ground, but logic had burned her before. Above ground was already a headache, but it could also include 'suspended halfway up a tree'. If someone was feeling particularly creative, it could even be inside the tree, with its little jammy tendrils creeping over the branches.

Technobotany aside, she had to come up with a convincing plan. She had found her predecessor's toolkit, which was surprisingly well-stocked with the sort of things she would recommend. She'd also found a laptop bag that included a handy space for said toolkit, so she was ready for a field trip. If only she knew where.

It turned out that cracking the code had been the easy part.

Chapter 25: Forty Winks

Lying awake, Jason felt intensely homesick.

He had sent Amy a message, but he had no idea if she had a way of seeing it – though the minimum he'd expect from her, after forty-eight hours, was hacking a security camera feed. Nikolai had watched him suspiciously, then rolled his eyes and left him to it, despite being under orders to act like his shadow. Jason thought Nikolai would rather he ended up dead, all told.

Like the heroine of a romance novel, he wondered if Amy was thinking about him. That she was worried about him was a given, but did she miss him? Was she thinking about what had passed between them, in that strange familiar apartment that hadn't ever really become their home?

He'd wanted to please her, to know her, but she'd felt distant that night. They'd been waiting for each other for so long that somehow it felt inevitable, how they'd fallen together, yet he felt like he didn't have her full attention. Had she been lost in her head, unable to drag her thoughts away from the danger they faced? He had also felt the urgency, the haste of it all. He hoped he hadn't hurt her. He hoped she wasn't overthinking it, like he was.

He felt restless, and thoughts of sex didn't help. He snatched up his fleece and crept over to the dormitory door, walking out into near-complete darkness. 'He took a leak, and then decided to explore the corridor. He had remembered to bring a cigarette and, old habits dying hard, he made his way to the door to smoke it.

It was locked.

He tried the handle but it wouldn't budge. There was no sign of a lock on the door, no keyhole or electronic pad to be seen. Did the Governor have some secret way of locking the door from his office? Had whoever was monitoring them really given him that much power?

'They locked it. They lock it every night.'

Jason whirled round. A figure stood silhouetted in the glaring brightness of the main corridor lights, and Jason could just make out the stiff clumps of hair trailing over his shoulders.

'Why?'

'Curfew's at midnight. That's one of the rules.'

'No one told me the rules,' Jason said.

'That's because it's need-to-know and you're clearly thick as shit.'

Jason felt his fist clench. He wanted to punch the dickhead, but as he took a step forward, his foot hit a patch of water and his leg skidded out from under him, landing him hard on the concrete.

Dreadlock did nothing. He just shook his head and walked away, leaving Jason lying on the freezing cold floor. Too proud to call for help, too stubborn to accept it anyway. This guy really knew how to push his buttons and watch him fail.

Pushing himself up against the wall, Jason tested his leg and glared at the pool of water leaking in from under the door. He slowly limped back towards the dormitory, no idea what time it was, though the night was dark as coal through the mess windows. The clock on the mess wall wasn't visible by night and Jason couldn't find a light switch. Was that also automated? Did they switch off the lights as a signal to disperse, to enforce their curfew?

Why were they given freedom in some areas and not others? The garden hadn't been an intended thing, he was certain. How many of the rules of the place, including the automatic lights and automatic locks, were features that came not from outside but at their self-appointed governor's request? Did Martin fear an uprising so much that he would keep them hemmed in by rules, routines, and restrictions?

Jason suddenly remembered the note he had given him. He dug it out of the pocket of his fleece, holding it close to his face and squinting in the dark at the pencil scratchings:

SAVE ME

That was unexpected. Jason absent-mindedly placed the paper inside his mouth and chewed it to a pulp before swallowing. What exactly did the Governor need saving from? Gareth had said that Mole and the Governor were close. Did he think that Mole's death meant they were coming for him next? Was this about a power-play in the compound?

If it was about power, then the elites were the likeliest suspects. They would be interested in being more than second-rate. Jason recalled how Nikolai had refused to leave during his audience with the Governor. Waiting for the man to deliver exactly this kind of message? Removing any possible allies from him before seizing control?

Jason wasn't 100% sure he wanted to get into bed with a serial killer, but he also knew he'd been sent in here not only to get Lewis out safely but to solve the murder and prevent any further harm coming to the prisoners. Including one Martin Marldon.

Turning away from the mess and its invisible clock, Jason caught himself once more looking towards the door. Lewis had told him that Mole had gone outside to dispose of the vegetable peelings but had been locked outside. It got dark outside well before dinner, but the lights in the mess would've been on. If he knew there was a risk of being shut outside, wouldn't he have looked at the clock before stepping out into the night? Couldn't the peelings have waited until the morning?

If he had looked at the clock, had anyone seen him do it? The clock wasn't that high. Maybe someone deliberately changed the time on it to trick Mole into leaving the compound when it wasn't safe to do so. Deceiving him into certain death.

The problem with this whole situation was that it required a driver asleep behind the wheel. Jason couldn't imagine that this death had gone over well with the overseers of the Project. The rules were the rules, but a dead man was much more trouble than a couple of bent regulations. If it was a choice between locking the door on time or breaking a rule to save a man's life, what would the operator behind the camera do? Or did they have strict instructions not to interfere with the affairs of the compound? If Jason started a fight club in the mess, would they just let it carry on?

Unless they weren't omniscient and omnipotent controllers of their fate. Maybe there weren't cameras. Maybe they didn't have any monitoring and it was all automated, right down to the choosing of prisoners and the perfectly-balanced meals of tins. Maybe they were just waiting for the dust to settle before they tried much beyond observation.

Sighing, he headed back to the dormitory, no closer to the answers and feeling more than a little closed in.

Better than freezing in the fresh air.

Better than freedom?

Chapter 26: You Can't Stop the Signal

Unable to sleep, Amy decided that night time made the most sense, as she was unlikely to run into Owain – the biggest obstacle in her path. She was confident no one else would question her closely.

She looked at her watch. It was just after one – time for the 'lunchtime' meal of the night shift. She thought maybe she could use the opportunity to get outside, disappear into the chaos of their movement and onward to her destination. No one would notice she was gone, but how would she get back in? Would she spend all day and night wandering the woods in only her hoodie? She hated the cold and it was freezing down in the bunker, let alone outside.

This was a stupid idea. How the hell was she going to find a signal jammer and disable it, when she didn't know where it was or even what it looked like? She crashed down on the floor of her office, barely noticing the sting of the impact, not caring about the laptop bag bouncing on the hard floor. She was out of her depth. Jason was relying on her, and she was drowning.

She felt her breathing speed up, her heart pounding, and she knew it was inevitable. Belatedly, she remembered that her tablets were unopened in the bottom of her backpack. She couldn't even get that right. What a lazy, stupid, waste-of-space she was.

She closed her eyes and she saw her parents, but not the hazy image of her childhood. The sharp images of just over a year past, staring at her with pity and revulsion. Knowing they had been right about her all along. She would never make anything of herself. She would never be able to survive life on her own.

Amy fought against the rising panic, but it had hold of her now. Her throat closed and her hands trembled in front of her, her shoulders and arms aching with tension. She was losing control and there was no one to catch her. She thought she was better. She would never be better.

She sucked in a breath, and then another. She held on to the breathing and nothing else, pressing her palms flat against the cold floor. *Focus. Breathe.*

Breath after breath passed, until her hands were chilled and the floor felt warm. She opened her eyes and stared at the closed door of her office. She was okay. She was alive. Standing on wobbly legs, she checked her watch again. It was quarter past two.

She had missed it, her one chance.

Kicking out at the door only earned her a throbbing foot. She swore, hauled the laptop bag over her shoulder, and threw open the door. Marching out into the corridor, she looked left and right for someone, anyone, who might be able to get her out of this mess of her own making.

Someone barged into her, sandwich in hand, and she reflexively grabbed for his sleeve.

'I'm fucking late, all right?' he snarled.

'Good,' she said, slightly breathless. 'I need an escort.'

The guard turned on his heel, swallowed his mouthful of bread, and flashed her a jam-smeared smile.

'Do you now, love?'

He looked her up and down, eyeing the blouse she had borrowed from IN3 that was too small even for her petite frame. It was disconcerting, being stared at so openly. It was a thing she had never experienced, not even from Jason. Was this how it was for other women all the time?

'I have to perform maintenance on the signal jammer,' she said, with barely a stutter.

'I'll take you out to the Hide now. You can be my cover with SN1 – he hates breaking the rules. I reckon you quite like it, don't you?'

'I have bent them a little in the past.' It felt awkward in her mouth, but the agent didn't seem to notice.

'I'm SN6, by the way. You must be the tidy little TD1 that's got the day shift in a twist.'

'I wouldn't want them to…lose focus.'

What was she even saying? The words were meaningless. She felt her face flush with embarrassment, but SN6 only took that as encouragement. He placed a hand on her back and started walking her towards the tunnel and the vault door.

'We keep Dodger in the Hide. He's meant to be out in the cold on the roof, but he just won't work out there – lazy bugger. I don't think it's bothered him much though.'

Amy was momentarily unsure whether Dodger was a signals technician or the jammer itself, but it seemed they viewed the jamming unit like one of the team. If the device was inside the security agents' base, she would struggle to conceal what she was doing from them – though she still had no idea what that was. Her quick thinking with the guard in the hall was different to carefully and competently disabling a jamming device without raising any alarms.

The tunnel seemed longer than she remembered, and she glanced back. Yes, it was further. They must've passed the ladder that led to the entrance she had used. This tunnel continued for almost double the length of the walk she remembered, lit by only tiny LED units stuck into the tunnel wall. She was suddenly aware that she was alone in the dark with this man and his pace seemed to be slowing. She tried to keep up her determined walk, but his fingers caught in her shirt, his hand drifting lower.

'What's the rush, love? No one out here but us. I thought you were after an escort?'

'Maybe later,' she said.

His hand was on her arse, cupping the cheek through her jeans. She felt uncomfortable and her instinct was to hit out, to scream, but she didn't. She didn't say anything, do anything. She just kept walking.

'Later, later,' he said, mocking the pitch of her voice. 'Maybe I'll come find you in the locker room, eh?'

Her mouth wouldn't work, but he didn't notice. He didn't notice much. Maybe he just didn't care. They finally arrived at another ladder, and he nudged her towards it with a slap.

'Up you go, love. I'll watch your step.'

He laughed at his own joke, as she made her way unsteadily up the ladder, her laptop bag swinging awkwardly against her thigh. She couldn't see what she was climbing towards, but the lights were coming closer together and that must mean she was near the end of the ladder.

Her head hit the hatch and she grit her teeth to stop herself crying out. She could hear laughter above her, but no one opened the way for her. She had to wait until SN6 had climbed up behind her, climbing over her body to reach for the keypad to the right of the hatch. *4-3-2-1*. The same idiotic combination that had been on her office door.

He pushed up the hatch and she scrambled up the ladder, almost falling out of the top in her haste to get away. As she was on her hands and knees on the concrete floor, she looked up to see five tall, broad men staring back at her, with the same generic white faces and brown buzzcuts and slight smirks on their faces.

'You brought us a friend, Sixy.'

'She says she's working, Number One.'

SN6 offered her a hand up, but she got to her feet without assistance, even though the laptop bag threatened to unbalance her.

'I'm here to service the signal jammer.'

Laughter echoed around her at her words, and she realised the innuendo too late. Her face was hot and red, but SN1 – or Number One, as he was up here – didn't say anything further. He merely gestured to a large black metal cube in the corner of the room. It was stuck with a pair of eyes someone had cut from a magazine, and a handlebar moustache. Newsprint letters, like a ransom demand, spelled out 'DODGER'.

Amy knelt down beside the signal case and took off her laptop bag, removing the toolkit from inside. She didn't turn around, forcing herself to stay focused and keep her back to them, filtering out their words and their laughter and their movements. She had no real sense of where she was, except that it was maybe the size of the Eye Room. She wouldn't look at them, at the room. She was going to do her job and get out.

She carefully opened up the external housing for the signal jammer with her Allen keys, noting that it had some scratches and rust along the edges. Inside, the black device with its upright signal antennas looked like a cartoonist's idea of a hacking tool, its fans whirring away to keep it from melting. It sounded like AEON on a bad day, when Amy's now-defunct computer had been pushed to her limits in the pursuit of knowledge and perpetrators.

The housing also contained a plastic wallet with what appeared to be a manual inside. The few typed pages were written in a disjointed English that indicated a non-native writer, the photographs showing that a colour booklet had been printed in black and white. This wasn't in-house army technology, but a foreign import. This operation seemed to operate in some nebulous grey area, in the same way she had for years, but this felt more menacing somehow.

Amy turned off the power and the fans whirred to a stop. She carefully cleaned the dust off the surface with a microfibre cloth, and considered her compressed air cannister, before returning it to the bag. However, the lack of noise was too obvious, and she could soon feel Number One looming over her shoulder.

'Are you going to be long?'

'I will be faster if I'm not interrupted.'

'That's what my wife says.'

More laughter, but she was forced to turn the power switch back on, and the loud whirring of the fans was restored. Any loss of power to the unit would be immediately obvious. Short of breaking it with her clumsy 'service', she had to find another way to disable it.

There were individual dials beside each of the antennae. She could turn them all down, which would surely reduce the gain, but she would likely still be too close to escape even that greatly reduced jamming field. As the jammer was surely designed to cover the compound, it would also be unaffected by such a minimal reduction. Maybe she could turn them all off? That would be easily discoverable though, and impossible to explain away.

She touched the nearest antenna and held it between thumb and forefinger, twisting slightly. The stalk wobbled slightly in its housing but didn't fall. Was that enough to disable it, or at least make it unreliable? She quickly worked her way through all eight antennae, carefully unscrewing them just the right amount.

When she was finished, she replaced the manual and secured the housing, working as quickly as she could without drawing attention to her haste. With the box done up, and Dodger's paper eyes looking at her dolefully, Amy packed up her tools and climbed to her feet, finally turning to face the room.

There was a table in the centre, where three of the agents were playing cards. Another pair were seated in front of two monitors, showing night vision shots of the world outside. Amy recognised the gate where she and Cerys were surrounded, from an angle that suggested the camera was up a tree. The other screen showed the edge of a metal gate and beyond it, at some distance, a one-storey building surrounded by a metal fence.

Where Jason was.

Amy was then painfully aware of the door in the wall, a way into the outside world, a way towards Jason. Of course, she would likely not be able to get to him, to even get beyond that gate and into the compound from the outside. She would have to make do with having *contact*.

'You in a hurry to leave us, pretty girl?'

'Have some respect, Threesome.' A younger agent got to his feet and gestured towards the hatch. 'I'll show you the way, ma'am.'

'What's with the fucking 'ma'am', Twofer? She's just the tech.'

'She fucking isn't. She's the one in charge when Jenkins is out.'

Threesome shut up after that and Sixy looked a little put out. Twofer opened the hatch for her and let her go down first, before following and closing the hatch behind him.

'Sorry about them,' he said, on the walk back towards the main bunker. 'They're not allowed to, uh, 'fraternise' with the Eye girls. It makes them cranky-pants.'

'It makes them dickheads,' Amy said, without really thinking.

Twofer laughed, a little nervous. 'I, uh, I guess it does. Sorry.'

'You already said that.'

Amy was tired from lack of sleep, from lack of Jason, and she hadn't been prepared for all this negative male attention. She found it exhausting. She wished she had just stayed in her house and never thought about coming out, not if this was what awaited her on the other side of the door.

'I can take it from here,' she said to Twofer, and left him standing in the tunnel, alone.

Back in the office, she slammed the door shut and sank to the floor. After a minute, she reached for her backpack and pulled her mobile phone out of its secret compartment.

Three bars of signal and GPRS. She wished she could feel happy about it.

Chapter 27: Top of the Tree

Cerys arrived for work at midday, discovered she was actually on a night shift, and went back home for a restless nap.

Twenty hours later, Cerys emerged into the grey Cardiff morning and found Catriona waiting for her with coffee and a McDonald's breakfast.

'You are amazing,' she told her.

'I've found something,' Catriona said.

On a bench in Memorial Park, Catriona opened up her laptop as Cerys swallowed down her mouthful of egg and sausage, washing it away with strong, sweet coffee. After waiting for Cerys to finish her breakfast and sipping at her own cup, Catriona played a thirty-second clip of treetops, before turning to Cerys in triumph.

'Okay...' Cerys said, slowly. 'Run that one past me again.'

Catriona played the clip back at half-speed, tracing her finger along an S-curve through the trees – and a glint of silver.

'What am I looking at?'

'I am 89% sure you are looking at a road – and a gate.'

Cerys pointed towards the silver glinting gate, but Catriona caught her wrist before she touched the screen.

'I've been around Amy long enough to know that,' Cerys said. *And Owain.*

He hadn't replied to her message. It was probable that he was subject to the jamming signal and that the NCA network didn't allow access to personal email, or anything extracurricular at all. She was definitely an extracurricular. Sometimes, she wondered if he was still sleeping with Frieda, even though she tried not to wonder that.

Catriona released her, turning the laptop back towards herself. Cerys watched her, head dipped in concentration as she moved her mouse around with quick, deft movements. Her hair was tied back tight, shiny with something that had smoothed out the curls, and Cerys found her eyes losing focus as she stared at the morning sun reflecting off her flaming head.

Catriona faced the screen, back towards Cerys.

'Here is the location of that clip on the area we covered.'

A red box was superimposed on the map, which already had a pale blue circle overlying it to represent the jammed area that had been covered by the drone's flight.

'If we assume that the gate is immediately before the area of interest—'

Catriona dropped a flag on the tiny spec of silver on the screen.

'—then this is likely the area that Jason is being held.'

She added a solid red circle just beyond the flag, closer to the entrance where they had been ambushed than to the farmer's field on the other side.

'This probably means that the signal jammer is not in the same location as Jason is.'

She pointed to a small dark blue dot in the dead centre of her pale blue circle.

'What about Amy?' Cerys asked.

'I've been thinking about that. We can't know how far the tunnels go under the woodland, but we can make a guess for the entrance that you were brought to.'

Catriona picked out the entrance gate on the map with another flag, then stretched out a line from that point which produced a measurement in metres. She swept it round in an arc through the blue-shaded wood, leaving a thin black line in its wake.

'That is the distance we estimated you walked that night. Notice anything?'

Cerys had to concentrate on the screen for several seconds before she realised how the walking line neatly swept through the flag Catriona had placed for the silvery-glinting gate.

'They're in the same place!'

'Ten points to Gryffindor. Why build two things when you can build one? I will bet you anything that Amy is directly below Jason – and he doesn't even know it.'

After his shower, before breakfast, Jason dared to check his mobile phone.

I got your message.

His heart leapt into his mouth and he felt like jumping for joy, despite his throbbing ankle from the slip yesterday. He knew Amy was watching over him, like a guardian angel with cables for wings. How the fuck she'd done it he had no clue, but he wasn't going to question his good fortune.

With everyone pointedly not looking at each other as they dressed, he fired back a quick message while supposedly digging through Lewis' backpack for a clean T-shirt. All he could find was a broken watch and several odd socks – typical.

Body was in the garden but died in the kitchen. They say he was locked out.

If Amy had access to the cameras, maybe she could also see the past footage. Maybe he wouldn't have to do anything more in here, and he could let it run its course until the cavalry arrived to shut this place down. Or, if the cavalry weren't coming but the mystery was solved, he could get him and Lewis out with a minimum of fuss.

'You lost something?'

Lewis bent over him, wearing nothing but a towel, fresh from the shower.

'I'm borrowing a shirt,' Jason said, slipping the phone into a convenient hole in the lining of Lewis' bag.

'The one on my bunk? Mate, you are losing it.'

Jason picked up his own discarded towel and whipped at Lewis' legs. He screeched and was seemingly on the verge of tearing off his own towel, when Bo stood up from his bunk.

'No more of that,' he said. 'This isn't a bloody stag night.'

Jason thought about talking back, about turning the towel on the elite, seeing if the broad, quiet man was capable of snapping. This was the most he had said since Jason arrived, and every instinct he had told him to provoke him, needle him. He could pretend it was to get information, but his blood was up. He was just spoiling for a fight.

'Are you just sad you don't get a tiara and a pretty pink sash?'

Jason saw the punch coming and dived to the side, rolling off the bed and onto the floor. He was caught in the tiny space between his and Dreadlock's bed, but he refused to be cornered like a rat. He just about got his feet under him before Bo took another swing, catching him in the ribs.

Jason reeled to the side, crashing into the board of Dreadlock's bunk. Bo was a big man and in peak condition. If he wanted to win this fight, he had to take him out fast. Head down, he surged forward, barrelling both shoulders into Bo's thighs to take him to the floor.

The large man toppled backwards with a roar, Jason landing on top of him in the middle of the room. He could feel all eyes on them now, tense with anticipation, silently placing their bets. Jason went for his head, jabbing him with a right hook two, three, four times, watching his head bounce on the floor.

Bo bucked his hips and pushed at Jason's shoulders, trying to turn Jason off him, but Jason dug his knees into his sides, keeping him down. He thumped Bo hard just below the breastbone, stealing his breath, before slowly getting to his feet and stepping away.

'Stay the fuck down,' he said.

Bo stayed down.

'Lewis, get dressed and get Bo cleaned up.' Dreadlock's voice came from beside his bunk – Jason hadn't registered his presence at all during the fight. 'Jay Bird, you're with me.'

Snatching up the T-shirt from the bed, Jason made a point of stepping over Bo – and not meeting Lewis' eyes. He knew his mate would be disappointed in him, but was having difficulty caring. With his adrenaline high, he felt fucking invincible.

The corridor was fucking freezing, and he yanked the T-shirt on, as Dreadlock strode away from him. As the cool air penetrated his brain and his body started reporting in just how unhappy it was, he realised he had been an idiot. Lewis was right to be disappointed. If Amy had seen that, she would be worried – and also disappointed. What the hell was happening to him in here?

Where was Dreadlock taking him? Was he going to throw him outside in his T-shirt, to freeze like Mole? Was he going to make him a cup of coffee and pat him on the back for taking out Bo, secret menace of the group? Or was he just making him half-jog up this corridor to knacker his twisted ankle before he beat him to a pulp in revenge?

When Dreadlock stopped, it was outside the Governor's office. He knocked and opened the door without waiting. The Governor was sitting at his desk, eating toast with jam, with an oversized mug on his desk. The only mug of its kind in the place and Jason knew that for a fact, because he'd washed them all.

'Jay Bird took out Bo.'

'Will he recover?' the Governor asked, with barely a pause.

'Probably.'

'Who started the fight?'

Dreadlock hesitated, and the Governor's gaze passed to Jason.

'Who started the fight?'

He was softly-spoken, but the quiet authority he exuded was unnerving. Especially as Jason had known him in his former, snivelling life.

'It was Bo, sir,' Jason said. 'He came at me.'

The Governor's eyes flicked to Dreadlock, who nodded briefly.

'Very well. Congratulations – you now enjoy elite privileges. Dreadlock, find him a uniform and update him on his duties.'

'Is he going into the Project Room, sir?'

The Governor regarded Jason for a moment, then shook his head with a smile.

'I think not. You and Nikolai can take the lead there.'

'Yes, sir.'

Dreadlock opened the door, making it clear they were leaving, and Jason nodded to the Governor before heading out into the corridor.

'You happy now?'

'Not really.'

'Good.'

Dreadlock stalked angrily towards the mess, as Jason tried to make sense of what had just happened. He had taken out Bo, which meant that the man now couldn't be relied on to police the rest. Therefore, Jason had to replace him. He was now one of the senior and more privileged members of the group, so he could go anywhere and do anything he liked.

Except he was now permanently attached to Stoker as his guard buddy and had rules to enforce and a higher-level game to play. He was also away from the kitchen, the scene of the crime.

Amy was going to kill him.

Chapter 28: Found Footage

Owain summoned Amy to the Eye Room, and she reluctantly appeared.

'P8 has been promoted to Enhanced status, displacing P5. Please update your analysis.'

It took Amy's sleep-deprived brain a few moments to decipher the code Owain was talking in, and then her brain filled in the blanks: Jason had done something stupid, again.

'Yes, sir. I will review the footage and—'

'No need for that,' he said, too quickly. 'All the detail will be in ID4's incident report.'

'Okay. What about maintenance, Agent Jenkins? We are behind on essential repairs.'

'No more than thirty minutes downtime on the main system and no loss of recording capabilities.' Owain sounded like he was reciting from something, which might have been one of Frieda's Word of God pronouncements

'Of course, sir' she said, as if speaking to a small child. 'You won't even notice it's gone.'

Back in her office, Amy looked for the footage she'd been told there was no need for her to see. The filing system was simple, yet effective: captured video from the current day was placed in a working folder in the archive, divided by camera. The cameras each had a random ten-character serial number, which was regenerated with each new day. When the day was over, the footage was archived in a new folder with a random fifteen-character label. Neither the main user interface or the archive folders appeared to have a way to search the index by date or camera. The footage was preserved for posterity, but it was impossible to actually view it in a way that made sense.

Thankfully, her current area of interest was the last few hours and it was relatively easy to find the punch-up in the dormitory. She winced as Jason took the blows, but silently cheered as he laid out the large hulk that was P5. She was pleased he had held his own, even if it now made their jobs a lot harder.

His movements were going to be more heavily scrutinised now, both inside and out, and she wasn't sure how she was going to keep Owain from discovering that Jason had a phone he could now use. At least he was aware of the cameras and would hopefully continue to be discreet. The time stamp on the message he'd sent her confirmed that it was just before the brawl broke out, and she couldn't tell from the footage where the phone was when he'd typed it. He was getting good at playing spy, despite his enforced hiatus while Frieda had Owain watching over them.

With every hour that passed, her desire for this to be over increased ten-fold. She didn't want to dig into the bowels of this system under the guise of 'maintenance' or run into SN6 ever again. She didn't want to find out from Owain what he meant by 'analysis', in case it meant she was supposed to be producing actual work instead of perusing the extremely boring notes for the days Mole had been in the compound. So far, nothing of interest had jumped out. She wasn't sure it ever would.

She had to find a way of searching the archive folders for video from 5th March. Given the inaccessibility of the archive, she doubted the footage had been removed – it had just been automatically filed and lost from view. She opened one of the folders and then a camera subfolder within. The files were each thirty minutes long – also labelled with random characters – and she played the first file. It was a dark shot of the dormitory at night. She fast-forwarded through it and nothing at all changed. The night shifts here must be very dull indeed.

She looked at the metadata on the files. To her surprise, nothing had been stripped away in the archiving. The information included the date and time of creation: 19th December 2015 02:00. She confirmed her suspicions by opening another couple of folders, and they all told the same story – the archive was created at 2am on the day after the recording, freeing up the 'current' folder for a new set of footage. She could identify the files for the 5th March, if she could only find the folder created on the 6th.

She checked the number of folders: 246.

She was going to need more coffee.

Halfway through her second cup, she found the folder she was looking for – and had two-thirds of the archive numbers recorded beside their days. She didn't want to go through all this only to find that all the important events happened on 4th March, and she couldn't remember which folder that was.

Watching the footage alongside the notes for various prisoners confirmed her suspicions – this was the right day, and the right night. After dinner, Mole left the dining room and headed down the corridor towards the kitchen – and entered a camera blackspot. The maintenance report from 6th March identified that the corridor and kitchen cameras both needed fixing. However, she only needed to know who entered the area at this stage. All the prisoners had been in the dining area, except one. He was presumably the mysterious G, lurking in his office, which was in the blank space without cameras. How convenient for him.

However, as the minutes ticked by on the footage, no one approached the blackspot. The prisoners all left the mess around midnight, heading straight for the dormitories. P4 entered the blackspot for about two minutes, then left again. The notes on his file from other days suggested he was saying goodnight to G. IN2 was a particularly detailed reporter and Amy knew all the details of P3 and P4's routines, right down to their dental hygiene and their favourite cereals.

Two minutes was no time to kill someone. She watched until 01:59, but no one entered or left the corridor. She moved on to the files created on 7th March, one of the days she thankfully already had listed. This was more of the same until around eight o'clock, when Lewis first entered the blank corridor and then immediately went out of the front door. She didn't have any outside views, but she suspected what he might find.

A few minutes later, Lewis ran back in, shouting for help. Everyone ran outside. About half an hour later, four men came back through the door, carrying a small body between them. Everyone was quiet, sombre. They took him down into the blankness of that corridor, and the darkness swallowed him whole.

Mole had somehow gone from being alive in a corridor at 7pm to dead in the garden by 8am the next day. He didn't seem to have been put there or walked there himself, not according to the continuous footage of the corridor she had just viewed. How then had it been achieved?

She needed Bryn. She needed Jason. She needed to share this fucked-up reality with them before she could even begin to make sense of it. She had forced herself to focus on the murder, because to question the sanity of the experiment was to question her own. They were operating so far outside normal society rules that she couldn't tell which way was up, let alone think about how she might describe it to her friends, how they might stop Frieda and her disturbing lack of ethics.

The murder was safe. The murder was solvable. Or was it?

How was she meant to solve the crime when she couldn't see all the scene, name the players, or understand the game?

Chapter 29: The Sky Is Falling

'Jay! The kitchen is leaking!'

Lewis skidded into the mess hall, his T-shirt drenched and his face splattered with rain. While the kitchen technically wasn't his domain anymore, Jason was always going to help Lewis out, and his brother guards were all various stages of drunk.

Saved from another round of death by poker, Jason followed Lewis out of the mess and down the corridor. The kitchen was certainly leaking, a pool of water spreading out into the corridor. Maybe the aging industrial dishwasher had breathed its last, or perhaps his theory about Mole's death was about to be knocked on the head.

Surprisingly, neither turned out to be true. Water was pouring in from the ceiling, a hole in the flat roof above them letting in the Welsh winter weather. Jason hadn't thought the wind was blowing that hard outside, but then this building had seen better days and probably no one thought to check out the roof before shutting in a bunch of prisoners.

'I'll get the ladder,' Stoker said from the corridor, before disappearing.

Where had he even come from? He hadn't been in the mess playing poker with the rest of them – and neither had Lewis. Jason thrust the thoughts away again, but they just kept coming back. Why couldn't he get Pansy's insinuations out of his brain? What the fuck was wrong with him?

'You all right?' Lewis asked, touching at his shoulder

'Is there a bucket around here?' Jason asked, voice tight, trying not to shrug away his best mate's hand.

'Yeah, there's one in the store. I'll get it.'

Jason squinted up into the rainy night, until his shirt was as soggy as Lewis'. The light in the room was off, so he was in darkness staring out into more darkness. He wasn't sure what he was trying to discover, but all he found was that water was wet.

He was too stupid to be an elite or for the Project or to help Amy with her work here. He was just stupid enough to stand under a leaking roof and get soaked without achieving anything at all. Which is exactly how his time here felt. He could feel Amy's disappointment deep in his chest.

What would happen about the roof? Would a repair team come in while they were all sleeping? Was it only the front door that locked, or did individual rooms in the compound do that too? How would they do it without their little roof mission becoming part of the Governor's escape plan? Unless this was the escape plan. Maybe someone had stuck the roof on purpose just to let them all run out into this cold and wet night.

Or maybe not. After all, Jason wasn't the brains of this outfit for a reason. He might have an active imagination, but his problem was always in the execution.

Lewis returned a minute later with Stoker, ladder, and bucket. Jason chucked the bucket under the biggest leak and then looked at the ladder.

'I don't think this will work from the inside.'

'Outside then,' Stoker said. 'I'll round up some help.'

Despite the freezing, sheeting rain and the vodka, Stoker rounded up Bo, Dreadlock, Nikolai, and Gareth to help them out. They chucked on fleeces and jumpers before their coats, none of which had hoods due to bloody prison regulations. Jason was planning on a hot shower after this. Well, a lukewarm shower that was barely a trickle over his head, but a man could dream.

'Your first elite job, Jay Bird,' Nikolai said, with a shit-eating grin. 'Up you go.'

Nikolai and Dreadlock held the ladder and Gareth held open the door, in case they took too long and the curfew lock kicked in. Stoker and Lewis went to the junk pile round the back to look for anything to secure over the hole. Not wanting to spend any longer outside than he had to, Jason tucked a torch into his waistband and climbed up the ladder, bracing himself against the force of the wind. He paused every few steps to hold himself steady against the gusts, feeling the ladder sway and hearing the two drunken men below wrestling with it.

On the roof, he pulled out the torch and, crawling across the wet surface, he located the hole above the kitchen – and the large tree branch that had done for it. Avoiding the edges of the break, Jason saw that the damage spread much further than he'd expected. Peering down, he could see the bucket he had placed in the centre of the kitchen, but the tear in the roof extended right to the edge of the building. Except, weirdly, the kitchen did not.

There was an extra metre or so to the building that wasn't accounted for by the kitchen. The cupboards were flush against the wall and there was no sign of a false door or anything that could conceal a heating system, or some other inner working of the building. Was it part of the surveillance? Jason recalled Amy's server room from their old house, but even he knew you couldn't just lock a piece of equipment like that behind a wall. He tried to look down into it, but he saw nothing but black. Darkness above, darkness below.

Shifting the branch out of the way, he tried to get a closer look – and someone pushed him towards the hole.

Jason yelled and grabbed for the branch as he overbalanced, jarring his old arm injury and sending a wave of pain through his upper body. He landed heavily on his back, the roof cracking ominously beneath him. He was mostly away from the hole but with one foot dangling precariously into the broken mess. He tried to kick himself back and away, but he only shifted a couple of inches.

A sharp blow to his cheek snapped his head back, and he lost his grip on the torch. He saw its light roll away across the roof and over the edge, leaving them both in complete darkness. The full weight of his assailant came down on him – and the roof cracked again. The branch was digging into his back, grounding him, reminding him that this was real and he wasn't floating in outer space.

One last shove, and the branch fell away. For a moment, he was suspended in mid-air – before crashing through the fragile roof and down into the kitchen below.

Chapter 30: Red Alert

As soon as she heard the alarm ringing through the compound, Amy knew Jason would be at the heart of it.

It was near the beginning of the night shift, most of the day shift finishing dinner or grabbing a shower before bed, and Amy emerged from her cupboard to find the corridor unusually full of people.

'Is he conscious and has he broken anything?' Owain barked.

Amy elbowed her way through the crowd, her heart clawing at her throat, threatening to choke her. She made her way to Owain's side, a single video feed occupying the whole screen. It took a moment for her to orientate herself – she was looking at the mess hall of the compound, where two tables had been shoved together and a man laid on top of them.

Jason.

'He's talking,' she said, without her brain really connecting to her mouth. 'That's Le – That's P7 who's got his hand.'

'Can confirm.' IN4 piped up from her station. 'Positive ID on P8 as the injured party, with P7 keeping him conscious.'

'Who has medical training?'

There was a slight pause, before IN3 answered him.

'P6 is the most qualified. P5 has basic training.'

'P3 also has basic training,' said IN2.

'Can we get sound?' Owain asked.

'No sound in the canteen. The microphones were damaged about six months ago, and we've been unable to access for repair.'

'Sloppy,' Owain muttered, earning him sour looks from those gathered.

'What happened?' Amy asked him, still breathless.

'We think he fell through the roof.'

She didn't even want to know how he'd got up there. However, she would be accessing whatever footage was available to find out. Though, as most of the corridor cameras and the outside cameras were busted, she would have pretty much zilch. In many ways, it was now easier to list the areas they did have covered rather than the ones that were missing.

She found her calm in her to-do list, taking each breath as it came, slowing down her heart rate as she took on more oxygen. Keeping breathing for Jason, who had just fallen through the ceiling, because he was colossal fuckwit.

'Let me the fuck through!' bellowed a voice from the door.

The day shift agents parted to admit an irritated-looking guard. Amy recognised him as Number One, in charge on the night shift.

'I have Control. Do we need an airlift?'

'Status of your prisoner, IN4?'

'P6 has completed his survey,' she reported. 'No treatment measures currently in place.'

At that moment, Lewis helped Jason to sit up and swing his legs over the side of the table. Amy felt the wave of relief ripple through the room, and there was a smattering of applause.

'Let Control know we have the situation under control, SN1.'

'Yes, sir.'

'Stand down Emergency Protocol 1. Day shift, get some rest. INs, as you were.'

The crowd at the door filtered away, leaving the surveillance room empty of everyone except the night Eyes, Owain, and Amy. She stayed to watch a little longer, taking in the way Jason favoured his right arm – the old injury where Stuart Williams had taken a pipe to it – and how he was struggling to weight bear on his left leg.

'Send crutches in the next requisition,' Owain said.

'We have a pair on site, sir,' IN2 told him.

'IN1, I need a report ASAP.'

'Yes, sir.'

Why was Owain asking IN1 for the report? Was it about the missing record for P1? She was now convinced that G was the man with the absent record. Did he have a mechanism for reporting in? Also, SN1 had 'Control' in direct contact – how were they able to send communications outside the bunker, when they thought the mobile jammer was still functional? Was there a landline lurking around here somewhere?

Amy thought of her own line of communication and wanted access to it right now. Jason needed her, and she was stuck in this stupid place with no windows and no way out, and he was hurting when she wasn't there. She hated watching him get hurt, at a distance, and not being able to do anything. She'd thought those days were behind them, but it seemed she had more sleepless nights to come.

On the feed, the crowd of men around Jason parted and a figure entered in a uniform she hadn't seen before. Was this G? He talked to Jason for a couple of minutes, before saying something to the tall man with dreadlocks standing next to him. Then, he turned to leave.

The Cardiff Ripper stared out of the screen at her.

She was back there, in her flat, struggling to breathe as she kicked out, tried to run, tried to escape him. She couldn't escape him.

She was there on the balcony, one toe in the outside world, and the gun was in her hand. But it was Jason bleeding, because she had fucked up.

'Agent Lane, I need you to walk with me.'

With a hand on her back, Owain escorted her from the room. She had sparkles across her vision and it was growing black around the edges. She wasn't breathing. Why wasn't she breathing?

She heard the beeping of a keypad and then Owain's office door was open, and he was trying to sit her in a chair, but her legs had given way and she was on the floor. Leaning against his desk and dying.

'The Cardiff Ripper is there.'

'Yes, he is.'

She wheezed out a laugh, near-hysterical, and sucked in a breath to stave off the blackness.

'You knew – and you didn't tell me.'

'Only when I got here. I'm not happy about it either.'

'He's going to walk, isn't he? That's how it works. They play the game and then they walk.'

Owain hesitated, then nodded.

She laughed again, the hysteria bubbling out of her mouth. It was hilarious, it was tragic, it was the worst day of her life.

'He killed all those women. He tried to kill me, and Carla. It doesn't mean anything to her, does it? She just wants to play games.'

They didn't have to name her to feel her spectre in the room with them, as they had often enough in Amy's flat, in the car on their way to Bristol.

Amy tried to breathe, but the laughter wouldn't stop.

'What was the point in it all?' she wheezed. 'He's just going to kill again. Maybe he already has. Nobody here cares.'

'I care,' Owain said, fiercely, the strongest sign of emotion she'd seen from him since he first defected to the NCA. 'I fucking care, Amy. We put him away forever, and now it's going to be undone, all of it. But that's not our job right now. Our job is to keep everyone else in there safe.'

'No one is safe in there. They're locked in with a serial killer! Jason is in there!'

'Jason can handle himself.'

'Someone just pushed him through a hole in the roof. That is not handling himself.'

Owain suddenly stopped and frowned. 'How do you know he was pushed?'

'It's not a coincidence, is it? Mole dies, Jason falls – it's all connected.'

Owain was looking at her with pity. She had seen that look on her sister's face, or her mother's. She hated it.

'You need to get some rest.'

'You need to listen to me. We all need to get out of here, sooner rather than later. There is a killer in that compound – and we already know his name.'

Owain offered her a hand up. She considered refusing, but she didn't trust her legs to support her without his assistance.

'It's been a long day—'

'One day, you will fucking listen,' she said, and walked out with the remaining shreds of her pride.

Chapter 31: Bed Rest

'I'm all right,' Jason said for the hundredth time, but no one was listening.

'Sure you are,' Lewis said, again, and helped him into the bed that had belonged to Anchor.

Above him, Joe was motionless inside his sleeping bag, giving a bad impression of sleep, but Jason didn't give a shit. Anchor had dug out some strong painkillers from a first aid kit and iced his ankle until it came out all pink and purple bruises. He was relieved of all his duties, because an elite who couldn't walk was useless and the kitchen was still underwater.

As Lewis was zipping up his sleeping bag, Jason caught sight of his friend's face.

'What the fuck happened to you?'

He leaned forward to reach for Lewis' split lip, but he jerked his head back.

'Fucking Nikolai,' he said under his breath. 'Leave it.'

'I will not—'

'Stoker has it in hand.'

Jason hadn't heard any disturbance at the bottom of the ladder, but that at least accounted for Lewis and Nikolai, maybe Stoker too. That left Dreadlock, Bo, and Gareth able to climb the ladder and punch him, assuming that someone else hadn't snuck out of the building to do it. Manning the ladder and the door wouldn't have been a high priority for them if there was a fight breaking out. Perhaps Nikolai had caused the disturbance on purpose, as a distraction.

'Get some rest.'

Lewis left him alone before his mouth could catch up with what was happening. His body was humming with adrenaline and really good painkillers, but he was struggling to think it through. Someone had tried to kill him, or at least injure him seriously enough that he would be removed from this place. The attacker hadn't counted on him grasping for a ceiling tile to break his fall, only landing awkwardly on his ankle and sparing the rest of him more than scrapes and bruises.

It had to be linked to Mole's murder. Had he been asking too many questions? The only person he'd really spoken to was Gareth, though he supposed anyone could've overheard him talking to Lewis in the kitchen. Or did someone think he was out of place, out of sync with the brainwashed culture, and think he was a copper or a plant? All were possibilities, but his head was spinning too fast to consider any of them.

Jason was jolted from his thoughts by what sounded like crying. Or, rather, someone trying to pretend they weren't crying because they didn't want anyone to know. He had heard its like in prison and had tried his hardest to forget the pitiful sound.

'You're all right,' he said, the words almost automatic from his times consoling Amy.

The sound died away.

'No,' a voice said, surprisingly strong. 'I'm not.'

It seemed to be coming from the bunk above and, as the rest of the room looked empty, Jason assumed it was Joe speaking to him – the man who thought he'd been poisoned.

'Is it the poison?' he asked.

'You must think I'm a wanker,' Joe said. 'Faking poison or whatever. I thought I was going to die. Still do, really. Any day now.'

'If you tell me who's after you—'

'He'll make sure I'm dead. I'll keep my secrets, thanks.'

Either Joe was experiencing a break from reality, or he knew who had killed Mole. Jason cursed himself for not being Bryn or even Owain, for having the right words to provoke a confession. He had no idea how to extract information except with his fists or a flirtation, and neither was going to work here.

'Is there anything I can do?' Jason asked.

'He's painted a target on your back now. You'd better watch yourself – and get out. When the vote comes around, tell them you want out. It's too late for me, but you've still got a chance.'

'It's not too late. You could leave here too.'

'He won't let me go. He doesn't know that I don't fucking know anything! I don't have the proof! Fucking Alby and his fucking light fingers. I could murder him. I really fucking could.'

The tears had started up again. Jason thought it was a terrible shame that any man was driven to tears by Alby Collins.

'What did he steal? Did he steal your evidence?'

'I can't—'

'It must still be here. He can't have left with it, can he?'

The crying abruptly stopped.

'What? Why not?'

'Because…' Jason paused, considering how to put this without giving himself away. 'Because he was a thief, wasn't he? They wouldn't have let him leave without searching him.'

'Shit. You're right.' Jason heard the bed creak as Joe sat up. 'What the fuck am I doing? I have to find it. I have to get it back.'

'What did he steal?' Jason repeated.

Joe was coming down the ladder on wobbly legs, bringing a smell of stale BO with him.

'My watch,' he said, giving Jason a slightly desperate smile. 'Only my watch.'

Chapter 32: Down the Rabbithole

Cerys woke up on a strange sofa in a strange room. What the hell had she done last night?

Downstairs, she could hear a man's voice singing in Welsh, a deep resounding tenor that made her hair stand on end. She glanced across at the nearby coffee table and saw a couple of empty cans of energy drinks and two tiny espresso cups.

She abruptly recognised the caffeine crash headache from an all-nighter after a night shift, her sheep in the pattern royally fucked. She ran her fingers over the crocheted blanket, picking out the grubby unwashed sheep, not able to remember how it had got there. Had Catriona made this? She was a deeply weird woman with hidden depths of weird.

Checking her surprisingly plugged-in, fully-charged phone, Cerys saw she had one new text message. When was the last time anyone had sent her a text instead of a snap or WhatsApp? The message was from an unknown number, and it said:

Find alby and ask about phone.

It took her a minute to realise what – or, rather, who – 'alby' was. Alby Collins had been a rat-faced dickhead who had worshipped her brother and tried to perv on her in the shower. He was also the reason Jason was currently locked up in the middle of a wood with his other so-called mate Lewis Jones.

Which meant that this message had to be from either Jason or Amy. The signal jammer was down, and they could communicate with them. Catriona would be able to get a precise location on them and they could confirm all their findings!

Cerys grinned. She was starting to feel just as nerdy as Catriona or Amy, getting excited over GPS signals. She hadn't spent much time with Catriona before these past couple of days, but she was beginning to appreciate her talents and her dedication to the task in hand. She had the same drive as Cerys, and they seemed to complement each other's working styles. When her training was over, Cerys wondered if she could go wherever Catriona was, to continue their winning partnership.

She climbed out from under the blanket, stretched into the chill air of the room, and went to find both towel and shower. When she returned wrapped in the towel, Catriona was seated at her computer, and a pile of unfamiliar clothes rested on the end of the sofa.

'I thought you might want something fresh to wear,' she said. 'Coffee's on the table.'

Cerys pulled on the cord trousers and soft knitted jumper, pleased to find they fitted her well, even if their sense of fashion was miles apart. She sat back down on the sofa and sipped at the strong, dark roast. The sleep-deprived, caffeine hangover clearly demanded more caffeine.

'I got a text from Jason,' Cerys said. 'Or maybe Amy. Probably Jason.'

'Oh?'

Cerys waited a few moments, allowing Catriona's brain to catch up with her mouth. She suddenly turned in her chair, staring at Cerys.

'From inside the compound?'

'Has to be. The signal jammer must be dead.'

'We can go out there and get an exact location now.'

'First, we have an errand to run.'

'We do?' Catriona frowned at her. Her coffee clearly hadn't kicked in yet.

'Find Alby Collins and shake him down for information.'

Catriona turned back to her computer. 'Do you have a phone number for him?'

Cerys stood up and swung Catriona's chair back round.

'Oh no. We do this the old-fashioned way.'

As Cerys parked her bike outside Dylan's garage in Canton, she could sense Catriona's regret at agreeing to be her wingwoman on this trip. They were both battered by the rain, Cerys' leather doing a better job of keeping out the elements than Catriona's denim. They trudged through the puddles in silence, Cerys resisting the urge to kick out at the muddy water and send it flying. Cerys' feet led them to her favourite no-go pub and the place to find out about any bad behaviour in the local area, probably because it was happening right in front of you.

'Welcome to The Black Sheep,' she said, ushering Catriona to a dark table in the corner, in a place filled with shadowy corners.

It was very early for a pub to be open, but then Cerys suspected the place didn't actually close. No copper was going to come and look too closely, not when he risked losing his good looks over it. They were probably the first police to set foot in there for years.

Cerys ordered them both bitter, and was pleased that Catriona drank deeply, even though it was first thing in the morning. They sat for a few minutes, saying little, as Cerys scanned the place for a likely target. Her eyes landed on someone she hadn't expected to see, someone she didn't want to see, but he would be able to give her the information she needed.

'Give me two minutes, then follow me in.'

Without waiting for an answer, Cerys got up with her pint and crossed the bar in a few strides, sitting down at the table with three Cardiff boys who were clearly hanging from more than caffeine, more than alcohol.

'Stuart,' she said pleasantly.

Stuart Williams looked up at her and mustered a shadowed grin, the expression pulling at the thick web of scars on his face. He had aged in the years since she had seen him, the confident and cocky gang boy fading into obscurity and a love of hard drugs. She couldn't believe she had once dated him. She didn't want to think too closely about how much that was just to piss off her big brother.

'Cerys Carr. I hear you're a pig now.'

'I am,' she said, owning it. 'But I'm off duty. You seen Alby Collins?'

'Yeah, I have. What's it to you?'

'He owes Jason.'

Stuart laughed. 'With four years of interest, is it?'

Had it really been four years? It didn't feel like so little time since Jason went down. Which meant it was less than three years since her and Stuart…

'Can you help me?'

'What's in it for me?'

The real question. She saw his eyes roaming her body and felt sick with it. Then, she realised he wasn't interested in her – just assessing her clothes, her look, her confidence, to see how much she was worth. How much she could give to him in cold, hard cash.

'I'll give you twenty.'

It was too low for Stuart's pride, but enough for a few bags. Enough to blow away another night. It was a sign of how much he craved the hit that he didn't even haggle, just held out his hand and twitched his fingers.

Cerys pulled out the twenty from her pocket, where she'd stashed it earlier, and held it out. He reached, and she withdrew – playing the game. His eyes never left the note.

'He's at his mam's place. Stuck in a K-hole for days.'

Cerys flicked the note into Stuart's hand, annoyed with herself that she'd had to give it up for such an obvious tip. His fingers brushed over hers, lingering, but she didn't let him take hold. She was up and leaving, just as Catriona was rising from the table. Cerys caught her arm and they swept out of the pub together and back into the rain. She walked quickly, trying to put some distance between them and Stuart, just in case he took it into his head to follow. Catriona didn't ask questions, just kept pace with her, until they were out of Canton and over the bridge into the centre of town, the Millennium Stadium on one side and Cardiff Castle on the other.

'Was that Stuart Williams?' Catriona asked, at last.

'Yes.'

Catriona subsided into silence again, which Cerys was grateful for. She wasn't in the mood to talk. She also wasn't in the mood to dwell on her past mistakes, or her more recent good fortune, but her brain took her there anyway. Without Jason and Amy, without Owain, she could've been sitting at that table with Stuart, never thinking further than the next hit. It had been two years, four months, and a handful of days since she'd dumped Stuart for breaking her brother's arm. It felt far too close. She felt right on the edge of that life.

'Do we need backup for this?'

Cerys suddenly realised she'd walked them all through town and out into Butetown, standing in the street outside Alby Collins' mam's house. Only one street over from where she lived. They'd spent a lot of time at Alby's house as kids, because Alby's mam worked shifts and therefore they had free run of the place all evening, all night.

'No, it's fine. Wait for me.'

Cerys walked up to the front door and knocked. She wasn't surprised when Mrs Collins answered the door in her dressing gown, bleary-eyed and taken aback by her presence.

'Little Cerys Carr. What do you want now?'

'I'm here to talk to Alby.'

Mrs Collins beckoned her in quickly, shutting the door before Catriona could mount the steps. She walked upstairs at a pace, with Cerys close behind her, noting absently that nothing had changed since she'd last been here a handful of years ago. She gestured towards the closed door of Alby's room.

'He's a good boy,' she said, sounding like she was desperately trying to convince herself, before retreating to her own bedroom and closing the door.

Cerys knocked and pushed open the door without waiting for a response. The wood pushed aside an empty pizza box and several discarded cans. The room smelled of stale sweat and cannabis. Alby was sprawled on his bed, staring up at the ceiling, nowhere near reality. Cerys crept towards him, watching his flickering eyes, before leaning in to give him a shove.

Alby lurched upright and grabbed for her neck.

'Surprise, bitch.'

Cerys tried to wrench his hands away, but he had secured his grip now, looking at her calmly and assuredly.

'You're my special gift, aren't you? I thought you'd come find me, but not so soon. Not so fucking soon!'

Cerys tried to kick out at him, but the man just laughed

'You're still a tiny twiggy thing, Cer. Don't fight it now. You'll pass out soon, and then we'll have fun. I've got a needle with your name on.'

Her vision was starting to go black at the edges. She had to do something. She grabbed for the nearest thing – an empty bottle – and threw it. The bottle smashed against the window, showering them in warm lager and shards of glass.

'Mam can't help you. She won't help you. She's so pleased that her little boy's home.'

Cerys felt her body go loose, saw Alby's grin widen, then saw him jerk once as glass rained down once more. She fell to her knees, gasping, as Alby crumpled to the floor in a bloody heap.

Catriona was kneeling beside her, rubbing her back, and radioing for police assistance and an ambulance. Cerys tried to tell her that she was okay, but it came out as a rasp.

'Shut up,' Catriona snapped, and Cerys did as she was told.

Chapter 33: Stairway to Heaven, Elevator to Hell

Sick of bed rest and being alone in the dormitory, Jason decided he was done playing the invalid. Lewis had found a pair of crutches lying around a store cupboard, and Jason used them to manoeuvre his way down the corridor and towards his old haunt: the kitchen.

The water was gone from the floor, but the place was freezing cold. The hole in the roof had been patched with a plastic sheet but nothing else, so it was draughty like some haunted castle on a crag above the sea. There was also a bucket acting as a trip hazard, collecting steady drips of water, even though it had stopped raining yesterday.

Jason started work on a bean chilli for lunch, chopping up the last of the onions and carrots, before getting the tomatoes, beans, and spices into the pot. With the rice simmering away, and his cover story firmly established, he turned his attention to the wall of the kitchen that was not, in fact, a wall.

He remembered clearly what he saw before he fell through the ceiling, and that was an extra space beyond where the kitchen should end. Carefully, he worked his way along the wall, tapping on the plaster and examining it for any marks or cracks. He opened the storage cupboard and inspected the back panel, as if it were the door to Narnia, but he couldn't see anything unusual.

He opened all the cupboards along the wall and, crouching painfully, checked them for any way into the space. Maybe there was access from the Project Room, but it was locked at night and he wasn't ready to share this theory with anyone else yet. From the chat around him in the mess after his fall, he realised the consensus was that he'd jumped, that Dreadlock had been right to put a watch on him, and that they should continue with that plan. No one realised that someone else had been up on the roof with him, not even Lewis, and he wanted to keep it that way.

Something happened to people when they stepped inside this place. He remembered the effect from prison, the crushing of questions, the swift kick if you stepped out of line. Everything was the routine and keeping your head down and getting on with business. This was like that, but twenty times worse. Because they had all just accepted the price of admission and so they didn't care about why or how or what happened next.

So, when someone died or got thrown off a roof, everyone took the easiest explanation and ran with it. No one wanted to openly rock the boat, to be the one that sank their chances. He had seen the relief in Lewis' eyes when Jason stopped asking questions. Questions could get you killed.

If he hadn't been hanging out with Amy for these past few years, he would've been exactly like them. Prison had taught him well. But Amy liked to question everything, and he had caught the bug. Yet even he found himself slipping into the habits of the place, the stupor of the convict, and he had only been here a few days. In a week or two, he might be just like the rest of them.

Opening up the cupboard in the kitchen island, Jason suddenly struck gold. Behind the pots and pans, there was a metal plate on the side nearest the false wall, about the size of the average letterbox. Jason gently pushed at it, and it opened inwards, with a draft of cold air spilling out. What the hell was it for?

He started to let go, then stopped. Very faintly, he could hear something echoing up from below, when it was half-open and allowing air to travel freely to his ears from wherever down there was. At first, he thought it was water or some kind of animal, but the more he listened, the more it sounded like talking.

Then someone laughed.

Shit, they're right underneath us.

'Jay Bird? Are you in here?'

Jason let the plate close with a metallic *snap*. He cursed under his breath and stood up slowly, holding onto one of the small pans.

'Alright, butt?' he said to Dreadlock, who was looking at him with something like panic.

'You're meant to be in bed,' he said. 'Someone was meant to keep an eye out for you.'

'I thought I'd cook,' Jason said. 'Do you like chilli?'

Dreadlock looked at the stove, then gestured at the pan in Jason's hand. 'What's that for then, if you're doing chilli?'

'I was thinking of some custard for afters.'

'You'll need a bigger pan.'

Jason looked at the pan in his hand. 'Yeah, you're right. Don't know what I was thinking.'

He looked at Dreadlock, waiting for him to leave, but it seemed he was making himself at home. Keeping up the suicide watch. Between his elite duties and this renewed concern for his wellbeing, he was going to have less than no chance at discovering anything worth finding.

Jason bent back down into the cupboard and changed the pans, staring longingly at the plate in the wall. If someone was down there, someone watching them, it meant the hatch was for someone up here. Someone to communicate with their overlords underneath.

They had a spy among them.

His mind jumped between the inmates, sizing each one up in his mind. It had to be someone who'd been in a long time, to get established. Maybe even from the beginning. He returned once more to the elite, the trusted few – and also to the Governor. He was their official overseer, but he was in formal communication with the controllers of this experiment. He didn't need a secret drop point in the kitchen.

Had it been Mole – by name and nature? The kitchen was his domain, after all. Had he volunteered for the post to gain a line of communication? Had he been murdered for being an informer? Had the killer now marked Jason as a grass, an outsider? It was not the first time the thought had occurred to him, but now it came back stronger, more insistent. He couldn't walk the walk anymore, and someone had noticed.

'Is that thinking hurting you, Jay Bird?'

Jason mustered a grin for Dreadlock and shook his head. 'Just thinking about how long this place has been going.'

'It's been 35 weeks,' Dreadlock said, immediately.

'That was fast.'

'We record it every eviction. 34 people gone. 35 weeks.'

'You've been here from the beginning.'

Dreadlock nodded, picking up a cutlery knife and tapping it against the edge of the work surface. 'A bunch of us have. When it works, it works.'

'The Governor, you...'

'Nikolai and Bo too. Stoker came a bit later, a few weeks in. Mole and Gareth are from around that time too. The others have all been pretty recent, in and out – we can't find the right people for the job.'

'And what job's that?'

'I could tell you.'

'But then you'd have to kill me?'

Dreadlock laughed. 'This ain't the Mafia. I guess you should know, as you're elite now. The mission we were given, when we came in, was to escape: all of us, outside the perimeter, no wounded or dead. Then we'd get our orders for stage two. Easy, we thought. If this was only the first stage, they must expect us to get on with it. We made half a dozen attempts in the first month alone.'

'What happened?'

'We realised it was a fucking waste of time. The odds are so stacked against us that we're never getting out of here. We might as well just make it into a half-decent place to live until the morons in charge get bored and let us out.'

'So, what happens in the Project Room?'

'The new boys throw themselves at the problem, over and over. Sometimes, they look like they're making progress, but mostly they're just retreading the same ground. Hijacking the prison transport, cutting the fence, arming ourselves with sticks and climbing trees. All of it's bollocks. The only way out of here is a vote or total shutdown.'

'If the game is rigged, why are we playing at all?'

Dreadlock laughed again. 'You're smarter than you look, you know that?'

He dropped the cutlery knife to the floor with a clatter, waiting until it had stopped bouncing and settled.

'It passes the time, don't it?'

Chapter 34: Collateral History

A severe panic attack could drain her energy for hours, even days. Without Jason to bring her chocolate and tea, to ground her, Amy felt like her anxiety was an entity that she had spent all night and all day fighting against, boxing at shadows.

It was past midday when she roused herself from the folding bed in the corner of her office. She shook off the cobwebs, the wrung-out feeling invading her muscles, like she had been drained of all energy. Was this how marathon runners felt after the finish line? She wished she felt a sense of achievement at surviving, rather than shame at falling down that hole again.

Five minutes without Jason and all her bad habits had kicked in. She needed to shower and dress, eat something with a vitamin, and drink a strong dose of caffeine, but she felt listless and drifting. What was the point? She couldn't stop Jason from getting hurt. She couldn't do anything to influence the outcome for him. She could only watch.

Belatedly, she remembered she hadn't taken her medication. Had she remembered it yesterday? She threw them back with some water, and immediately felt better. Not because the tiny white tablets had started working within seconds, but because she was taking a step towards control. She wouldn't break down without Jason. She would survive.

Next stop was a shower and clean clothes. The water was too hot, too loud, too sharp on her skin, but she got through it. Defying the dress code, she dressed in jeans and a burgundy T-shirt emblazoned with the goddess Brigantia. She made a cup of coffee, with a generous portion of milk, and found a tin of peaches in the back of a kitchen cupboard.

After a bit of self-care, Amy started to feel the beginnings of functionality. She opened her laptop and checked her phone. She had two messages from Jason, and one from Catriona.

Jason's first message simply said:

Don't worry xx

The kisses were important. They made her feel less inclined to murder him.

The second one was more confusing. The miniature phones they had were difficult to type on and didn't have the same predictive text as a smartphone, so each letter had to be typed individually. The message read:

Def a snitch in here secret hatch in kitchen were up above you find the longest players and joes watch.

After spending a couple of minutes puzzling over it, Amy decided to write it out on a piece of paper, filling in the blanks and separating out the points:

- Definitely a snitch in here
- Secret hatch in kitchen
- We're (?) up above you
- Find the longest players
- And Joe's (?) watch

The first point confirmed her suspicion. When Owain talked of receiving a report, he had someone on the inside. A secret hatch in the kitchen, though? Was that the method of communicating? Maybe it wasn't a coincidence that the cameras were out in the kitchen.

The third point was difficult to fathom, but the last two were easy enough to understand. Jason wanted her to find out who had been in the compound the longest and to find a watch belonging to Joe. Unfortunately, while they were easy points to understand, they were pretty much impossible to carry out.

With each prisoner inheriting the number from the one before him, the only way to find who had been there longest was to read each individual entry. Or, at least, the entries on exit and entry days. She did a quick calculation – it had been just over 35 weeks, so that was 350 entries to find and read. Assuming there weren't blanks, and not counting the prisoner record that she had no access to.

The record for G – aka The Cardiff Ripper. He was now her number one suspect. He was in the same camera blackspot as Mole when he died. If she could only work out how he got the body outside, they could pack up and go home.

Though, was he also the snitch? He seemed to have some kind of position of power there, and that must involve officially communicating with the agents – about supplies and who was leaving, if nothing more. It had to be someone else.

If she looked over the records and footage for the past week, if she could remember what had happened during the incidents, she might be able to work out which prisoner was assigned which number. Then, by process of elimination…

Then, there was Joe's watch. Who the hell was Joe? If she asked Jason to describe him, that might narrow it down, but a lot of these boys were similar build, similar hair, similar attitude. Even if she could accurately identify him, how was she meant to find his missing watch? She could try to follow him between cameras, but for how long? If he'd lost the watch in the last couple of days, she might have a chance. However, if he was unsure, if it could've been a week or a month ago, she didn't have a hope in hell.

Setting aside Jason's five impossible things before lunch, she looked at Catriona's message. There was a link to a picture message, which her crap phone couldn't handle and couldn't access the internet to see. The text said:

Thanks for restoring the signal. We have a location. You're underneath Jason.

With repetition, Jason's message suddenly became clear. They were literally on top of each other, his surface compound mapping to her underground bunker. With all the missing camera angles, she hadn't realised that the layout of the compound almost perfectly resembled the bunker, but now that it had been brought to her attention, she could see the obvious resemblance.

The kitchen hatch now also made a certain amount of sense. Were the kitchens in alignment? How did they receive the communications in the bunker? Amy checked her watch. It was between mealtimes, mid-shift – this was the emptiest the corridors would ever be, and she was unlikely to find anyone but Owain in the kitchen.

Entering the corridor, she took her empty mug back to the kitchen. Once inside, she closed the door and set her mug down by the sink. She hadn't paid attention to the stark metal of the kitchen before, but it was full of identical cupboards, all dull silver. She opened one at random and found more tins. She opened the next one – and a folded sheet of paper fell into her hand.

Glancing up at the door, she unfolded it and read, before returning it to the cupboard and closing the door. She washed up her mug in the sink, her mind whirring, trying to keep the panic under control.

The note said:

Communication compromised. Will find new drop point. Disregard further messages.

It made sense that once Jason found the hatch in the kitchen, the snitch would sever that line of communication. That he would warn his handlers that he had been compromised, that he might target the person who had unmasked him. All those things should make her panic, make her breath catch in her throat so that she couldn't draw another, slowly suffocating with anxiety. But it wasn't that which caused her to fret.

The thing that panicked her was that the note was in Jason's handwriting.

Chapter 35: A Splitting Headache

Watching Catriona pace was making Cerys feel very sick. She was practically vibrating with tension, getting in the way of the nursing staff and making everyone very nervous. It was like being escorted by the canine unit.

Gwen had arrived about half an hour ago and was sitting next to her, gripping her hand as if it would disappear at any minute. Cerys felt a tiny bit guilty for the shit they put their mother through, but then decided it was Jason's fault for setting a bad example.

Her neck was a mess of red marks and blossoming bruises. She'd been given an ice pack to help with the swelling, but the coldness made her breath catch, reminding her of being choked all over again.

One of the attending officers stopped Catriona in her pacing and asked for her statement.

'PC Carr entered Mrs Collins' residence by invitation. She was assaulted by Alby Collins and raised the alarm. I forced entry and neutralised him.'

Catriona's clipped words were punctuated by the burning intensity of her eyes. Cerys hadn't heard Catriona's voice take on that particular coldness before, at odds with her knitted sweater and her fiery red hair. It wasn't that she was detached or emotionless, but something was wrong in the way she spoke, the stiffness in her body. Had she been hurt?

The officer closed his notebook and crossed the Majors department, standing outside a cubicle and conferring with another constable there. That's where they were keeping Alby then. She saw Catriona have the same revelation, saw her rise up on the balls of her feet, as if ready to run.

'Mam, can you get me a cup of tea? And maybe some chocolate?'

Gwen squeezed her hand, frowning down at her.

'Are you allowed that, *bach*? Won't it make your throat sore?'

'It's like a cold, isn't it?' Cerys blagged. 'Hot drinks are soothing.'

'I'll pop down to the coffee shop then. I won't be long now.'

As soon as Gwen was out of sight, Cerys swung her legs over the side of the bed. Catriona watched her warily.

'Where are you going?'

'If you're going to question Alby, I want in.'

Catriona shifted her weight, looking away. 'I never said—'

'Come on,' Cerys said and, without waiting for an answer, crossed the A&E department.

There was only one PC outside now, and Cerys recognised him from training. His eyes caught on her neck and she watched his eyes flood with sympathy. She hated that. The last thing she needed was her colleagues to think she was weak because a perp had got the jump on her.

The curtain hadn't been fully closed, and she could see Alby Collins sitting on the edge of the bed. The doctor with him stepped back to admire her handiwork. Alby's face was covered in spiderwebs of blood, the front of his head shaved to reveal a network of lines that had been recently glued shut. The tray on the side had a few slivers of glass in amongst the bloody cotton pads. Catriona had really done a number on him.

'I'm done for now,' the doctor said. 'You'll need an appointment with plastics. I'll ask the consultant to check you over before you leave.'

It was amazing how many doctors believed curtains to be sound-proof. She cleared up her tray and stepped outside, bypassing them all without a second glance. The PC sighed quietly.

'Be quick,' he said, and jerked the curtain aside.

Alby looked up at them both and flashed a lazy smile at Cerys.

'Nice tattoo you got there. That one's on the house.'

Cerys took hold of Catriona's arm, unsure of what she might do. Always the quiet ones.

'You'll be back in prison before you know it,' Catriona said, in that same hard, cold voice.

Alby stretched his free arm behind his head, settling back on the pillow. The other was secured to the bed rail with handcuffs. As was proper when he had just committed assault. An assault on a police officer, an assault on *her*. Cerys felt her own blood begin to boil.

'Nah, see, I've got immunity. The Governor himself sent me out here to find Jay Bird. That NCA bitch made her promises too. You should look into that.'

'Oh, we have.'

Cerys turned to see Bryn walking through the open curtain. It seemed that coppers shared the delusion that these conversations were private. However, he didn't try to force them out, just sat at the end of Alby's bed and smiled like a shark.

'I think you're a bit unclear on the terms of your arrangement. You had a clean slate, a second chance. Then, you assaulted a police officer, and what do you know? Your record suddenly reappeared on my screen, as if it had never been gone.'

Alby sat upright, his shoulder jerked back by the tether on his wrist. 'What? That can't be right. She said we were going free!'

'Free if you kept your nose clean. But here you are, back under arrest, and nowhere to hide. You're going back to Swansea, boy. It'll be like you've never been away.'

She saw Alby's frightened eyes in the rictus mask of his face, barely able to breathe as his world crashed down around him. *Good.* He should know what it was like to suffocate. Catriona's fingers gripped Cerys' sleeve, and she saw the perverse pleasure on her friend's face. She was sure the expression mirrored her own.

Bryn allowed his words to sink in, let him really understand the consequences of what he had done. He waited until he was sure Alby knew he was drowning before throwing the lifeline.

'Of course, it might've been self-defence. Someone coming into your room, unexpected-like, and startling you when you were coming out of your K-hole. A sympathetic judge might leave you with a suspended sentence and a bit of drug rehabilitation. But it's a big ask, isn't it, with a history like yours.'

Catriona made a small noise of discontent beside her, but Cerys shushed her. She was a bigger picture person. If this deal helped them now, she didn't really care what happened to Alby. He'd go back to being an irritating memory in her past, and that suited her just fine.

Alby swallowed, quickly sizing up his options. He looked at his wrist, the chafed red skin beneath the cuff, opening and closing his hand to watch the tendons move beneath the skin.

'What is it you want?'

'Information on your country retreat.'

The panic was back. 'I can't. I signed a thing. I'll lose—'

'You already lost it, all of it. The only person who can help you now is me.'

'You don't understand. They're not like ordinary cops. They're gonna come after me if they know I talked.'

'Who's going to know, Alby? It's just us in here, and a judge who took pity on you and your poor mam.'

'I don't know anything though!'

'You know where the watch is,' Catriona said.

Cerys knew Alby of old. She expected him to grin, to smirk at how he had pulled off the petty theft and kept his prize away from everyone involved. He had always been a show-off, taking his little victories when he could, enjoying the patronising praise of the others. But now he shrank back onto the bed, suddenly looking young and lost, even more frightened than when he had been faced with Swansea again.

'You don't want that watch. Not really. Whoever's got that watch, on the inside – they have a target on their back.'

'What's so special about the watch?' Cerys asked.

'It's not the watch. It's what's on it. It records reminders, see. If you've got a lot to remember, it records a lot of shit. Half an hour of shit, or something.'

Cerys saw Bryn have the same revelation as her, felt Catriona press her arm tightly.

'Someone was using it to gather information,' she said.

'Joe was recording stuff. But he wasn't doing it for his ownself, see. He was doing it for someone else.'

'Who was he doing it for?' Bryn asked.

Alby shook his head, clamming up and trying to sink further into the bed, as if it would swallow him up. 'No, I can't. They'll kill me.'

'They're locked up in a compound in the country,' Catriona said.

Alby laughed then, hollow and desperate.

'Not for long.'

Chapter 36: The Black Knight

Amy went to fetch a cup of coffee around half-eleven, her eyes tired after a long day of staring at video footage and trying to link shapes on the screen to a prisoner code.

The minimalistic diary-keeping was driving her insane. Every prisoner showered, ate, worked – day-in and day-out. She had divided them quickly into those who went to the Project Room and those who did other odd jobs around the place, and the enhanced prisoners wore a uniform that marked them out. She recognised Jason and Lewis, of course, and she remembered the one with the anchor tattoo had tended to Jason: P6. Scrolling back through his entries didn't take long, as she worked out he had replaced Alby Collins by the eviction dates.

The rest was a muddle that was nearly impossible to decipher. Even the prisoners who were distinct on screen weren't obvious in the paperwork – no one bothered to note if they were short, stacked, or White Welsh in their sparse documentation. Jason hadn't responded to her request for information on his fellow prisoners, nor her message asking him what the fuck he was playing at with that note. She would have to wait a little bit longer to bollock him.

She was frankly furious with him. He hadn't sent her anything reassuring, coordinated any of his increasingly dangerous 'plans' with her, or even had the decency to let her know what was going on with him. That was before she even considered that she had shared her body with him, and the most she had got from him since was a row of crosses via text. The anger and fear jangled inside her and she felt constantly on the edge of a panic attack. She wished she had more diazepam to calm her the fuck down. Instead, she had to rely on exhaustion to settle and caffeine to work.

As she entered the canteen, she realised it wasn't as empty as she'd hoped. Some guards from the day shift were playing cards and drinking something that definitely wasn't coffee. She recognised them from her excursion to the Security Hide: Twofer, Threesome, and Sixy. Not exactly her favourite people.

She went over to the drinks table, dumped a tablespoon of coffee granules in a mug, and filled the mug to the brim. Turning towards the door, Sixy suddenly loomed in front of her, cutting off her exit.

'If it isn't TD1. Shouldn't you be in bed, love?'

'I'm working,' she said, not meeting his eyes, trying to step round him.

Threesome appeared next to him, blocking her way again. 'Why don't you take a break? It looks like you need a little bit of relaxing.'

'I'm fine. Excuse me.'

'Will not,' Threesome said, as if this was a childish game.

'You should join us,' Sixy said, reaching out to touch her shoulder, to hold it and try to steer her towards their table.

'I said I'm working.'

'All work and no play,' Threesome sang to her.

Sixy put both of his hands on her shoulders and pulled her towards him. She tripped forward, dropping her coffee cup with a smash, as he smothered her with his body. She could hear Threesome cackling like an unhinged witch, as she was suffocated, unable to move or breathe, her whole body on fire with shame.

'Fuck off, Sixy!'

The weight was suddenly off her, and a hand was gently pulling her back, steadying her when she slipped on her spilled coffee. She focused on her breathing, on the air moving freely in and out of her lungs, trying to remember her mindfulness exercises. She could feel the coffee warming her leg through her jeans, the trickle of heat into her trainer. She knew her cheeks were burning and the hand on her arm hadn't let go, searing her skin through her T-shirt. She heard raised voices, loud and up close, but she just had to keep breathing.

'Clean this up. If I catch you doing shit like that again, I'll put you on report.'

'Who the fuck do you think you are?'

'I'm the one who's telling you to back the fuck off.'

The hand left her arm. The breathing continued. A minute passed, as she heard the broken china clinking against the floor, the gush and hiss of the hot water machine, and the warm pressure of a hand returning to her back.

'Hey? Let's get you back to your office.'

She walked as she was pushed, her vision slowly swimming back into focus, the corridor appearing beneath her feet, and her office door materialising in front of her. Her fingers found the code automatically, opening the door, and letting them in. The door shut and she sank back against it. *Focus. Breathe. Focus. Breathe.*

'Are you all right? Did he hurt you?'

Twofer was still here. Why was he still here?'

'Thank you,' she said, but her voice sounded strange and far away.

'That was bang out of order. Those dickheads make me so angry.'

She looked up at him, at the intense righteous indignation on his face.

'I'll be all right.' *I've survived worse things.*

He reached down and smoothed her hair, setting it back into place and sending a shiver down her spine.

'I hope so,' he murmured, and leaned in to kiss her.

He tasted of coffee, of something else bitter and unfamiliar, and his hand was so gentle on her face, handling her as if she might break. He moved closer, pressing her up against the wall, trying to deepen the kiss, but she held up a hand to his chest, pushing him away.

'Are you okay?' he said.

'I have to work,' she repeated, the only words that would come to her mouth.

'You can't work after a shock like that. You need to relax.'

Relax.

He tried to kiss her again, but she pushed him away, hard. Twofer looked confused, then tried to kiss her again, but she stepped aside, wrenching the door open. Anger was fuelling her now, setting every nerve alight as her body screamed DANGER DANGER DANGER.

'Is this a game you play?' she said, furious. 'Are you trying to make me your damsel in distress? You came to rescue me so you could… so you could…'

She couldn't even say it. Twofer started to protest, then thought better of it, stepping out into the corridor. She guarded the gap, her body swinging wildly between the desire to punch him and the desire to run and hide forever.

'They really wanted to hurt you,' he said.

'So did you,' she said and slammed the door in his face.

Chapter 37: Burn

Jason had slept badly, second-guessing himself into the early hours of the morning.

It had seemed like a good idea at the time, sending a message to the folks down-below, cutting off the lines of communication and making them doubt everything that followed. Even if they didn't accept his message as genuine, they would know that someone else had found the hatch and that they couldn't be sure which messages that followed were legit.

But if they had another way of communicating with their agent up here – and they must do, because that hatch was surely only one-way – they would be letting him know that there was someone who was onto him. Which made Jason a big fat target. What the fuck had he been thinking? He'd already been pushed off a bloody roof!

As he was waiting for the shower, balancing on his crutches on the wet tiles of the bathroom floor, he tried to think of a way to salvage this. Of course, he should let Amy know what he had done so she could help him figure it out, but he knew she would be pissed off. If he was honest with himself, she probably had a right to be. They were meant to be a team, but he had continued to run solo, even though he had a way of checking in with her. He hadn't even replied to her messages from yesterday. She was probably worried sick about him.

Gareth came out of the shower, adding to the puddle on the floor, and nodded to Jason as he went past. Maybe there was an opportunity there to drop a few hints about there being someone dodgy on the inside. Dodgier than everyone else because they weren't meant to be there. It was a risky strategy, because he was also a plant and he didn't want there to be a general suspicion about that. But he needed this guy flushed out, needed to know how a member of the team running this place had let a murder happen on his watch. He had to wake the sleeping dragons inside the compound and force them to ask the hard questions.

A piercing scream cut through his thoughts, the shower curtain flung open before him. Bo was standing in front of him, pale palms reaching out blindly, the top of his head covered in white foam that was dripping down over his eyelids towards his open, screaming mouth. Red angry welts were rising in its stead, blistering on contact with the air.

Jason leapt forward, shoving him back under the shower spray and reaching up to wash the foam off. Bo tried to fight him, pushing at him, but Jason held fast, even as his own palms burned with the contact.

'Fucking hold still!'

'You fucker! You're killing me!'

'I'm trying to fucking help!'

Jason turned the dial down to freezing, physically holding Bo's head beneath the spray. As the white froth washed away, Jason saw red blistering marks, but the skin was pale beneath the burn. On the shelf, the shampoo bottle was still open, the strong smell of bleach filling the room.

Bo got his hand up and caught Jason in the face, knocking him out of the shower and onto his backside. Two bodies rushed forward to take his place, keeping Bo under the stream of water.

'It's bleach,' Jason yelled. 'Watch out for the bleach!'

Anchor knelt down beside him, and Jason held up his bright red palms for inspection. He nodded, then moved past him and into the shower with the others. Lewis helped Jason to his feet and over to the sink, where he rinsed his hands under the freezing water until they went blue beneath the red.

Bo continued to scream.

Jason heard Dreadlock's voice behind him, as his hands shook beneath the icy water.

'Who the fuck did this?'

'We should ask the man with the proof on his hands.'

A hand caught Jason's shoulder, jerking his smarting hands out from under the water. It was Nikolai, face unnaturally red, scowling at him. Jason saw him draw back his hand.

'Jay Bird's burned because he dived in to help Bo, he did,' Gareth piped up. 'He was just waiting for the shower. I don't see you helping no one but yourself, Kolya.'

Nikolai rounded on Gareth, turning his punching arm on the towel-clad gang boy. Gareth put up his hands, ready for a fight like all good Canton boys – but he wasn't quick enough, Nikolai's punch laying him out on the floor.

A klaxon suddenly wailed from the ceiling, filling the confined space with deafening noise.

'On the ground!' Dreadlock yelled. 'Hands on heads!'

He grabbed Jason's shoulder and leaned in, voice loud in his ear. 'Keep your hands up.'

Jason watched the dominos fall, ten men lying down on the wet bathroom floor while Bo cried in the shower and Jason closed his eyes. Waiting for whatever to hit them.

Within a minute, armed men in black opened the bathroom door. The masked leader pointed his gun at Jason, who raised his hands higher.

'Status?' he barked.

After a long pause, Jason realised he was talking to him.

'He has bleach on his face,' he said, as loud as he dared. 'It's on my hands.'

The soldier-like figure nodded briefly, before lowering his weapon.

'Lock down the inmates,' he shouted to the others. 'First aid for these two right here.'

One guard stepped forward to Jason, examining his hands, as another went towards Bo. The rest shepherded the prisoners out of the bathroom, as the klaxon abruptly stopped and the only sound remaining was water dripping on tile and quiet sobs.

'These are superficial,' the man in black said to Jason, tapping the back of his hands. 'We'll order in some cream.'

'Thanks,' Jason said, clenching and unclenching his fists – and then wincing.

'Stop that too, idiot. Come on – time for beddy-byes.'

Jason followed the man out into the corridor and back down towards the dormitory. He was directed to the left side, his side, and he heard the door lock shut behind him. They really did have eyes on them all the time, total control over every aspect of the environment. Except when someone tried to bleach someone's face – or when someone was murdered.

'What the fuck happened?'

Jason turned round to find Dreadlock and Lewis staring at him. Joe was lying on his bunk, apparently uncaring, and – the Governor was sitting on Dreadlock's bunk, staring at his own hands as if they were also red-raw.

'He just started screaming. I think there was bleach in his shampoo bottle – that's what it smelled like. It's burned him, burned me too.'

'That's convenient, isn't it?' Joe's voice drifted down from his bunk. 'No one will suspect you then.'

'You and Bo weren't exactly friends,' Dreadlock said, carefully neutral.

'I punched him,' Jason said. 'I do my business upfront. Not sneaking around putting bleach in little bottles, to burn a man in the shower.'

'It's not how he does business,' Lewis agreed.

'You'd know, wouldn't you?' Joe said. 'You're best pals from back in the day. You want to bum him more than you want Stoker.'

There it was again – the insinuation, the sneering. Lewis scowled, skin tinged red, but didn't argue. Maybe his recent zen outlook made him feel all 'live and let live' about the mockery. Jason didn't want to think about it. He didn't want to be here either, with his stinging hands, and everyone thinking he'd probably done for Bo.

The minutes passed, slow and silent, until Jason heard the door unlock with a loud *click*. Dreadlock barged past him and out the door. They followed after him, as he led them to the mess. The others were already gathered there and, as Jason scanned their faces, he realised Bo was missing.

'Fuck, it must be bad,' Lewis murmured next to him. 'I don't think they've ever taken a prisoner out before.'

'Except in a body bag,' Joe said, loud enough for everyone to hear. 'It's the way we'll all be going if this carries on.'

'Shut the fuck up, Joe,' Pansy said. 'You're such a fucking downer.'

'I'm a fucking realist, Pansy. Mole's dead and now Bo's been bleached.'

'It was this Jay Bird. We know this.' Nikolai was still after him, it seemed.

'Yeah, whatever. How did I kill this Mole before I was even in here?'

'Perhaps your little partner did – little Lulu did a murder.' Nikolai laughed at his own pathetic joke.

'It was an accident,' Dreadlock said. 'Or we would've all been sent back to lock-up.'

'Would we?' Roshan said, the first time Jason had really heard him speak. 'Wouldn't they just cover it up? Keep Calm and Carry On, they say.'

'They are fucking sick,' Joe said, with venom. 'What the fuck do they want? For us to kill us all like dogs? Is that what this is?'

'Calm the fuck down,' Dreadlock growled. 'All of you.'

'Burning Bo was not an accident.' Nikolai was still angry, spoiling for a fight. 'Bleach in a bottle is not an accident.'

Gareth rubbed at his black eye, taking another step back from Nikolai. 'It doesn't mean it was Jason. Bo wasn't exactly anyone's favourite – except maybe yours, Kolya.'

'I am not one of them!' Nikolai yelled, and stormed out of the room.

'What the fuck do we do now?' Pansy asked, sounding a little scared. 'We're all going to die in here, aren't we?'

'You heard Roshan,' Dreadlock said. 'We do the keep calm thing. We carry the fuck on.'

Chapter 38: Familiar Faces

Amy took the lead in the Eye Room while Owain rang through to Control to work out what to do with a prisoner blinded by bleach.

The guards had quartered P5 in the Hide, constantly rinsing out his eyes with sterile fluids from an IV bag. She'd learned that each Security team had two first-aiders and the Eye teams had one each, which was good to know if she ever needed something stronger than paracetamol. The response was immediate, ordered, and effective. She now understood why SD1 thought she was an idiot for failing to raise the alarm properly about the drone. When it counted, the security team was a well-oiled machine, and she watched them remove the inmates, treat the wounded, and evacuate P5, all in under five minutes.

It was impressive. It was terrifying. She didn't want to cross them.

Something strange had caught her eye, though. When the prisoners were being moved back to the dormitories, one of the guards had acted oddly around an inmate. It was P6, the man who had replaced Alby, the one with the sailor's tattoo. They had spoken at length, seemingly about P5's condition, but the guard had placed a hand on his shoulder. Like a friend, a close friend.

Surely the NCA would've checked everyone's background, ensuring the agents had no connections to the prisoners, even the newer ones. Had someone somehow slipped through? Though, if they had, why was this guard comfortable letting everyone around him know that he knew the guy? Sure, his friends were busy, but secretive people were generally more cautious than this. This guard knew P6, and he wasn't afraid to show it.

Maybe this man wasn't P6 at all. Maybe he was actually the snitch.

The more she thought about it, the more it made sense. If a guard acknowledged a prisoner, he didn't care who was watching, on camera or in person. Because he knew him professionally, and perhaps so did everyone else. It was an open secret that this man was undercover.

If that was the case, why was the record for G locked? What was it about him that needed special protection, when an operative inside the compound had his movements recorded just like everyone else?

Or did he?

Amy brought up the previous day's footage on her laptop. Zipping through the frames, the day log matched exactly with the evidence before her. But the night…

She watched P6 rise from his bunk and walk casually down the hallway at 03:24. Yet the log said he'd done nothing but sleep soundly all night. The night shift was dull, but surely that just made every little thing that happened more memorable? P6 walked down the corridor and into the blank area at the end. The area that contained the kitchen – and its chute for secret messages.

Something didn't sit right with Amy. Were ID3 and IN3 recording two versions of their logs – a public one and a private one, the second sent directly to a higher power? If so, why was the information that an agent was on the ground being kept from everyone else? Though that made no sense, because the security agent knew him…

Amy's head was beginning to hurt. She massaged her temple and took a large slurp of lukewarm coffee. Around her, the room was starting to return to its usual function, the prisoners released and Jason narrowly avoiding another fight.

She was worried, of course, but something kept her from looking directly at him, even though he obviously couldn't see her. Would he know what she had done, kissing another man? Just thinking about Jason kissing another woman raised her blood pressure and had frequently pissed her off in the past.

Not that she had wanted to kiss him. But the shock and the emotion had been too much – which is what Twofer had been counting on. She knew it was his fault, but she still felt guilty as hell. Detonating a bomb over their relationship before it had even got started.

Not that Jason knew, or needed to know. Would she tell him? Should she? She didn't know, and she knew there were more important things to be thinking about, but this was the one that lodged in her mind and prevented her from giving her full attention to the other hundred things needing her oversight.

She forced her attention back to her laptop screen. P6 was still frozen in the corridor, with the log calmly lying about it. Something wasn't right here, and there were only two people who could explain it to her: P6 and IN3. As P6 was currently out of reach, it would have to be IN3, currently sleeping in the dormitory down the corridor.

Amy tried to think of a reason for rousing her but couldn't see a way to do it without alerting all the other sleeping agents to her suspicions. She would have to wait until the night shift, several hours away. In the meantime, she had to do some investigation work. Everything in IN3's logs was now suspect, but the footage didn't lie. She would have to watch night after night of video, finding out what P6 was really up to in the compound.

Owain entered the room, flustered with red right up to his hairline, his cheeks scarlet. He was furious, she could tell.

'Contact prisoner transport for emergency transfer.'

ID1 looked at him curiously, his head slightly on one side. 'Not an ambulance?'

'You heard me.'

ID1 nodded and left the room.

'Agent Lane, you are relieved. You will be supervising the night shift from now on – get some rest.'

'Yes, sir,' she said, scooping up her laptop, and quickly following ID1 out into the corridor.

She caught sight of the agent at the end of the tunnel, stretching away from her. It was hard to see through the gloom of the poor lighting, but he seemed to be climbing the ladder to the Hide. That was where the landline communication was, then – inaccessible to ordinary agents unless they had a specific task to complete.

Still carrying her laptop, Amy ducked into the locker room, her old sleeping place. She reached deep into the pocket of her jeans and pulled out a tiny key attached to a plastic label that read LOCKER MASTER. It was good to be tech support in a high-security building.

Finding IN3's labelled locker, Amy inserted the key into the underside of the combination lock and released the mechanism. It opened easily, and Amy stared into IN3's black-and-white life. Her clothes were neatly hanging from the rail at the top, her bedding absent due to currently being wrapped around its owner. The holdall at the back was empty, the items at the bottom of the locker arranged in labelled plastic tubs – makeup, hair products, snacks.

One tub was unlabelled, and Amy immediately seized on it. There was a diary, written in a language Amy couldn't read, and a sheaf of papers of various sizes and materials. She opened the first one:

Nothing to report. IN0

IN0. She had been right, there was an undercover agent in the compound and, by his designation, a former member of the night surveillance team. Their supervisor? Owain didn't have a label though, so perhaps this was just a made-up label to suit the purpose. An agent that only the night Eyes knew about? Perhaps the guard recognising him had been a genuine surprise, agent-to-agent acknowledgement without knowing the whole truth of the matter.

'What are you doing?'

Amy held herself still. She had been caught rifling through someone's locker. Or had she? She couldn't see the person, the locker door between her and the exit. Which meant they couldn't see her. She carefully dropped the papers back into the box, shutting its lid as she peered around the open door.

'Oh, hello!' she said, a little too brightly.

It was ID1, returned from his trip down the corridor, to fetch something from his locker before he resumed his post.

'Is that what you do, when your master takes you off the leash? Steal people's secrets?'

'I'm testing the lock,' she said, feeling her face redden, as she clumsily gestured towards the master key. 'IN3 reported a fault.'

'Where's your oil then? Your tools? You're full of shit.'

Amy closed the door and turned the master key to lock it. 'It was fine,' she mumbled, tongue tangled up. 'It must've been a mistake.'

'A mistake. Yeah, a big mistake. Not even Jenkins can save you from this, you little creep. You're worse than the last loser we had here.'

ID1 marched towards the door, just as Amy's tongue came loose.

'How can I be worse than him?' she squeaked, too high, too faint. 'I'm here and he's not.'

ID1 shot her a withering look.

'Because he got a promotion to the Eyes and you're going to be busted out of here.'

He was gone in an instant, and Amy knew she had no time to fix this. She opened her laptop and called up the maintenance log. It was impossible to forge properly, not with such short notice, but she could refine it later. She backdated a log with IN3's designation, requesting maintenance of the lock, and placed it high up her queue. She then saved it, before editing to add a note about how maintenance was not required. The last update would then show the current date and time with her login attached. It was crude and wouldn't hold up to close scrutiny, but it would buy her time before Owain was forced to throw her out.

Taking a deep breath and then another, Amy slowly made her way back down the corridor towards her small office. She had no time to rest, no time to think about Jason – she had to find out who knew what, and what they were hiding.

She had to find out their secrets, before they discovered hers.

Chapter 39: Soldier, Spy

Standing in front of the Governor's desk was like being back at school, hauled up in front of the headteacher for a prank or a punch. Jason hadn't missed that feeling at all.

The Governor looked straight at him. 'What happened?'

'I was waiting for the shower. Bo started screaming, covered in all this white foam. The place stank of bleach. I got him under the water, burned my own hands. Then the cavalry arrived.'

'The shampoo bottle was the delivery method,' Dreadlock said, holding up a freezer bag containing the offending item.

'Dispose of it,' the Governor said.

Dreadlock hesitated.

'It was in the shower,' Jason said. 'You won't find a print on it.'

'It is very convenient,' Nikolai said. 'That you know this and that you were there. So convenient – for you.'

'You remember how you were sent down,' Jason said, and left it at that. He knew no one would ask for more, not in here.

'I will not work with this man,' Nikolai said. 'He is the one who has burned out Bo's eyes. I will not give him the power to do the same to me. He must be locked up, voted out.'

'If Nikolai won't work with Jay, then he has to be the one to go.' Stoker spoke softly, but his words were strong and filled with conviction.

'You will not do that.' Nikolai's eyes bored into the Governor's. 'I have been with you since the beginning.'

'Shut the fuck up,' Dreadlock said. 'Who else is there?'

'There's Lulu,' Stoker said.

'Oh, your piece of ass,' Nikolai said, sneering. 'Of course you want him, cosy-cosy together. It makes me sick to my stomach.'

'What about Gareth?' Jason said. 'I think he'd be handy in a fight.'

'I have hit him,' Nikolai said, grinning. 'And I hit the Lulu boy. They cannot be respected.'

In a flash, Stoker turned just before Jason could, and punched Nikolai in the nose. He crumpled to the floor, clutching at his face, as blood streamed from his nostrils.

'Kolya's not fit for work,' Stoker said, still perfectly calm.

'Yes, I can see that,' the Governor said. 'Please promote the one with the first aid training – Anchor, is it? He has proven himself useful and will be respected because of it.'

'Yes, sir,' Dreadlock said, though he didn't look happy about it.

None of them really knew Anchor. He kept himself to himself and, while he'd been helpful with Jason's ankle and responding to Bo's bleaching, he was also unknown. Could he handle himself in a fight? It looked like it, but looks weren't everything. Jason had been caught out by blokes half his size, and seen big men toppled by a glancing blow. If he was truly a navy boy, then he at least had some discipline – not that it seemed to matter much here. For all the look of military efficiency, it was still managed by whoever had the fastest fists.

Nikolai was still kneeling on the floor, blood dripping from between his fingers.

The Governor looked to Stoker. 'Tell Anchor the happy news, and then ask him to see to… this.'

'Yes, sir.'

Stoker gestured to Jason and, together, they hauled the unresisting Nikolai to his feet and out the door. He shook them off in the corridor, splattering red as he went, swaying down the corridor towards the bathroom and the relief of cold water.

Taking pity on him, Jason headed for the kitchen to retrieve an ice pack. While he was there, he ducked his head into the cupboard – and found that the plate was stuck fast, blocking any access. Someone had received his message.

As he stood up, he heard the kitchen door close. Anchor was standing there, looking at him with a perfectly neutral expression.

'I'm just fetching an ice pack for Nikolai,' Jason said, crossing quickly to the freezer.

'You're Frieda's man, aren't you?'

Jason stopped, looking at Anchor with new eyes, and trying to think of the right thing to say. 'That's Agent Haas to you.'

Anchor nodded and offered a brief smile. He had passed the test.

'You weren't briefed about me,' Anchor said. 'I was an emergency deployment, after the death of P8. The former P8. It was a local decision.'

Which meant that Frieda Haas and the NCA higher-ups knew nothing about it. Jason just nodded at the agent-speak, retrieved the ice pack, and handed it over.

'I asked for the hatch to be closed,' Jason said. 'I thought it was compromised.'

'It's all right. They're always watching.' Anchor waved his hand in the air. 'Not down here though. These have been out of action for weeks.'

It seemed Anchor knew about this place long before he'd arrived here. Was he originally part of the monitoring team? Jason had so many questions, and no way to answer them without looking entirely ignorant.

'The report about the murder was…brief.'

'Murder? It was an accident.'

Jason saw something flicker in Anchor's eyes, before he got his expression locked down again. Was it surprise? Anger? What was he hiding from Jason?

'Suspicious death, then,' Jason said. 'How'd he lose track of time like that?'

'It's easily done,' Anchor said, quickly. 'Look, we can't talk long. Someone will come looking. But let's keep close on this, yeah? Keep each other updated.'

'Updated. Sure.' Jason had a sudden thought. 'All of us?'

'I'll pass on anything relevant,' Anchor said, his voice brooking no argument. 'You haven't…made yourself known?'

'Those weren't my instructions.'

Seriously, how many undercovers were there in here? How many were actually supposed to be in the place at all? Jason began to wonder if this was all a farce, with twelve agents locked in a compound together, all spying on each other. If it weren't for Lewis and the Governor, he would be putting money on it.

'Right, of course. I'll keep the lines of communications open. Who, uh, who are you reporting to?'

'Classified,' Jason said, with a little apologetic shrug of his shoulders.

'Right, right.' Anchor waved the ice pack. 'I'll get back to my new duties then.'

He waited for Jason to walk with him, and they left together. Stoker and Lewis were standing in the corridor, and Stoker gave them both a suspicious look.

'Ice pack was hiding down the back of the freezer,' Jason said by way of explanation. 'What's up with you two?'

Anchor carried on down the corridor to his patient, whose swearing was echoing in the confined space. Stoker placed a hand on Jason's shoulder to stop him following.

'I didn't know you and Anchor were mates.'

'We're not.'

Jason didn't try to shake off his hand, mostly because he wasn't sure he could.

'Spending an awful long time in there for men who aren't friends.'

'Chatting shit about Nikolai.'

'Fucking Kolya,' Stoker said, immediately and vehemently, and Jason knew he had found the thing that would bind them together: uniting against a common enemy.

'How's your mouth?' Jason asked Lewis.

'I'll live,' Lewis said, sucking the injured lip into his mouth. 'I hear Stoker did a number on Nikolai's nose.'

'Nothing less than he deserved.'

The even, reasonable voice was somehow more frightening than any fit of temper. Jason imagined that Stoker could kill a man without thinking twice, if it made sense to him. No emotions, no regrets. Just death.

'Do you think Anchor can do the job?' Lewis asked Jason.

Nostalgia struck him, and he was suddenly hurtled back to four years earlier, with the two of them huddled close in the dark making plans. Stupid, childish plans, to rob that shop with some makeshift weapons that Alby had scared up from somewhere. But it was Alby that gave them cause for doubt. Could they really trust him? Was he going to bottle it at the last minute? *Can he do the job?*

'He's quiet, level-headed.' Jason looked to Stoker. 'Just gets on with business.'

Stoker looked away, seeming uncomfortable. 'Yeah, don't trust those blokes,' he mumbled.

Judging by Lewis' frown, the reaction was out of character, but Jason didn't have time to dwell on it. Midday was approaching and they hadn't found anyone as good as him in the kitchen.

If he wanted to communicate with the 'higher-ups', this was his chance.

Chapter 40: Come Into My Parlour

Cerys had been confined to her bedroom by her mother, like a child sent home from school with a stomach bug. At least she'd brought her hot buttered welsh cakes and tea, with the promise they'd order in pizza as a 'special treat'.

Her phone buzzed with a message. It was probably Catriona checking up on her – *again*. It didn't matter how often Cerys told her that it wasn't her fault, Catriona still seemed determined to feel guilty about it.

She reached for the phone, wincing as she turned her head and aggravated her bruised neck. The message was from Catriona, but it wasn't asking her if she'd taken ibuprofen or if she could breathe. Instead, her breath caught in her throat, though it had nothing to do with the pain:

Meeting with Frieda 5pm Amy's flat. Could use some backup.

Cerys had never met Frieda Haas, not really. She had heard a lot about her – her manipulation, her use of power, her need for control. The closest she had come was seeing her in an upstairs window when she'd gone to confront Owain about spying on her. That's when she'd known it was completely over between them. Except for falling into a bed of regret every now and then.

She didn't really want to meet with Frieda now. Firstly, despite her protests to her mam, she felt absolutely shocking. The fight with Alby had taken it out of her and her sleep had been uneasy and broken. Secondly – closely related to firstly – she looked shocking too, and she didn't want to face the current 'love interest' of her ex on such a bad skin day.

Thirdly, she would have to somehow get past Gwen Carr.

Just as she was pondering climbing out of the window, her bedroom door opened, revealing both her mother and Catriona.

'Your friend's come to see how you are. She wondered if you might want to go for ice cream down the Bay, but I thought it was a little too far.'

'Taxi door-to-door, I promise,' Catriona said, meeting Cerys' gaze, then looking down at the phone on the bed. Cerys resisted the urge to roll her eyes.

'She said.' Cerys picked up her phone and waved it. It had been barely thirty seconds since that message had come through. Had Catriona sent it from outside her house? 'I think I might fancy an ice cream, mam.'

'Only if you go careful,' Gwen said, though she had obviously pegged Catriona as a sensible young woman, in her sturdy boots, jeans, and knitwear. 'Come straight back home after.'

'We won't be more than an hour,' Catriona said.

'Let's make it two. Ice cream and then coffee.'

Gwen pursed her lips and said nothing, her trademark expression of disapproval. Still, she escorted Catriona downstairs to wait, while Cerys found something to wear that wasn't a onesie. She had one faded polo-neck jumper in navy blue that covered the worst of the bruises, with the slight red mark protruding above easily passing for a love bite. She styled her hair with product and put on enough makeup for the 'minimalistic' look, with a swipe of lip gloss at the end.

Admiring herself in the mirror, she now looked less like a walking corpse and more like a woman who could say 'my ex used to have me, so he can do way better than you'. It was petty, but it was important to go into these critical meetings with the right attitude.

Coming down the stairs, she realised the polo neck was going to irritate the shit out of her injured neck, but it was an inconvenience she could bear. Catriona stood up from the table as she entered the kitchen, shoving the last morsel of welsh cake in her mouth. Gwen could never resist feeding any person who passed through the door.

'The cab's waiting,' she said.

With a quick goodbye to her mam, Cerys was free – and stepping out into the unseasonable warmth of a Cardiff March. They ducked into the cab, which would be down into the Bay within minutes, but Catriona was smart to suggest it. Cerys wasn't sure she could manage much walking right now.

'Where to, love?'

Catriona gave the address of Amy's flat, then leaned close to Cerys so they couldn't be overheard and handed over her phone. 'This is the message I had from Amy.'

After an exchange about the technicalities of map locations, the most recent message read:

Send a message to Frieda Haas: P6 is an agent and your staff are faking records.

'Why are we sending a message in person?' Cerys said.

'It puts her on our territory. Or, at least, Amy's territory. We might learn something from how she responds.'

'Or she might get more from us than we want to give.'

Catriona shrugged. 'We don't know an awful lot, do we?'

At Amy's flat, Cerys realised she'd left her wallet at home, but Catriona paid without asking. She'd also forgotten to pick up her mam's key to the building, but Catriona had that too, letting them in the front door.

'I didn't know you had a key.'

'It's Bryn's. I said I needed something from Amy's.'

'Who knows we're doing this, exactly?'

'Just us.'

Catriona opened Amy's flat door and gestured for Cerys to go in first. It was coming up to half-four, which gave them time to have a cup of tea before Frieda—

'I wondered when you were going to show up.'

Frieda Haas was sitting on Amy's sofa, a steaming cup of black coffee in front of her. By the window, a woman in a black suit was lurking, her face inscrutable.

'You're early,' Catriona said.

'I arrive exactly when I intend to,' Frieda countered.

'I'll make some tea,' Cerys said.

'My time is precious, girls. Shall we get on with this?'

Cerys ignored her and topped up the kettle. Catriona sat on the futon, a lower and lumpier seat, immediately putting her at a disadvantage to Frieda. However, Cerys was able to use the tea to keep Frieda waiting, checking the milk hadn't expired and digging through the cupboards for sugar.

When she finally came back to the coffee table, she set down mugs for her and Catriona, before moving Frieda's mug to set it on a coaster. She enjoyed the perturbed look on the NCA agent's face, but her victory was short-lived.

'Your brother is in violation of our agreement. He's going back to prison.'

Cerys resisted the urge to fling the cup of scalding tea into Frieda's face.

'Jason is doing the Agency's work right now,' Catriona said, voice soft. 'As is Amy.'

'I don't think they're working for anyone but themselves.'

'Maybe you should ask Owain about that,' Cerys said, acidly.

Frieda smiled like the Cheshire Cat. 'Please, let's be adults about this. It was just sex. Agent Jenkins is my employee now, and all that is behind us. We can be civil professionals, can't we?'

'Civil professionals running a secret experiment in the woods?' Catriona asked.

Frieda clenched her jaw. 'That is classified. If classified information has been leaked—'

'You have a rogue agent,' Cerys interrupted.

'I am well aware.'

'Not Amy. P6. They've gone rogue. Entered the compound without your permission. Your staff are filing false reports.'

Frieda's smile was frozen, like a Snow Queen. 'You don't understand a word of what you just said, do you?'

'It's you who doesn't understand,' Cerys said, trying to bluff her way through this. 'You've lost control of the situation. None of your agents are working for you anymore. They've all got their own agenda. Amy isn't the exception – she's the rule.'

Frieda was silent for a couple of seconds, but that smile was still in place. She wore the dead eyes of a predator, of a shark swimming towards the blood in the water.

'Agent Lane is many things, but she's not a liar. It's her one failing as an agent. If my agents are all running wild, as you say, I will start disciplinary proceedings. For some, that will mean a demotion, or expulsion from the service. For others, it will mean serving time in prison.'

Catriona inhaled sharply and Cerys felt the floor fall out from under her. Shit, they had made things worse. They had come here to score points, to goad Frieda into giving things away, and instead they had brought down the sky on Jason and Amy. *And Owain.*

'Of course, the situation might still be salvaged. Communicate with your…handler, in whatever way you've established, and tell her this: she will solve my little problem, with this "P6" and with Carr – the older Carr, of course. She will take command from Agent Jenkins, and we will see if she can do any better.'

'What will happen to Owain?' Catriona asked, saving Cerys from losing face by asking.

'As I said. We have disciplinary proceedings. If he has truly gone against my wishes in this matter, he will be demoted. If, however, he has lost control of the situation or acted out of ignorance – well, then he is a hopeless case, and I have no further use for him.'

Frieda stood up, and her shadow by the window moved to stand beside her. The threat in the air was palpable, the implication that she could target any one of them at any time.

'I am sure you will make this perfectly clear to Agent Lane. And if she has deceived me…well. I'm sure she knows what happens next.'

Chapter 41: What Goes Around

The compound was full of wanderers.

Amy could well believe that rates of insomnia were high in prisoners, but the corridors were a constant source of traffic. She learned that P6 had roamed the corridor every other night since his arrival – always around half-three in the morning, disappearing down the far end. Two or three times a week, P12 sat in the mess hall after everyone had gone to bed and scribbled in a battered notebook for hours and hours, until he gave into sleep in the early hours.

And every night, without fail, P10 got up just after 1am to use the bathroom. Amy put it down to the hot drink he always took to bed with him, but it was notable because it happened every single night. Something about it was bothering her though, and she couldn't quite place what it was. He was otherwise unassuming, a short South Asian man who was part of the Project Room crew, and seemed to get on with everyone without having a single close friend. He was perfectly dull. So why was she so obsessed by his 1am ritual?

There was a knock at her office door. She got up to open it, and Owain was standing there, once more red in the face. She checked her watch.

'It's too early for changeover,' she said.

'I need to talk to you.'

She let him in and sat back behind the desk, feeling better for having the solid wood between her and him. Highlighting the divide between them.

'What did you say to Frieda?'

'Nothing.'

While it was technically true, Amy knew exactly why Owain was raising this now, exactly how she had been instrumental in causing it, and how she had told Frieda something even if she hadn't spoken to her.

'Amy, come on. We're…'

'Handler and agent,' she said, bluntly. 'What I told her had nothing to do with you.'

'It has everything to do with me! If there's something happening in the compound, I am responsible for it. You undermined me by going further up the chain.'

'I went to Frieda because I thought she already knew about it and was playing her usual games.'

She hadn't meant to undermine him or cause him grief, but she couldn't bring herself to apologise for it either.

'You could've told me. Why the hell wouldn't you tell me?'

'I don't trust you.'

The words had already left her mouth by the time the truth of them hit her. She didn't trust him. She could never trust him. It hurt to suddenly feel so certain about that, after they had been friends. But now they had been whatever-they-were longer than they had been friends, and she couldn't change how she felt. She could think about the emotions that led to her behaviour, but these feelings weren't based on lies from her depressed, anxious brain. They were simply reality.

'But you trust Frieda.'

She could tell she had upset him, but she stood her ground.

'Of course I don't trust Frieda. I know every deal with her is a deal with the devil. She has never pretended to be my friend.'

'When will you get over that?' Owain shouted, slamming his hands down on the desk and causing her laptop to shudder.

'It will never happen,' she said, keeping her voice steady and trying to control her rising heart rate. 'You viewed us as your ticket out of the police, and now here you are. I hope it was worth it.'

'Now that I've been relieved of my position? I'm being sent home in disgrace and you've got my job. Is that what you wanted? Because I don't think it is. I think it's the absolute last thing you wanted.'

Amy gawped at him, a rock falling into the bottom of her stomach. 'Frieda's given me your job,' she said, in faint horror.

Owain shook his head. 'I hope it was worth it,' he echoed, and left her.

The evening was cool and crisp, and Jason stepped outside for some fresh air. And a cigarette.

While they were technically allowed to smoke inside, the Governor didn't like it, which meant that everyone smoked outside or spent the night hours hanging out of the bathroom window like they were still in school. Jason had technically quit, but old habits died hard, especially in the company of old friends.

He found Lewis and Stoker sitting on a felled tree together, sharing a cigarette and laughing by the security light. The wind whipped away their words, but Jason could see they were relaxed, comfortable with each other. Stoker stood up, touched Lewis' shoulder, and turned back towards the building. He hesitated when he saw Jason, but merely nodded as he continued on his way.

Jason took his place on the log, the wood warm beneath him. Now that he looked closer, he noticed that the wood had been carved and treated, to make a proper bench out of it. It seemed those prison woodworking courses had been put to good use. Jason reached towards Lewis and was rewarded with a cancer stick for his troubles.

'Where are yours?' Lewis asked.

'I quit,' Jason said.

'These things will kill you,' Lewis said, waving his own cigarette

'No sooner than this place.'

They looked out into the darkening woods, the chill of the night waking Jason after the heavy lamb curry he had cooked for dinner. They were never going to let him out of the kitchen. He would have to start poisoning some people.

He shivered. Not poisoning people. He had seen the suspicious looks he had earned today, from more than just Nikolai. The others feared him now, doubted him. He'd been the last one to tangle with Bo. He was the prime suspect. If he were Bryn, he'd haul himself in for questioning.

As he knew he was innocent, even if no one else did, he had been mentally pointing the finger all day. The only motive he could see was that someone was trying to turn the compound against him. Nikolai was the obvious choice – he'd made clear that he wanted him out, and that feeling had only intensified since Stoker broke his nose. Nikolai was also a candidate for having pushed him off the roof, except that he'd been busy punching Lewis at the time.

Other possibilities were few and far between. He was as likely to accuse Lewis as he was Pansy or Gareth.

'Penny for 'em?'

'Thinking on who set me up.'

'With the bleach?'

'Yeah. I reckon that's got to be the reason.'

'Bo isn't the most popular,' Lewis said, taking a drag of his cigarette. 'Too quiet for that. Maybe his fall from grace was an opportunity for someone?'

'It's a pretty harsh attack just to gain an edge.'

Lewis blew out smoke in a long, smooth line, his cool breath adding to the effect.

'It may look soft in here, Jay, but it's still a prison.'

It was hard to think of it as a prison, with the woods in all directions and his best mate sitting here with a cigarette, like they were free again, and young. Except they weren't and this place was suffocating him every day. He didn't like what he was becoming within this stifling cocoon.

'Is that why no one asks any questions?'

'What's there to ask? "Why are we here? What's it all for?" I go to a minister for that shit, Jay, not the Governor.'

'You don't care about what comes next? About the 'second stage'?'

Lewis didn't ask how Jason knew about that, and just shrugged instead.

'I care about what comes after that. When the dust settles, when it's all over. I've always been about ends over means.'

Jason nodded to himself, knowing Lewis was right, that Jason could've said the same. He wanted to know how the Governor came to be on top, but he otherwise just wanted to survive and get out. That could be the motto of this place.

'What are you going to do after?' Jason said, aiming for distraction.

'I thought I might train as a mechanic. Mess around with cars, like we used to do. I'd need help though. I couldn't set up something like that on my own.'

Jason knew what he was asking and knew that he couldn't give it to him. Could he? He had to look after Amy, solve mysteries with her, find out where this thing with her was going. Except she could pretty much take care of herself, she was only solving NCA-approved mysteries, and he reckoned they could figure it out better if he wasn't hovering over her all the time.

'Could you give me some time to think about it?' Jason said.

Lewis laughed. 'We've got a lot of time and nothing to do but think.'

Jason finished his cigarette and stood up, reaching down to give Lewis a hand up. He stubbed out his own end, and accepted Jason's hand. Hauling him up, Jason realised how much muscle he had gained, how he had grown into his long limbs, how they were now more similar than ever. It would be something, to run a garage with Lewis, to make something of themselves together.

He just had to explain it to Amy.

Heading back to the compound, Jason noted the lack of stars and thought they might get frost tonight. Stoker would be pissed off, because his baby vegetables would all freeze to death and he'd have to start over. Jason smiled at the idea of the grown man's tantrum, stomping around his garden and hauling up the shrivelled leaves to fling them onto the compost heap.

Lewis reached the door and pulled at the handle. It didn't open.

'What's wrong?'

'The handle's stuck.'

Jason froze. 'Shit, what time is it?'

Lewis checked his watch. 'Just after eleven-thirty. Why?'

'It's too early, too fucking early. What the fuck is going on?'

Lewis grabbed his shoulders and shook him. 'Jay! What are you talking about?'

Jason looked him dead in the eye, hating that he had to tell him this.

'Some bastard has locked us out.'

Chapter 42: Déjà Vu

Still in a daze, Amy walked into the Eye Room at the start of the night shift and announced, 'I am now in charge of the compound. Agent Jenkins has departed.'

The Eyes looked at her blankly. It could be for any number of reasons – they didn't understand what she was saying, they didn't give a shit about Owain, or they had all been trained into responding with studied neutrality to anything out of the ordinary.

'Therefore, I will be supervising the day shifts directly,' she continued. 'I will expect a report from…IN1 in the morning.'

The mask on IN1 slipped, and he looked frightened, out of his depth. Amy recognised that feeling well, because it was the one currently oscillating in her chest. *You have no idea what you're doing and people are going to die.* The only way she was getting through this was by roleplaying with a Frieda mask on and hoping it stuck.

'I have seniority here,' IN2 suddenly said. 'I can do the report… ma'am.'

Amy had been under the impression that IN1 and ID1 were senior by default, but she hadn't really had a chance to look through the personnel records. She merely nodded in acceptance of IN2's offer and watched IN1 sink back in his chair with relief.

'IN3 – where are we with the incident report for P5?'

'ID3 has completed the contemporary record,' IN3 answered. 'I'm going to review the footage from yesterday to determine who contaminated the bottle.'

'Come to my office when it's done.'

IN3 looked at her in surprise, but Amy didn't let her dwell on it. Let her think it was some stupid quirk of the new boss. She just needed to get the woman on her own to find out what the hell was going on with P6. Catriona had sent her an update on their disastrous meeting with Frieda. She should've warned them not to get too close to the ice queen.

'IN4, please prepare an update on the status of P8. We don't need any more evacuations.'

'Yes, ma'am.'

'As soon as you know—'

'I will come to your office – yes, ma'am.'

Amy was suspicious of anyone that keen to please, but it would only serve to reinforce her request to IN3. Also, IN4 sat next to IN3 every night – she might be able to shed some light on the whole affair. It was easier to find an informant than a confessor.

Amy left them to it and made her way down the corridor. She hesitated, leaning towards her old office, before opening the door to Owain's. It was almost exactly the same size as the server room, but significantly less cluttered. The desk and the folding bed were the main features, with an end table bearing a kettle and mug with a personal stash of herbal tea and digestive biscuits. They weren't Owain's usual choices, so it must've belonged to the previous incumbent. The bunker was certainly getting through its leaders.

It was going to be strange here without Owain. She had avoided him most of the time, but at least she knew she had an ally here. For all she hated him and couldn't trust him, she could rely on him to take her concerns seriously. He would've had her back, if only to keep Frieda sweet. Operating alone was going to be much more challenging.

'Challenging' was a good word. It masked the absolute blind panic that was bubbling away under the surface. If only she could keep focused on 'challenging', she might make it through the next few hours without screaming, before retiring to another folding bed to stare at the ceiling and freak out.

But that was for later. Now, she had work to do.

She'd kept the technician's laptop, but her security access had been immediately upgraded. She clicked on the new directory, hoping to find the records for G. Instead she found file after file of protocols and policies, each dozens of pages long. Everything from emergency evacuation to flowcharts for plumbing failures, the NCA – and the Army – had provided a text that she was meant to absorb and understand.

She hadn't been given the opportunity to ask Owain for guidance, and she knew she would've struggled to ask for help even if she'd had the chance. She was stubborn and she was proud, and while she could sometimes appreciate her own tenacity, this was not one of those times. She had persisted in hating and mistrusting him, and now she was all alone in this place with no idea how to steer the ship.

Retreating to the familiar, she looked again at the video of P10 leaving the dormitory to visit the bathroom. She watched the latest version a couple of times over, trying to work out what was bothering her about it. Did she think he was the one who had spiked P5's shampoo with bleach? That made no sense though, because toiletries were kept in the dormitories and they slept in different rooms.

What was wrong with this picture? What was she missing?

There was a knock at the door, and IN4 entered without waiting for her invitation. Amy gathered herself, put on her Frieda mask, and gestured for her to sit.

She merely nodded at Amy's laptop. 'I've submitted the report.'

'Thank you,' Amy said. 'Take a seat.'

IN4 was perplexed. 'It's not…complicated. He's recovering fine from his injuries, doing all the usual things. There's nothing to report.'

'Take a seat.'

IN4 let the door fall closed and sat down across from her.

'I need to get back to my station.'

'Tell me about P6.'

Now IN4 was even more confused. 'That's not my place, ma'am. IN3 monitors P6.'

'I know that. I want your perspective.'

IN4 looked flustered. Because she was being asked about her colleague? Or because she knew something she wasn't supposed to?

'No one is in trouble,' Amy said, soothingly. 'I just need an update on the situation.'

IN4 was a deer in the headlights. 'S-situation?'

Amy decided to take the plunge. 'Handling an agent is outside IN3's training for this assignment. I need to know if the partnership is working smoothly.'

IN4 visibly relaxed. Now that Amy had let on that she knew the secret, it was easy to tell the rest. 'Oh, very well. They knew each other before they came here. IN1 – I mean, IN0 has seniority, of course, but I don't think it's causing them any problems.'

'I trust the line of communication has been secured.'

'IN0 reported yesterday that the second hatch is still operational.'

'You are very well-informed, IN4. It's good to see someone so diligent working here.'

IN4 beamed with pride at a job well done. It was easier to get people to confirm or deny things, rather than questioning them. She'd learned that piece of knowledge from Jason. She'd just continue saying things as statements and see where IN4 landed.

'I am looking at candidates for the IN1 position. Do you have the skills for that role?'

IN4 looked dumbfounded. 'IN2 has seniority—'

'Seniority isn't everything. There's also merit to consider. IN1… well…'

'It's not his fault,' IN4 protested. 'Under the circumstances, I think he's doing well. We were going to reshuffle the room, but we thought it would draw too much attention – from the day shift, you know. People who weren't "in the know".'

The more Amy learned about IN0, the more concerned she became. This wasn't one or two bad apples – this was a conspiracy among the entire night shift. They were all in on it. Who was this IN1? Why had he been thrust forward like this? To replace IN0, yes, but why him?

Suddenly, the timings of the whole debacle clicked into place and Amy couldn't help the smile that came to her lips.

'It's merely a lack of experience and training,' she said.

'Technicians can make very good agents,' IN4 said, earnestly. 'I mean, I don't have to tell you that, do I? But he really isn't up to speed on the handling of G and P2 – it's a difficult assignment for anyone.'

'I don't think it would be too difficult for you.'

Another blush, and a demure nod of her head. IN4 knew she was in with a good chance here, if she played her cards right.

'Until I can formally review the positions, I don't want the news getting out that I'm considering a reshuffle. I can count on you to keep this conversation confidential.'

'Yes, ma'am.'

Content that she had bought IN4's silence, Amy let her go, and let her Frieda mask drop. It was exhausting, acting as if she were this competent, cool operator instead of a nervous wreck threatening to shake apart at any moment. Maybe Frieda was also a constant ball of anxiety beneath her icy exterior. *Or maybe not.*

The knowledge that there was a conspiracy among the members of the night shift, particularly within the Eyes, opened up a series of interconnected doors that would take Amy days to explore. For now, she stuck to the important details: IN0 had previously been IN1 and was now P6. The new IN1 was the former TD1, the missing technician that Amy had supposedly replaced. This change had been organised within the night shift, not by the external agency. Maybe the agent who'd held Owain's job – *her* job – had known about it, but they weren't around to ask.

Which begged one very important question: *why?*

Why would this group of NCA agents conspire to send one of their own into a den of prisoners, at least one of whom was a murderer? Why would they pick the technician, of all people, to replace him? She could see that he was forgettable and expendable, but was that the only reason? What did they need this IN0 to do on the inside that they couldn't do from the outside?

After working for the Agency for a year, Amy could only think of two reasons: he was in there to investigate the crime, or he was protecting someone or something. If he was investigating a crime, why wasn't he doing it officially? Frieda had sent in Owain to look at the murder – it would've helped him to know there was someone on the inside. So, what was he protecting?

Then, it hit her. He wasn't protecting an object or a person. He was protecting *the truth.*

They knew who had murdered Mole. All of them. They knew, because they had watched it happen – or as good as watched it. Then, instead of raising the alarm, they had decided to send an agent in to make sure the truth didn't get out. To silence the killer, or merely to make sure he didn't say or do anything stupid?

Yet she had seen the footage from 5th March, and she hadn't witnessed a murder. The footage she had watched perfectly corroborated the idea that Mole had died of exposure in the garden. The footage she had watched…

She pulled up the footage again and fast-forwarded to the dormitory section of the corridor, just after 1am. She ran the tape at double-speed and waited. Waited, and waited. She stopped the tape at 3am. P10 had never visited the bathroom. On this one night, of all nights. Why not?

If she looked at the file properly, she was sure she would find evidence that the video had been tampered with, the same few seconds or minutes looped continuously to replace whatever had been there before. It was likely the same for the other end of the corridor and the exit door – it was easier to mass-replace the problematic section of hours instead of just the troublesome spots. The technician had probably worked flat-out to fix the video – and she was sure it had been the technician now – and so time was of the essence. He wouldn't have known about P10's little bathroom ritual and so he edited right over it.

She now had evidence that agents in the compound had witnessed a murder and covered it up. They would carry on covering it up until the day the experiment ended, and beyond. Did they believe in this scientific torture method that much? Or did something else drive them?

Amy had no answers that could help her understand them. What she did know is that this was dangerous knowledge, and she had just told IN4 that she knew all about it. If they found out that their cover-up was in jeopardy, she didn't know what they would do to save their own skins.

And Amy was standing directly in their way.

Chapter 43: Baby, It's Cold Outside

Jason needed gloves and a hat. Also something to break a window.

The outside light had switched off at midnight, the time the doors were supposed to lock, leaving Jason and Lewis with only a watch backlight to see by. The moon was stubbornly hiding behind a thick cloud, which meant the temperature was marginally above freezing but it was also pitch black. They had edged their way round the building a couple of times, but the windows were all too high to reach, and finding a missile in the late winter darkness was all but impossible. That didn't stop Jason digging through the rubbish heap to find something.

'Now I know what Mole felt like,' Lewis said humourlessly.

'Mole didn't die out here,' Jason said. 'Neither will we.'

Jason heard Lewis sigh.

'You're still on about that then.'

'We've just been locked out of the building. Bo's eyes are full of bleach. Someone threw me off the fucking roof. How much more proof do you need?'

Lewis suddenly seized his shoulder. 'What the fuck? What roof?'

Jason hadn't meant to tell him like this, but it was out now.

'I guess it was technically *through* the roof, not *off* the roof—'

'Fuck!' Lewis was angry. He always got angry when he was upset. 'Someone pushed you? Why the fuck didn't you say something?'

Jason didn't know how to say, 'Because Stoker is always attached to you like a pathetic puppy dog', so he said nothing and kept searching. He winced as his frozen fingers snagged on a piece of wire or fragment of glass.

'Who was it?'

'I don't know. It was dark.'

'Nikolai couldn't have done it. He was there the whole time. After that… I guess the fight was a pretty big distraction.'

'He could be working with them, or they just knew what he was like.'

'Why didn't you tell me? I'm not smart like Amy but—'

'It's got nothing to do with that.'

'Then what's it about?'

It was a good question. Why was Jason holding back from Lewis? They were best friends, and he would trust him with his life. While he did want to talk it all over with Amy, it was exactly Lewis' way of thinking that he needed in this situation. Yet he'd barrelled on alone, making his decisions solo, and only complicating the situation further.

'It's Ben, isn't it?'

'I haven't got a problem with Stoker,' he said, hotly. 'I just don't know if I can trust him.'

'I trust him.'

'Do you? Have you told him about me then? That I'm spying?'

Lewis' silence was telling. Jason snorted, and picked up a long metal pole. It might've once been a rake, but now it was going to be a smasher of windows. Or, at least, a tapper of windows until someone found a way to let them in.

'I wanted him to like you.'

'Everyone likes me. It's my face.' Jason hefted the rake and grabbed Lewis' arm. 'I've found a pole.'

'Ben doesn't like you. He thinks you're…uh…'

Jason stopped and resisted the urge to press the freezing metal into Lewis' arm. This was worse than trying to figure out why Amy was in a sulk, which could be anything from 'you forgot my sister's birthday' to 'this coffee is cold'.

'Thinks I'm what?'

'Homophobic.'

Whatever Jason had been expecting, it wasn't that.

'I am not,' he stuttered.

'You're awkward around gays.'

'I am not,' Jason repeatedly, stupidly. 'How would you know anyway? What gays?'

Jason could feel Lewis staring at him through the veil of darkness.

'Us, Jay. Me and Stoker.'

Jason felt everything in his brain lurch to a sudden stop. It wasn't just banter. It was real. Of course it was real. Only an idiot would deliberately miss every single sign since he'd walked into the place – if one of them had been a girl, he'd have clocked within five minutes, and not just because his mam liked romcoms. He hadn't really wanted to know. Because it didn't sit right with him, and he couldn't exactly say why.

'Oh,' he said.

'It's probably only an inside thing,' Lewis said, hurriedly. 'Stoker, that is, not me. I'm gay. Like…really gay. Sorry.'

'How long have you been…y'know…?'

'Gay? Fucking men? Use your words, Jay.'

Jason shook his head. They didn't have time for this now. They needed to get inside before they both froze to death, and he could have his little freakout later.

'Not now,' he said, and started them forward, carrying his pole under his arm like a lance.

'Yes, now. We can't start this now and not finish it.'

'We can finish it once my balls are less brassic. Uh, I mean…'

'I don't want to shag you, Jay. Not anymore.'

Lewis laughed nervously. Jason tried not to think. He shoved the pole blindly towards the building, and it scraped against the wall. He took a couple of steps closer and probed along the edge, until he hit the metal edge of the windowframe.

'I've got the window,' he said, his voice tight.

He was so glad he couldn't see Lewis' face right now. He'd have that slight pink tinge of embarrassment that he always got when talking about sex, the awkward, hunched-up shoulders, and that look of disappointment that reminded Jason keenly of his mam. Yeah, he was glad of the cloudy night.

He banged the pole against the metal windowframe, the clanging sound seeming to echo through the woods. Yet nothing changed inside – no curtains opened or lights came on, no running feet coming to their rescue, or vodka passed through the slight opening of a window. Nothing.

'Maybe it's the bathroom window,' Jason said, and shuffled them along a few feet until they heard the next metallic *clang*.

Still nothing. The blackout blinds didn't shift an inch, and the room beyond seemed unusually quiet. Surely even the best-glazed windows couldn't block out all the sound, not of a group of grown men drunkenly playing poker. Had they lost more time than he'd thought? Had they all gone to bed immediately after curfew?

'What time is it?' Jason asked.

Instead of Lewis' voice, a perky young woman with an RP accent said, 'The time is twelve-twenty-one a.m.'

'That is a fancy-arse watch you've got.'

'I didn't pick it,' Lewis said, defensively. 'I won it off Alby in a poker game.'

Jason almost dropped the pole. 'Off Alby? What was Alby doing with it?'

'He said his mam had bought it for him for his birthday.'

'Lulu, you idiot,' Jason said, exasperated. 'That's not a birthday present. It's the missing watch – the one Alby stole off Joe.'

'Fuck,' Lewis muttered. 'Of course it bloody is.'

Tired of waiting, tired of his mate being an arse, and tired of his own brain making him doubt his integrity, Jason rammed the pole into the corner of the window pane. It shattered with startling ease, raining down shards of glass which glanced off his thick coat and fell onto the hard earth. Jason cleared out the edges of the frame with a crude sweep, before tossing the pole aside.

'Give me a leg up,' he said.

Lewis boosted him up onto the windowsill and then Jason was in the mess hall – which was pitch black. He turned and reached down for Lewis, who gripped his forearms and dug his toes into the brickwork to get himself up and over the sill. Jason crossed to the doorway to turn on the lights, but nothing happened.

'Looks like the power's out,' he said.

'Oh shit,' Lewis said, a note of dread in his voice.

'What? Are you hurt?'

'No, it's just – this was the first step.'

Jason felt his own heart rate increasing, the sudden knowledge that he was about to be shoved straight into a situation he had no idea how to handle. 'The first step of what?'

'Of Pansy's plan. For the Project. This is how we break out of the compound.'

Chapter 44: All Your Base Are Belong To Us

The first warning was the loss of video from the compound.

IN3 crashed through her office door, slightly out of breath from running.

'We've lost all the feeds.'

Amy was about to joke, to ask if she'd tried turning it off and on again, when the lights went out and the laptop switched to battery. The power was gone.

An alarm started wailing. IN3 opened the door, revealing the red lights on the corridor floor – emergency lighting. Amy crossed the corridor to the Eye Room, where everyone was on their feet, all eyes looking to her. For leadership, for certainty.

She had nothing to offer them. She was a fraud.

'This is not a drill,' she said, because it felt like a good idea. 'We need to…leave.'

They continued to stare. Then, IN2 clapped his hands together.

'Evacuation procedure now! Wake the sleepers, and head for the Hide. You heard Agent Lane – we are evacuating.'

Amy was pathetically grateful that he had taken charge, that one nod from her was enough for them all to cascade out of the Eye Room and down the corridor to wake their colleagues who hadn't already sleepily stumbled out at the sound of the alarm.

For a reason she couldn't quite name, Amy returned to her office to pick up her laptop. Maybe she felt secure with the technology beside her, like a comforter, or perhaps she thought it might be useful. When she got inside though, it was her bag she reached for, and her phone. Her connection to Jason. Was this the real reason she'd come back?

And then they came.

The walls of her office shook, a shock vibrating through her bones. She gripped the back of her chair and then, without thinking about it, threw herself under her desk. Isn't that what they said to do in earthquakes and hurricanes? To take cover?

She heard shouting and someone screaming. She heard her door slam open – and then the invader moved on. Ran on, into the mess in the corridor. Had anyone made it out? Was the Hide also exposed, or had they refused to open the hatch?

How long could she hide under the desk? They would find her eventually. Her vision started to go dark around the edges, and she realised she was breathing too fast. Panicking. She was under attack, and she was panicking.

What a leader. They were counting on you. Look where you are. Pathetic.

She tried to breathe, but the fear gripped her whole chest like a vice. They would hear her breathing. They would hear her panicking. She was only making things worse by trying to fight it. Her heart was beating so loudly that it would give her away, like a poem by Poe.

Amy squeezed her fists, seeking the pain of her nails digging into her palms, something to break the cycle. But there was something in the way, something in her hand. She looked down at it, her brain struggling to recognise it. *A mobile phone.*

She still had her phone. With trembling hands, she unlocked it, and began to type. Painstakingly slowly, but she was trying not to hear the crying and the swearing and something heavy hitting the floor.

She checked the message and hit send. The reply was immediate: *ACKNOWLEGED. ACTION INCOMING.*

'There you are.'

Someone yanked on her hair, pulling her out from under the desk. The phone spilled from her hand, skittering across the floor and into a dark corner. The man was tall and pale, with an Eastern European accent. Amy recognised him as P4, one of the enhanced prisoners – well, formerly. He had been demoted during the day shift. It seemed like it was a lifetime ago.

'Come then, little girl. Come along with the others.'

Amy was manhandled back into the Eye Room, where a group of agents were kneeling on the floor in front of the empty dark screens. She counted ten people – all the Eyes from the day shift and four from the night shift. IN3 and IN5 were missing, as were the day shift security agents.

'Tell us how to override the bedroom lock,' her captor said, shaking her. 'Tell us or I start killing these people.'

'I don't know,' she said, quickly, immediately.

'It can't be done,' IN2 called, from the floor. 'The bedroom lock-down can only be overridden from the inside.'

'I wasn't asking you!' the man shouted, his grip increasing on Amy's shoulder. 'I was asking this little bitch.'

'She's new,' IN2 continued. 'She doesn't know anything.'

P4 pushed her to the floor and snorted. 'Of course she doesn't.'

Amy rolled onto her knees, like the others, and counted the prisoners in the room with them. She identified seven people, most of whom she knew by designation. But the one that immediately leapt to the forefront of her mind was a man she had been staring at for most of her waking hours: P6 aka IN0.

He was holding a makeshift club, so they obviously thought he was one of them. Nothing in his expression or posture gave him away – he was prisoner, not agent, and he was going to play his part until the end. Not that he could do anything to help the situation by revealing himself, but Amy also thought that he didn't want to. That the night Eyes were trying to preserve this experiment at all costs, up to and including murder.

'Ask her about the reward!'

It was the lonely journal writer who asked – P12, the one who spent his nights writing screeds in his notebook for no one to read. His comment was addressed to one of the enhanced prisoners, an exceptionally tall black man with dreadlocks, known to her as P2.

'When do we get the reward?' he asked, wearily, as if it was the last thing he wanted to ask.

Amy had no idea what they were talking about, but she tried to blag it. 'You'll get it when you meet the criteria.'

She heard IN2 snort behind her and hoped she hadn't said something ridiculous.

'We have met all the ones that count!' P12 whinged.

'There is only one,' IN2 said, sneering. '*Get everyone out* – and 'everyone' isn't here and you're not even out.'

Only one? Amy remembered Owain telling her this was only the first stage of the experiment. Did the men even know that? Or was it

Owain who had been deceived? And IN2 was right – everyone wasn't here, even counting the men out in the corridor. She'd heard their voices and there were three at most. That meant nine prisoners in the bunker. P5 was on his way to a hospital, which left two people unaccounted for. It wasn't rocket science to work out who.

'Where are P7 and P8?' she asked. 'Jason and Lewis – where are they?'

'I told you we needed them!' one of the enhanced prisoners shouted. 'You wouldn't fucking listen, Pansy!'

'I don't give a fuck about your boyfriend!' Pansy screamed back.

'Both of you shut the fuck up,' the dreadlocked man said. 'Someone needs to go up and get them. That's it. Then we go.'

Pansy put up a token protest, but it soon fizzled out.

'I'll get them.' The other man in the argument was grim now, determined. 'I need a light. And for you to open that bloody door.'

Pansy sighed deeply but opened the laptop he was carrying under his arm. It looked like it might've been Owain's. Amy watched him enter a login, start their system, and open up a menu she hadn't seen before. He had accessed high level clearance beyond even her new powers, possibly on a par with Frieda's. She wished now she had focused her attention on access instead of surveillance.

'It's done,' Pansy said, sulkily.

The man nodded, and left the corridor, presumably going back the way they'd come – from somewhere near the kitchen. She had a strange echo of Pansy's words in her mind – *your boyfriend* – and knew he had to mean Lewis. She'd never met Lewis, but she'd seen photographs, heard Jason talk about him endlessly, and, of course, seen his criminal record. She found the idea that he was someone's prison boyfriend surprising, but then checked herself. Who knew anything about anyone without asking?

'What are you going to do with us?' IN2 asked, and Amy realised that had been her line.

'Nothing.' The dreadlocked man seemed to be in charge, or at least in charge of the talking. 'You wait here until we're gone. Someone will check up on you eventually.'

Sooner than he thought, if Amy's message had gone through. With Pansy's command of the computer system, it was likely he'd cut off

226

the line of communication to Control, but he didn't know about the mobile. How quickly could Frieda get someone down here? If she tried official communications and found them disabled, she would act fast to retrieve her agents.

Or would she?

A cold feeling settled in Amy's chest and her eyes drifted towards IN0. He was protecting the experiment at all costs. Was Frieda? Had she known about all of this and wanted it to continue to its natural end? She might estimate the risk to the hostages as low, especially if she knew she had an agent on the inside.

Maybe no one was coming. Maybe they were on their own.

Chapter 45: Through the Looking Glass

'Tell me the plan again.'

Jason's voice was taut like a guitar string and he felt drunk on adrenaline. He fished his phone out of his bag, but there were no messages. Amy hadn't texted him. Maybe Amy wasn't able to text him.

'Jay—' Lewis started.

'Again, Lewis. How do they get out of the compound? What happens next?'

Do they kill the agents?

'Pansy didn't get that far. He thought there would be some kind of release system on the inside, a manual one that wasn't networked. He said that just made sense, from a security perspective. We all just went along with it.'

'And if there isn't? What then?'

Lewis shrugged helplessly.

'Why now?' Jason demanded. 'Why go now?'

'When the signal jammer dropped, Pansy could access the internet for the first time – not the network in Hell, but the actual internet. He arranged all the onward stuff, like transport and safe houses, that kind of thing. He didn't trust Them to keep their promises.'

'Smart fucker,' Jason said, who wouldn't trust Frieda as far as Amy could throw her. 'Wait, what's 'Hell'?'

Lewis pointed downward. 'That's where they are. Torturing us from down below. Hell seemed appropriate.'

'How do we follow them?'

Jason saw Lewis hesitate, and felt his heart harden against him. Did he not trust him anymore? Had he reacted that badly to Lewis' revelation that his best mate now couldn't tell him the truth?

'Lulu?'

'I know I said you were barking, Jay, but maybe they left us outside for a reason. It's not part of the plan, but then I wouldn't be in any plan to leave me behind, would I?'

Jason exhaled, trying not to show his relief. Lewis was upset with Stoker, not with him. His…partner, or whatever he was, had left him behind and he was smarting. Jason was in the clear.

'I thought we had to get everyone out?'

'How do you know that?' Lewis asked.

'Loose lips, sinky ships. Let's get out of here.'

He could see Lewis was still not quite with him, caught up in his betrayal. Jason grabbed his shoulder and bodily hauled him out of the dormitory and into the corridor.

'Where can we get a weapon?'

But Lewis had stopped. Charging down the corridor was Stoker, red-faced and out of breath, some mixture of panic and anger in his expression.

'I've been fucking looking for you! I went round and round this fucking place five fucking times!'

Lewis stumbled forward and Stoker kissed him, a rough full-body kiss that Jason realised he was staring at before he hurriedly looked away. Yeah, that was going to take some getting used to.

'You got a problem?'

Jason turned back to him, trying to ignore the pink on Lewis' cheeks and focus on the angry bulk of Stoker. He held up his hands.

'No problem, me. Just want to get out of here.'

Stoker took a step towards him. 'I haven't got a problem with Lewis having exes, you know. I just don't want them interfering in my business.'

Jason couldn't help himself. He laughed out loud, staring at Stoker in disbelief.

'I'm not his ex, Stoker. I'm just his mate.'

Stoker looked like he'd been slapped with a fish.

'Then why do you act like you own him, huh?'

Jason looked to Lewis, who was staring at Stoker. Did he act that way? He'd come in here with the aim of getting Lewis out, of saving him from the Big Bad NCA. Maybe because he hadn't been able to save Amy from Frieda, or maybe because he'd felt so useless to her this past year. Whatever it was, he hadn't been treating Lewis like an equal in this, but some damsel in distress.

How the hell did he tell Stoker all that without him getting the wrong idea? 'Oh, Lewis just reminds me of my kinda-girlfriend and I babyed him because I can't do it for her.'?

'He came in here to get me, Ben,' Lewis said, pre-empting him. 'He's not a con – not anymore. He's working…well, he's working against the people running this place.'

Working for them, working against them – Jason wasn't entirely sure what he was doing anymore, but the explanation seemed to make Stoker look even more uncomfortable. At least he wasn't in angry-panic mode any longer.

'You the law then?'

'Not me,' Jason said, using a phrase of Amy's. 'Just an interested third party.'

That didn't seem to help matters. Stoker shuffled his feet and moved away from Lewis, before suddenly meeting Jason's eyes intensely.

'It was me,' he blurted. 'It was me what pushed you off the roof.'

In his mind's eye, Jason replayed the scene on the roof, inserting Stoker into the narrative. He was the right build, and he had the strength. Jason had just assumed he'd been on the ground with Lewis when Nikolai had punched him, but then Nikolai probably would've ended up in a body bag. Now that he thought about it, it was probably Stoker's absence that gave Nikolai the confidence to take a swing.

'What the fuck, Ben?' Lewis said, horrified.

'I don't know!' Stoker wailed, in the biggest display of emotion Jason had seen from him.

Lewis turned away from him, tight-lipped and shaking with fury.

'We need to get out of here,' Jason said, making sure he included both Lewis and Stoker in his gaze. 'The rest is for later.'

'It was Pansy,' Stoker said, unable to stop confessing. 'He said we should leave you behind. But the agent, the girl in charge, she said we all needed to get out for us to, y'know, win.'

'What girl?' Jason said, suddenly intensely focused on Stoker.

'I don't know – a girl? Brown hair about here.' Stoker gestured at his chin. 'It's got this odd pinky bit in it.'

'That's Amy,' Jason said, marching up the corridor. 'We have to go now.'

'How do you know where to go?' Stoker called.

'I found out when you pushed me off the roof,' Jason called back and kept walking.

The kitchen cupboards had been dismantled, revealing the gap between the kitchen 'wall' and the external wall. A rope ladder had been constructed from knotted sheets, like in the best prison escape movies, and was still suspended into the dark hole. Between the hole in the wall and the hole in the roof, the place was basically an ice box.

Jason turned to Stoker and gestured down into the abyss.

'After you.'

Stoker nodded and started down the ladder. Lewis caught Jason's arm.

'Jay, I'm sorry. I've really fucked up.'

'Not now, Lulu. We've got to get out of here.' *Find Amy. Save Amy.*

Lewis went down the ladder, and Jason forced himself to wait. Count to ten. Deep breaths, in and out, in and out. Just like he'd gone through with Amy, back when she was fragile, when she needed him to breathe for her. How did Amy even get in there? Why did Stoker think she was in charge? What the fuck was going on?

He reached ten, and his foot was already on the first rung. It was a wild, bucking thing, but he felt it go taut. Lewis must've caught hold of it. He scrambled down as fast as he dared, alert for the sound of tearing cotton, before red light appeared below him. His foot hit the ground sooner than he expected, and he sensed Lewis next to him. The main lights were out down here too, with only a red floor-level glow to see by. How the hell had Pansy managed that? *Why wasn't Amy stopping him?*

He turned to see a white light some distance in front of them, giving him night blindness in the low-lit corridor. Lewis groped for his arm and, together, they stumbled drunkenly towards the light. As they approached the beacon, Stoker's features became clearer beneath the light. He was standing in front of an open door, about where the mess door was upstairs. It was an exact reflection of the compound, merely subterranean, and it was freaking Jason out.

Further down the corridor, he heard someone shouting and banging against one of the doors, with another beacon of light flooding his vision. Stoker nodded towards the door, and they stepped through together.

'Took your time,' Dreadlock said.

'They had wandered,' Stoker said, and said no more.

'Are you happy, Dreadlock?' Pansy said, sounding on edge. 'Can we go now, miss?'

'If you can.'

Her voice came from near the floor, coming out of a sea of shadowed faces attached to kneeling bodies. It sounded alien, harsh, but he would still recognise her anywhere. He tried to control his expression, even though he doubted anyone could see it, because that would be one small step to something very stupid.

'Where is the release for the hatch?' Pansy demanded.

Silence.

The sharp *thwack* of impact had Jason leaping forward, but Lewis had a tight hold on his arm. They had already been left behind once. They couldn't afford to be enemies again. But what was the use of being here if he wasn't protecting Amy?

'You like hitting women, Pansy?' Jason said, sneering. 'Are they the only ones who won't fuck you up?'

'She needs to know her place. Why's she even playing the game? She's already lost!'

'The house always wins.' Dreadlock sounded distant, almost dreamy. 'They set this up to watch how we'd do it. Either way, if we escape or we don't, they still get what they want.'

Chapter 46: The Charge of the Night Brigade

Cerys was startled from sleep by her ringing phone. What time was it?

She tried to reach for it, but something was weighing down her shoulder: Catriona's head. The DVD logo was bouncing around the television screen – what had they even been watching?

The phone was still ringing.

Mumbling an apology to Catriona, Cerys reached forward with her clumsy left hand and answered it. ''lo?'

'Cerys, it's Owain. Something's gone wrong at the compound. I need you.'

The words caused her stomach to flip-flop, in that way she hated. She wished she could hear his voice and feel nothing at all.

'Is Jason hurt?' she said, her voice shaking. *Get a grip, Carr.*

Catriona shifted away from her and ran a hand through her messy ginger curls, an expression of curiosity on her face.

'I don't know. The prisoners have taken over the bunker and communication has been lost. Frieda won't intervene, but I think it's… well, it will go to shit. It was a powder keg when I left. Amy can't handle it. I nee—You—We have to help them.'

He was going to say it again, but he stopped himself. She was glad he didn't. She needed to think about this with her rational head. Not that there was anything to think about.

'How soon can you be here?'

'I'm parked outside.'

Cerys hung up on him, resisting the urge to throw her phone. The presumptuous twat!

Catriona was still looking at her, a blanket falling off her shoulder and dark smudges under her eyes from lack of sleep. 'What's going on?'

'The compound has been taken over. Owain wants to save everyone. You in?'

'I'll get my coat.'

If Owain was surprised to see Catriona with her, he didn't say anything. She climbed into the back before Cerys could insist she take the front, leaving Cerys riding shotgun with the dickhead she was still in love with. He pulled away without waiting for her to fasten her seatbelt.

'What are you doing out here?' Cerys said.

'Frieda relieved me of duty. Amy's in charge now.'

Cerys knew that was down to them, but she said nothing. The streets flew by too fast, empty in the early hours of Friday morning, before Owain headed out of the city. The silence was weighing on her, but she wasn't prepared to break it. Afraid that any fracture in it would force her to confess a hundred unsayable things.

'How do you know what's happened?' Catriona asked.

Cerys could've murdered her.

'Amy sent an SOS text to the duty desk. I intercepted it. The private line to the compound is dead and all the Eye logins are disconnected. That's impossible, unless they've been cut off from the network somehow.'

Cerys only understood half of what he was saying, but it didn't sound good.

'What's the plan?' she asked.

Owain just gripped the steering wheel tighter.

'Of course you don't have a fucking plan,' Catriona said, quietly furious. 'You never think things through.'

Caught in her own pain, Cerys had forgotten how much Owain had wronged Catriona too. How she had lost her dream job because he had run off to the NCA.

'If you have something to say, Cat, just say it.'

'Don't call her Cat, dickhead.'

The words were out without her thinking them through, but then they hung between them, echoing in the silence. *Dick-head-head-head.*

'You don't have to come with me,' Owain said, jaw tightly clenched.

'We're here for Jason and Amy. That's it. We're not friends, Owain.'

'I know that. Let's just get the job done.'

They spent the rest of the journey in absolute silence, Owain only slowing his breakneck speed as they came closer to their destination.

'I…I don't know the exact location.'

'Take the next right,' Cerys said, remembering her way. 'We'll go in the back.'

'There's only one—'

'Just trust me.' *For once, Owain, just trust me.* 'You want this left.'

Owain took the turning and then stopped suddenly. 'This is a farmyard.'

Catriona opened the back door. 'I'll be right back.'

She ran across the yard, leaving Cerys and Owain alone in the car.

'Is it too late to say I'm sorry?' Owain said.

'You can say it,' Cerys bit out, damping down the piece of her heart that leapt at the apology. 'It doesn't mean I forgive you.'

'I am sorry. I fucked this up, all of it. I've lost…pretty much everything I cared about.'

'I don't care about your sob story.' She heard the harshness in her voice, swallowing against the lump in her throat. 'Jason and Amy are basically under house arrest because of what you did.'

'I tried to save you! She was going to take away your career!'

Cerys recoiled from him in horror. 'Tell me you didn't. Tell me this wasn't about me.'

He looked young again, miserable and lost. She hated that it still affected her.

'I thought I could protect you all from the inside. I was wrong about that.'

'You've been wrong about a fucking long list of things, Owain. Now, my brother is in danger—'

'That is nothing to do with me.'

'Will you take responsibility for fucking anything?'

The back door slammed.

'He says it's fine.'

'Reverse out of here and head further down the road.' Cerys was pleased that her voice was mostly under control again. 'You want the gate on the left.'

'He said to block it.'

'Who is this man?'

'The farmer who is kindly doing us a favour.'

Owain pulled into the gateway, almost knocking off the passenger-side wing mirror. Cerys resisted the urge to shout at him and clambered through the back. She scaled the gate, took the bundle Catriona handed her, then waited for her to climb over. The blanket-wrapped object was long and, as the wind gusted past, the cover blew back and her fingers touched metal.

'What's this?' she asked warily.

'Shotgun.'

'What? Cat, you – Catriona, you have to take that back.'

Catriona lifted it out of Cerys' arms, leaving her with the blanket. She flicked on a torch attached to a carabiner on her jeans, lighting their way across the field towards the deep, dark wood.

'Let's go.'

Cerys dumped the blanket and followed her closely, glad when Owain chose to keep his distance. She didn't want to continue their arguments with a shotgun in the mix.

'Do you know how to use that?' she asked, under her breath.

'Yes,' Catriona said, curtly.

'All right then!' Cerys clapped her hands. 'It's a party.'

'Can't you take anything seriously?' Owain complained.

'Can't you just fuck off?'

It was a shame the shotgun would get in the way of a high-five.

'Neither of you are behaving professionally.'

'This isn't a work trip, Owain. We're doing you a favour, to save our friends. I'll be as unprofessional as I like.'

Cerys felt absurdly proud of her, squeezing Catriona's shoulder in solidarity and leaning in to her warmth. They reached the edge of the woodland, the torchlight bouncing off the thick trunks of the trees.

'What now?' Owain asked.

'Now we go in,' Catriona said and, raising the gun, she walked into enemy territory.

Chapter 47: Divide and Conquer

Amy's cheek was smarting from where Pansy had slapped her. She was both surprised and hurt that Jason hadn't murdered him.

Pansy hadn't tried to get any more information and was now sulking in the corner with Owain's laptop. However, if Frieda wasn't coming to get them, Amy was just prolonging the agony by refusing to cooperate. They might as well get this experiment over with. Yes, a murderer would walk free, but that was the entire point of Frieda's bargain. Why had she even sent Owain in if she wasn't interested in justice?

Martin was lurking in the background, saying and doing nothing. It seemed like no one had a plan about what happened next. She wished she could come up with something, but her attention was caught by her stinging skin and Jason standing in front of her. He looked as stressed as she felt.

'Jason – bring the leader to my office,' Martin said. 'Let's settle this.'

Jason took a moment to respond, before lurching forward and dragging Amy up by her arm.

'Let's go,' he said, voice rough.

Amy put up some token resistance, while enjoying the warmth on her arm. If she wasn't being walked to her doom, she would be pleased at the contact. Her brain tried to cobble together some kind of defence to whatever Martin was going to say, but she had nothing. Jason was here and everything would be all right.

The door to her office was ajar. The man with dreadlocks was staring at the screen intently. He looked up and shut the lid as they came in.

'No luck with the password,' he said.

'Leave that to Pansy. And leave us please.'

He looked between them all, before leaving without a word, shutting the door behind him.

'Amy,' Martin nodded to her. 'Jason. Don't let me get in the way of your reunion.'

Jason dropped his hand from her shoulder, though their arms were still touching.

'What do you want?' she asked, forcing her voice to stay calm. *Be like Frieda.*

'I want to get out of here. Like Pansy, I don't trust anyone to keep their promises.'

'Who killed Mole?' Jason asked, as if that still mattered.

'I didn't see his face,' Martin said, deflating. 'But he...he dragged Mole past my office. Then presumably out into the garden, before the doors locked.'

'He was killed in the kitchen then,' Jason said, sounding triumphant. Amy would be proud if she wasn't also sick with dread.

'What do you *want*?'

Martin collected himself, assuming his mask as she assumed hers. They were playing the game again, except it was deadly and desperate.

'I want you to open that door.'

'I can't,' she said.

'And I believe you. But my young men won't, I'm afraid. You need to arrange some way for it to open. Quickly, please.'

'You'll want to take hostages.'

'Of course.'

'Take me and release the rest.'

'I need more than that.'

'You can have three.'

'Ten.'

'Five.'

'Done.'

Amy felt her skin come out in goose pimples. She had just bartered with five people's lives, as if they were nothing. They could all die and it would be her fault. The mask was starting to stick.

'If I persuade the agents inside the dormitory to open the door, I want them to be allowed to leave with the others.'

'I said I'll only keep five – including you. The rest can enjoy the facilities in the compound, as we have enjoyed them for the past few months.'

Amy nodded, feeling drained. This should be Owain standing here. It was her fault that it wasn't. He would've known how to conduct a hostage negotiation. Instead, she was just winging it. This was not the kind of thing she wanted to be blagging.

'I will allow you five minutes,' Martin said, unexpectedly. 'Jason will have to come with us to avoid suspicion.'

He stood up and left them, closing the door behind him. Jason hauled her into his arms, crushing her ribcage and her lungs and her heart – but she didn't care. She kissed at his neck, hands pressing hard into his back, as if she could keep him this close just by the force of her effort.

Then, she broke away, feeling his kiss glance off her bruised cheek, as she looked for the phone she had dropped into the shadows

'Cerys will answer her phone,' she said, searching through her contacts.

'I've missed you too.'

The phone didn't ring. She checked it again – no signal.

'They've reactivated the jammer,' she said, her heart sinking. 'We're really on our own.'

'This will work,' Jason said, with certainty. 'You'll get the hostages to safety and then we'll walk out of here. We'll all go our separate ways and I'll meet you back in Cardiff.'

He made it sound so simple, and not like every word was loaded with a thousand ifs, ands, or buts. It had been so much easier when she had lived inside her flat, only speaking to people on her terms, not responsible for anybody – barely responsible for herself. Bad things happened when other people's lives were in her hands.

'What about the second stage?' she said.

Jason looked at her, uncomprehending. 'What second stage?'

'There should be another set of tasks after this – that's what Owain said.'

'Owain was here?' Jason looked even more confused.

'Never mind. We'll figure it out.' She hesitated. 'What about the murderer?'

She'd convinced herself she didn't really care about that, but she did care. The prisoners were her responsibility as well as the agents. She couldn't let them out only for them to kill each other in the woods.

'Don't worry about that,' Jason said, but Amy saw something in his eyes.

'He pushed you off the roof!' she said. 'And he's blinded a man.'

Now Jason definitely looked uncomfortable. 'He didn't push me – well, I know who that was. He, uh, said he was sorry.'

Amy looked at him in disbelief. 'Well, that's okay then,' she said, sarcastically. 'I'm glad we cleared that up.'

'Let me take care of the cons,' Jason said. 'You concentrate on the hostages.'

Amy nodded, though she didn't agree. She stuffed the phone in her pocket and opened the office door. Jason placed a hand on her arm, proprietorially, but she was glad to have it back. He walked her back to the Eye Room, where she surveyed her team.

'IN1, IN2, IN4, IN6 – you're with me. Everyone else is moving up into the compound until the experiment is terminated.'

She met the gaze of the four people she had condemned with her, but only IN1 looked scared. IN2 nodded to her, as if he was proud. She felt like she might not be totally fucking this up after all.

'Gov, what's going on?' Pansy whined. 'I wanted all these girls.'

'The hostages are not to be touched,' Martin said, with finality.

'Stoker and Lewis – with me,' Dreadlock said. 'We'll escort the rest up to the compound.'

'Anchor, will you give us a hand with the dormitory?' Jason said, to one of the remaining men. 'Nikolai's down there.'

'I'm reading you,' Anchor said, nudging Amy with tip of his club. It was P6. The undercover agent. 'Off we go then.'

Amy led them out into the corridor and down towards the dormitories. One man was holding a faltering flare, while the other repeatedly kicked at the door with no results. The flare-holder held up the light to Amy and whistled.

'You brought us a tasty treat, Jay Bird?'

'Shut it, Gareth. We're releasing hostages.'

'Why would we do that?'

The Russian accent of the door-kicker was sneering, and he looked at her suspiciously. It was P4 again, the one who had dragged her out from under the desk by her hair. Her scalp smarted just thinking about it. He was probably the one Jason had called Nikolai.

'Governor's orders,' Jason said. 'Show of good faith, all that shit.'

Nikolai snorted but said nothing more. Jason gestured Amy forward towards the door. She took a hesitant step forward and quietly cleared her throat. She had no idea if the security guys would listen to her, but she had to try. Of course, if they wanted to stay locked up in here, that was their choice. She didn't have time to free people who didn't want out.

'Attention, SD1. This is Agent Lane. You are being moved as part of a hostage negotiation. Will you open the door?'

After she'd said it, she realised she should've made the question an order. Given the prisoners the impression that she expected to be obeyed, that she really was the one in charge.

'Override code, Agent,' SD1 called back.

Shit. She didn't have a code. If there was a code, Owain hadn't given it to her. What the hell was she supposed to do now?

She looked behind her, at Jason – and at Anchor. He was IN0. He had to know the override code. But he said nothing, did nothing. He wasn't going to help them.

The door burst open. Gareth dropped the flare.

Amy was flung back against the wall, her head banging hard against it. She bit down on her tongue, tasting metal, and belatedly realised she was sitting on the floor. Someone tripped over her legs and went flying. Further down the corridor, someone shouted and another person cried out. Bodies collided, punches connected, and soft squishy bodies hit hard surfaces.

Amy tried to get her legs under her, but someone was calling her name, someone she loved, and she had to stay where she was. Then, there was only silence.

'Pansy, put the lights on!'

'Gov—'

'Now!'

The strip lighting flicked on, blinding her and causing an ice pick to lodge in her temple. Jason was hovering over her, staring frantically into her eyes, as if checking to see if she was alive.

'Up,' she said, her voice thick, her bitten tongue too big for her mouth.

Jason helped her to her feet, and she looked down the corridor. People were lying on the floor, prisoners and agents. And there was blood. A lot of blood. What had happened? What had she done?

She counted two female agents, supporting each other to stand, and a couple of prisoners staggering to their feet. But one remained motionless on the floor, a dark puddle spreading over the corridor floor from beneath him.

Jason half-carried her down the corridor, and they stood over a young man who was lying on the floor, staring at the ceiling with sightless eyes, as blood sluggishly flowed out of his neck, from between Pansy's fingers. Amy numbly recognised him as P10, her regular wanderer. *He won't wander anymore.*

'Roshan…' Jason said, sounding as if he'd been punched in the gut.

The Governor looked at her, eyes cold and hard, more terrifying now than he had ever been to her – even when he wanted her dead.

'You did this,' he said. 'Tell me why I shouldn't kill every one of you.'

Her tongue stuck to the roof of her mouth, her head spun, but she had to answer him. She had to speak for the remaining lives under her care, even if she had failed this one.

'Because They will never stop hunting you,' she said.

Chapter 48: Opportunity Knocks

They wrapped Roshan up in a blanket and placed him on a bed in one of the dormitories. Joe insisted that he wanted to stay with him and Jason pretended he hadn't seen him crying.

The injured were kept in the other dormitory, prisoner and agent, with Anchor doing his first aid, and Jason and Lewis standing watch. Amy was being held separately from the others now, and Jason and Anchor were being kept away. In disgrace, for having fucked up so badly.

Nikolai had dislocated his shoulder and had passed out from the pain. The two agents were women who had been taken out by prisoners as they tried to escape, but they only had cuts and bruises to show for it. Jason didn't know what was happening with the other agents, but he needed to find out. Amy's plan was up in smoke, so he needed to step up. He was the master of getting out of tough scrapes, after all.

He turned to Lewis. 'You all right here if I go check on Joe?'

Anchor looked up but said nothing. He was fucking good at that, wasn't he? Jason hadn't confronted him, but he had seen how Amy had looked to him for help and got nothing in return. Was Anchor trying to get them all killed so his fuck-ups weren't discovered?

'Yeah, we're good,' Lewis said.

Jason crossed the corridor, glancing along it to where Gareth was standing watch. Gareth nodded to him, so he wasn't a complete pariah. Here they all were, playing soldier, as if that suited them better than cook or gardener or Project man. Did Gareth feel as out of his depth as Jason did, guarding a corridor, pretending they knew how to do this?

Joe was sitting on the bunk opposite where Roshan was laid out, hands clasped together, staring at the floor. Jason perched next to him, as if they were mourners at a funeral, huddled into the pews.

'He should be cremated,' Joe said, suddenly. 'He was Hindu and they burn their dead.'

Jason didn't think they were really in a position to set fires, so he just nodded.

'He was nice to me. Just…nice. No agenda to him at all. Apparently, he'd been done for smuggling counterfeits – can you believe it?'

'He seemed nice,' Jason added, though he hadn't really known Roshan, just been suspicious of how quiet he was.

'I don't know how this happened.' Joe held up his hand, to forestall an explanation. 'Not with those bastard agents – shit happens, y'know – but with Rosh. What the fuck was he doing in the corridor? The last place you'd find him in a fight was in the thick of it.

'Maybe—'

'Pipe down, all right? You didn't know him. He would never have been out there, not if he had a choice. There was a reason for it. There's a reason he's…he's…'

Jason tried to look past the grief, the ashamed tears, the quest for his death not to have been pointless. What Joe said did have a flavour of reason to it. Why was Roshan in the corridor? Pansy had been there too – another unlikely candidate for a fight. Had Dreadlock forced them out into the melee? That didn't seem like his style.

Stoker and Lewis had been out of the way, escorting agents up into the compound. That left Roshan and Pansy in the Eye Room with Joe, Dreadlock and the Governor. Jason had seen the latter three in the doorway as they'd stood over Roshan, not out in the corridor proper. Would Dreadlock send Pansy and Roshan out into the darkness, when he hadn't gone himself?

An uncomfortable thought entered Jason's mind. What if Roshan had known something? What if the fight had been an opportunity to silence him? It would be the perfect time – what if someone had seized the moment to remove quiet, inconvenient Roshan?

Jason mentally calculated who was left in the corridor. He had stayed down the dormitory end, knocked aside when the agents had come storming through. Anchor, Nikolai, and Gareth had pursued them. Including Pansy and Roshan, there had been five prisoners in that stretch of corridor at that time. If he assumed Roshan hadn't slit his own throat, he had four suspects.

Nikolai was the most obvious candidate, his name cropping up in every suspect list – though Jason now knew he hadn't pushed him off the roof. He'd also been on the other side of the corridor when they'd found him, shoulder wrenched out of joint, and completely dead to the world. But he could've cut Roshan before he'd been taken out.

Jason was more concerned about Anchor. He was supposed to be one of the good guys, but what had happened with the dormitory negotiation? He could've done something, shouted something so they recognised his voice without giving himself away. Maybe Roshan's death wasn't 'seizing the moment' as much as 'creating the moment'.

'If there's a reason, I'll find it,' Jason heard himself say.

'You were meant to find my watch,' Joe said. 'Look what happened there.'

Two things sprang immediately into Jason's mind. The first was that he had found the watch, but because of Lewis' revelations and breaking through the window, he had completely forgotten about it. The second was that Joe knew who had killed Mole – maybe now that Roshan was dead, he would feel enraged enough to point the finger.

'Could Roshan's death be linked to Mole's?'

Jason expected to be told to shut up again, but when he looked over at Joe, he seemed puzzled.

'I thought Mole was… I don't know anymore. What happened to Bo and Rosh – that don't make any sense. Maybe you could say what happened to Bo was just a bit of a prank that went wrong – unless it was you?'

'It wasn't,' Jason said evenly.

'Yeah. When I thought about it a bit, I realised it weren't you. But we haven't had nothing like that the whole time I've been here – and I was here after the first month, or so they tell me. Now we've got two dead men and one carried off, all in just weeks. If they're not related, it's a hell of a coincidence.'

'So…' Jason said slowly. 'If you told me who did for Mole, we could—'

'It's not him. It can't be. Leave it, will you?'

'You want to be next, Joe?'

Joe's expression was hard, the tear tracks fading.

'If I talk, I will be.'

Chapter 49: Self-rescuing Princess

Amy's head was killing her.

She could feel a lump forming where she'd hit the wall, the swelling causing her hair to stick out and the whole room to swing in lazy circles. The last thing she needed was a concussion, when her only asset was her brain.

She was being held in the canteen area of the bunker, but she wasn't being guarded. There was someone in the corridor who occasionally walked up to peer through the door, then left again. She had just been left alone with an endless supply of caffeine and biscuits. The privileges of rank.

When she could stand up without swaying, she made herself a cup of tea and rammed half a dozen chocolate digestives in her mouth. The feeling of sickness intensified, but she kept them down. What now? Her plan had been a disaster. She had a second chance to get it right, but how?

First things first – she needed access to a computer. She felt completely vulnerable without it and she would think so much better with keys beneath her fingers. If Pansy had Owain's laptop, the only other options were her laptop in the office, the computers in the Eye Room, or the computers in the Hide. The laptop in the office seemed like the only viable option, but how would she take out the corridor guard?

Where she wanted to be was the Security Hide. It might feel like abandoning ship, but she would be leading the free agents and able to coordinate a rescue attempt instead of playing the hostage. But the prospect of reaching that little hatch at the end of the darkened corridor filled her with dread. It wasn't just the corridor guard, but all the prisoners in the Eye Room too. She had seen what had happened to the agents who had tried to run past there, bruised and battered women laid out on the floor – and they'd had darkness on their side.

Darkness. The power had gone out just prior to the invasion. Which meant that above her, in the compound, there was a way of taking out the power. It might be in Pansy's super-charged access account, but she could find a way in if she had enough time. Even if she didn't have quite enough, she could still move freely and perhaps make contact with the agents who had been sent up.

She looked up and saw the guard looking in. She picked up the throw from the back of the threadbare sofa and made a show of laying it out, stacking up cushions at the end nearest the door. As he walked away, she stuffed a few more cushions under the blanket and headed for the exit. It would hopefully survive a second glance, but she didn't need the illusion to last for long. Any time it could buy her would be well-spent.

She opened up the door, saw the guard still had his back to her, and stepped across the corridor into the kitchen. The pantry was wide open and a ladder was hanging down made of sheets, leading into a dark narrow space above her. *No time to panic.*

The ladder swayed violently as she stepped on it, competing with the spinning of her head. She stopped, closed her eyes, and waited for her body to settle. She counted to thirty before, eyes still closed, she began to climb. She counted 42 cloth rungs, before light surrounded her eyelids and her head brushed the top of a cupboard.

She stretched her foot backwards and found the floor, reaching up to haul herself back and into…another kitchen. She didn't have time to linger and marvel at the similarities, though. Opening the door, she crossed the corridor into the room straight opposite.

This room was not the canteen. It was more like a conference room or the boardroom of a run-down company from the 1980s. The large table was tattooed with ink, and the chairs were in a state of disrepair. There were ageing sheets of paper tacked up everywhere, with crude maps and checklists and fragments of at least half a dozen different plans for escape.

In the corner, there was her prize – an ancient desktop computer.

She crossed the room quickly, aware that the camera in this room was just above the door and that someone might be monitoring the feeds. The computer was off following the power cut, but it booted relatively quickly for such a doddery old piece of tech. It was running Windows 98 and Amy couldn't believe the NCA portal even allowed a login from such an outdated operating system. Maybe Pansy had found a workaround.

Amy found herself admiring his ingenuity, as the portal loaded automatically – and logged her in. She blinked at it, then glanced across at the computer tower. No USB slot, only floppy disk and CD. She got up and circled the tower, checking the back. In one of the old school USB ports, she found an NCA passport.

It looked like an ordinary USB drive, except it carried the tell-tale imprint of a white crown. Amy verified the logo and shook her head. How had Pansy got hold of an NCA passport? Unless Anchor had given it to him, or there was a second agent in the compound – perhaps even Pansy himself. Though if he was working undercover, it was a pretty deep cover from what she had seen.

She returned to the computer and found the account's access was essentially unlimited. Everything from environmental controls to the minute details of human resource files, this account could access them all. Had Pansy's fellow prisoners known he had this kind of access on them?

The temptation to read was very high. All those answers at her fingertips. But anyone could be watching her right now, so she needed to move fast. Reluctantly, she tore herself away from the prisoner files and went back to environmental management.

She found the emergency power breaker. One button press and it would be done – lights, camera, exits. At the last moment, she instead went into settings – and restricted account access to passport-only. She wished she could be there to see Pansy's face when he tried to reactivate the power and failed to even log in.

Amy grinned and shut down the power.

Chapter 50: The Darkest Hour

The room was plunged into darkness and a woman screamed.

'Shut up, bitch.'

Jason heard Nikolai's shout from across the corridor. Joe gripped onto Jason's arm and they stood as one, edging towards where they thought the door was. Once the door was open, the red emergency lighting showed them their feet if nothing else. Across the way, Anchor and Lewis lurked in the doorway.

'What the fuck is Pansy playing at?' Lewis asked.

'The fucking NCA are here!' Gareth shouted from down the corridor. 'We're under attack.'

'They can't be!' Pansy screeched. 'They fucking can't!'

It looked like Frieda was going to show after all. Jason wasn't sure if he was relieved or more worried by her presence. She was ruthless and he had no idea where she stood on this whole situation. Was it more important to keep the secret or more important to get her agents out alive?

"That boss girl is missing,' Stoker shouted, his deep voice carrying easily. 'She can't have gone far. Who's with me?'

Lewis looked at Jason, but he quickly looked away. The urge to hunt for her was overwhelming, but he had to trust that she knew what she was doing. With that new piece of intel, it was much more likely that she had shut down the power and was working against Pansy's computer skills. Jason would bet on Amy any day.

'Everyone stay calm and stay where you are.' The Governor sounded weak after Stoker's booming shout. 'We'll restore the power soon.'

Nikolai shoved Lewis out of the way and stepped into the corridor, hand massaging at the bruised muscles around his shoulder.

'I have had enough of this,' he declared. 'Governor doesn't trust me. I don't trust him.'

He stepped back into the room and returned with a torch and one of the agents, dragging her by her long dark hair. She was trying to hold it together, but there was fear on her face. No amount of training could prepare a person for this.

'What are you doing, Nikolai?' Anchor asked him, a warning tone in his voice.

'I take this girl to the hatch and I shout until they let me out. If they don't, I break a finger, and I break more until they open the hatch. Very simple. Very effective.'

He didn't wait for their response, just started down the corridor with his prisoner. Jason stepped forward, but Anchor was faster. He brought his club down on Nikolai's head at full strength, felling him instantly and splattering blood on the terrified woman he was holding.

'What the fuck are you lot doing down there?' Gareth shouted.

They waited, all frozen in shock at what had just happened.

'I'm looking for my glasses,' shouted Joe.

Jason remembered to breathe. They were all on the same side now, united in hiding Nikolai's unconscious body and protecting the agents. Joe bent down to collect the torch, while Jason dragged Nikolai into their makeshift morgue. He heard Anchor talking softly to the girl in the corridor, his hands cupping both her shoulders, and coaxing her back into the dormitory where she'd come from. Jason wondered if he knew her.

Joe followed Jason with the light and they both peered at the wound on Nikolai's head. It wasn't bleeding much and he was still breathing, but he probably needed an A&E department. Wordlessly, they shut the door and left him in the dark, returning to the other dormitory.

'What's the plan?' Jason asked, the light beside him meaning he couldn't see beyond his small circle of light.

'Do you know the code to get into the…place where the guards are?' Anchor asked.

One agent sniffed. 'Why should we—'

'Yes.' The woman who Nikolai had taken looked straight at Anchor with unwavering conviction, despite the other woman's furious signals.

'Good. We'll cover for you and wait at the end of the corridor.'

'We are not opening the hatch for you.'

Jason had a lot of respect for the feisty one.

'I didn't ask you to,' Anchor said, voice calm.

'We're not getting out of here, are we?' Joe asked, sounding resigned.

'Not yet,' Anchor replied.

'Yeah, save the girls, seems legit. Let's do it.'

'The torch will keep the others night blind,' Jason said. 'Me and Joe will walk up with it. You two stay back, pretending to be on guard. We'll join you when we can.'

Jason couldn't see any expressions, but he heard Anchor's hesitation. As an NCA agent, he was used to giving the orders, not following them. He could pretend in a situation where he was undercover, but he must find it galling when Jason knew his identity and still took charge.

'Are you girls ready?' Joe asked.

'Keep a couple of feet behind us,' Jason added. 'Stay out of the circle of light.'

'Will this work?' She was still staring at Anchor, looking to him for answers.

'It's the only idea we've got,' said the feisty one. 'Let's go then, before you all change your minds. I've had enough of macho men today.'

'Try living with them for six months,' Joe grumbled.

Jason turned towards the door again, with Joe beside him, and stepped out into the corridor. It was like that old Greek myth, about the guy who led his girl out of Hell but couldn't look at her.

'I hope the Eurydices are following,' Joe said under his breath, and Jason grudgingly admitted that he'd misjudged him.

'Stay where you are!' Gareth shouted. 'The Governor told you to stay put!'

'I need to talk to him,' Jason shouted back. 'It's urgent.'

There was a small conference by the others, which Jason and Joe couldn't hear. He felt someone draw nearer to him, and he reached back to touch her arm.

'Not yet,' he murmured.

'Come on up then. Be quick about it.'

Jason and Joe started moving again, and Jason lost contact. They had to be following. They had to trust him. As they drew closer, Jason saw that it was Gareth and Pansy who were standing out in the corridor now. Joe stepped past them and stood more towards the kitchen, his light close to Gareth. Jason stood opposite the door of the room with the computers, hoping he was giving enough room for the women to pass behind him.

'What's this urgent business then?' Gareth asked.

'It's Nikolai,' Jason said. 'He must've been hurt worse than we thought, hit his head or something. He can't stay awake.'

'Fuck Nikolai,' Pansy said, with surprising venom. 'NHS wouldn't touch him anyway.'

'What the fuck are you talking about?' Joe asked.

'We can't get him out is what I'm saying,' Jason said. 'We'd have to carry him.'

'We'll have to fight our way out,' Pansy said, intensely. 'All guns blazing.'

'Except they're the ones with the guns,' Gareth said, wincing.

'That's why I need to talk to the Governor.'

'Good luck with that,' Gareth said, lowering his voice. 'He's quiet as a church mouse, hanging out in that dark canteen place by himself.'

'He's lost it,' Pansy said, bluntly. 'That's what Gar's trying so hard not to say. The boss has fucking lost it.'

Suddenly, out of nowhere, Jason saw Amy's face appear out of the darkness. He somehow avoided calling out – and then she was gone. Was he hallucinating? Or was she emerging from hiding, taking advantage of their double pool of light to make her escape? On one hand, he was glad she was getting herself to safety. On the other, he felt like he was on his own, even though Lewis had his back and Anchor was undercover. Amy was his other half, his partner against crime. He needed her.

'Jay Bird? Are you listening?'

He shook his head. 'Sorry. I…uh…I just thought…'

Gareth nudged Pansy. 'It's catching.'

'Maybe there's something in the air,' Pansy said, only half-joking.

'I'm fine,' Jason said, firmly. 'Let's go see The Wizard.'

Chapter 51: Into the Woods

The wood was haunted by shadows.

Cerys kept close to Catriona, holding up the map. She could hear Owain's footsteps behind them and saw a hundred creatures leap and swoop and scurry out of the blackness. At least Catriona seemed to know what she was doing with the gun, holding it level and not swinging it towards everything that moved.

Until a man ran straight at them.

'Fuck! You're armed!'

'Stand down, agent,' Owain said, firmly.

The man deflated, panting as he put his hands on his thighs. 'The SDs have gone crazy, sir. They think they're fucking commandos.'

'Are they in the Hide?'

The man laughed weakly. 'Oh no. They're out in the woods, forming a perimeter for when the prisoners leave the compound. SD1 said he wanted to hunt them like dogs.'

Cerys had never felt more frightened. Men with guns were going to hunt down her brother in these dark and twisted woods. He would never get out alive.

'You escaped from them?'

'SN1 wanted us all to wait, to stay together. But SD1 and the rest decided to go it alone. So SN1 said he'd escort us out of the woods – some of them had gone ahead to contact Control. But we…well, it sounded like there was a gunshot and we all ran like hell.'

'Keep going straight through the woods. Wait ten minutes for other agents, then retreat to the farmhouse.'

'Tell them Catriona sent you.'

The agent looked at Catriona and her gun, before nodding slowly. He then left them without a word, loping away through the woods as if his colleagues were on his tail. Fuck, this was a mess. Cerys had always known the NCA was batshit, but this was another level.

'Let's keep going,' Catriona said, and as Owain didn't contradict her, on they went.

They saw the compound first, a hulk of a building in clear open space surrounded by a chain-link fence. Again, there were people moving around it, but the darkness made it almost impossible to recognise anyone.

'This is where my map ends,' Catriona said.

'I can take us from here,' Owain answered, taking the lead.

They moved silently along the fence, but a voice hissed from behind it.

'Agent Jenkins! Over here!'

Owain took a few steps back, Catriona and Cerys keeping their distance. Cerys wanted to get on with this, not tend to the masses who Owain had let down. She needed to stop Jason catching a bullet.

'Where are the others?' the woman asked him, sounding desperate.

'We're the…the advance party,' he said, but it wasn't particularly convincing. 'What are you doing out here?'

'We were sent up into the compound as 'freed hostages', but Agent Lane told us to get outside, that the negotiation had broken down.'

'She was right. Stay away from the door and the fence. Keep together.'

'We can follow our training, sir.'

The woman's voice was cold, but then she was only wearing a cardigan. Cerys felt sorry for her, following orders from Owain and Amy. Not exactly a pair to inspire confidence.

Owain left her with a nod, and the three of them carried on, continuing to use the fence as a guide. Cerys wondered why they were sticking to it when Owain had just told the other agents to stay away. Maybe he didn't care as much if they got shot by rogue agents. Frieda probably didn't value cop lives as highly as agents'.

'We're close to the Hide now,' Owain said. 'Look out for—'

They were swiftly and completely surrounded within seconds. Cerys grabbed Catriona's shoulder with a yelp, which somehow didn't stop Catriona from pointing the shotgun at some agent's head.

'Put that toy away,' the man said.

'Are you a cop killer now?' Catriona replied.

'Stand down, SD1,' Owain said, in his voice of command.

The agent just laughed. 'You're not in charge anymore, Jenkins. Get your pet cop to put away her little gun.'

'Agent Haas has sent me to recover the situation after you all fucked it up,' Owain lied, calmly and confidently. 'Stand down.'

'Even if I believed she would trust you again, I don't buy that she'd send you in with a couple of WPCs.'

'This is a joint operation and we are an advance party only. It's hard to find trained NCA agents in the Middle of Nowhere, Wales, at short notice. At least, it's hard to find ones who can follow orders.'

'Fuck you, Jenkins.'

'After you put down your gun, Onesie.'

'Back off from the bitches, boys,' the agent said, trying to hide the anger in his voice with a laugh. 'They're both dykes anyway.'

'You need to escort—'

'You might be Haas' good dog, but I'm her fucking pitbull. I am going to lie in wait for those prison boys and then I'm going to take them down. Fuck the experiment. They are endangering agents.'

'Like you're not,' Cerys said, her mouth engaging before her brain. Maybe she shouldn't be so willing to taunt the man with the assault rifle.

'I can tell a piss-pants agent from a hardened thug, yeah. And I don't report to either of you. Write me up or whatever. I'm here to save lives, not earn commendations. Back to positions, boys.'

The men with guns melted away into the darkness as if they'd never been there. Cerys found that even more terrifying than being surrounded by their real and immediate presence. She wanted to know where the bullet with her name on was coming from.

'Let's go before they change their minds,' Owain said urgently.

They didn't need telling twice.

The Hide was little more than a shack, like some cabin in the woods that featured in a horror movie. It had been camouflaged with branches, but Owain made a direct line for the door and found an oddly-juxtaposed keypad under the foliage.

The door opened and the warmth of the room spilled out. There were two women standing in the middle of the room, out of breath and carrying a set of minor injuries that had been tended to. At the back, a man was leaning over to help someone up out of a hatch in the floor – and that someone was Amy.

She looked pale and worn, but surprisingly with it. She tried to remove her hand from the man's, but he was holding on tight, leaning in as if he was about to kiss her—

'Amy!' Cerys yelled, before she saw something she couldn't unsee.

Amy jerked away from him, freeing her hand, and looked as if she was seeing a series of ghosts. She eventually smiled and gestured for the man to close the hatch behind her. He looked disappointed, but Cerys didn't want to dwell on that.

'The cavalry's here,' Catriona said with forced cheer, setting down her shotgun on the table and closing the Hide door.

'Good,' Amy said, with feeling, 'because it's about to go to shit down there.'

Chapter 52: Downfall

In the canteen of the bunker, he made for a sad figure.

They hadn't seen him at first, the beam from their torches too powerful, but Jason suddenly made him out in the corner and swung the light on him. He didn't give any sign that he'd seen them, just continued staring down at his hands. Jason set the torch down on the table with the beam up towards the ceiling, the light spilling across the room.

'Look on my works ye mighty and despair,' the man formerly known as the Governor said. No one could possibly call him that now, not like this.

'What, you giving up?' Gareth said, but this was not a pep talk. His voice was filled with horror, disdain.

'I have ruined everything. Mole is dead. Roshan is dead. If the agents outside have their way, the rest of us will die very soon. I think that might've been their plan all along.'

Lewis looked at Jason to deny it, but he had nothing to say. Amy would protect them as best she could, but he didn't believe the NCA knew the meaning of compassion. Frieda certainly didn't. This could be their exit strategy.

'Let's leave him,' Pansy said, already backing away. 'Nothing for us here.'

He pulled on Gareth's sleeve and gestured to Joe, beckoning him. They came to him without a word, retreating into the darkness of the corridor. Jason could hear them whispering.

'What are our orders?' Anchor asked.

'I lied to you,' Martin said, sounding very far away. 'We were meant to get out of here and then we had...we had to do something terrible. I couldn't let that happen. I'm not a monster. Whatever you think of me, I'm not that. It was all for her, only for her...'

Anchor and Jason exchanged glances. If Martin wasn't able to lead, it would only lead to more chaos. Jason needed to find Dreadlock and persuade him to assume command. He'd never given the impression he wanted it, but he was also a natural leader who people respected. The others would listen to him.

They backed away from Martin without discussing it, without really deciding. It was a natural repulsion. Jason took the torch with him, leaving their former leader in darkness once more. He led the way out into the corridor, where the others were waiting for him.

'What now?' Gareth asked.

'Where is Dreadlock?' Anchor asked. He'd obviously had the same thought Jason had.

'We don't need him,' Joe said, quickly. 'We've got this.'

'Got what? No plan, no resources, no nothing.' Lewis sounded increasingly anxious.

'We could go back upstairs and pretend like nothing has happened,' Gareth said. 'Send the agents back down, seal up the walls.'

'We're not going out like that!' Pansy yelled. 'We're gonna fight 'til the end!'

'With what?' Anchor said, voice harsh. 'They have guns. We have clubs.'

'We could—'

Jason was interrupted by running footsteps along the corridor. But they weren't coming towards them. They were there, and then they were fading. Suddenly, Jason realised they were all standing there, all six of them – and only Stoker was guarding the hostages.

He started to run down the corridor, carrying the light with him. He burst into the room to find the agents gone and Stoker lying on the floor, his face bloody and his legs tied with a belt. Lewis pushed past him and knelt beside Stoker, begging him to wake up. Jason knelt down to untie the belt, calling for Anchor to help him.

Fire burst across his vision and he threw himself down, over Stoker, trying to get away from the sudden intense heat. Another searing blast of flame erupted next to him, catching the edge of his jeans and singeing them. Without thinking, he rolled Stoker over, moving with him towards the far wall of the room.

But where was Lewis?

Jason looked around him, struggling to see through the thickening clouds of black smoke. He ducked down and took a breath near the floor, where the air was still clear, before restarting his search. His eyes were drawn to a flaming computer chair and, pinned beneath it, Lewis was desperately trying to wriggle free.

Pulling his hoodie sleeves down over his hands, Jason pushed off the chair and helped Lewis up. He pushed him towards Stoker, before looking for a way for them to reach the door. He saw too late that the chair he'd thrown was now spreading its flames to the nearest computer desk, the fire licking along the surface and engulfing the computers.

The explosion sent him flying backwards, the last thing he saw was a figure in the fire, before everything went dark.

They were all going to die.

Lewis watched helplessly as Jason was sent flying across the room, broken glass scattering from the exploded monitor. He hit the wall monitor, cracking it with his hard head. He slumped down the wall, unconscious, his face flecked with blood from a hundred different cuts.

Ben wouldn't wake up. The agents had hit him hard, or the smoke was getting to him. Lewis could feel his lungs burning, the hot air and smoke starting to cook them from the inside. His brain wanted to ask questions like 'who threw the firebombs?' and 'why can't we breathe?' but Lewis had more important things on his mind. Like surviving long enough to find answers.

Lewis closed his eyes and concentrated. This was just like planning a robbery. A little more pushed for time, sure, but otherwise just the same. He had to visualise the space, know where all the players were. They only had each other. The only people outside were Bad Guys who wanted to stop them. That was the state of play.

The room was large, the same size as the mess upstairs. There was one door, no windows. A whole lot of electronics. Lewis counted at least six computers, including the exploded one, and that massive screen that now had a massive crack down it. This room was a hoard of flammable things and would be absolutely airtight with the door closed. Which would be great, except that they were all on the wrong side of it.

Something was irritating the back of his brain, but the smoke was making it hard to think. He laid himself down on the floor, trying to find some good air beneath the smoke, but it was all pretty smoky. It was nice to lie down though, almost peaceful. At least the smoke would take him before he burned alive.

He pinched his own arm hard enough to bruise and managed to shake off the lethargy – just a fraction, just enough. He was missing something. Something was missing. What was missing? This high-tech room, merrily burning, and it didn't even have a tap or a bottle of water. Were you meant to throw water on computers? Probably not.

How did the firefighters do it then? Did they just wait for it to burn out? Lewis pinched himself again. His thoughts were so slow and stupid. He was smarter than this. He was smart enough to live.

Fire extinguishers. Special ones, in lots of different colours. A room like this had to have one, or even several, didn't it? Lewis crawled his way along the floor, dragging his lethargic body towards the corner of the room. He couldn't see his own hands now and he really wanted to nap. But he had to get to the wall. Find an extinguisher. Hope it was the right one. Figure out how to use it. Then he could nap for a really long time. A really really really…

He had stopped moving. Lewis shook his head, shook his limbs and moved forward – head-first into the wall. The pain roused him, a spike through his head that told him he had to act or die. He groped his way up the wall and his hand touched metal. A big metal cylinder with a rubber hose. He couldn't see what colour it was or if there were instructions, but he yanked it away from the wall and stumbled towards the fire.

The desks were all alight now, the computers surrounded by flames – but Lewis didn't care about that. He found the glow from the middle of the aisle, the fire blocking his escape, and he guided the nozzle towards it. The handle wouldn't squeeze though, and he fumbled with it, dropping the extinguisher.

It rolled away – and he threw himself over it, as if it were his beloved dog. He clawed it back, standing up again and swaying drunkenly. He could hear shouting from beyond the fire, but he couldn't think about that. His fingernails caught on some plastic bit, which came loose in his hand. This time, the handle moved and a cloud of white came out of the end.

He pointed it at the fire and walked forward, the white fighting against the black, the white floating down onto the flames. Another and another, the fire raging all around, but the steps forward he was taking were moving him further and further along the room. Suddenly the way ahead was clear – but for how long?

He didn't have to wait. Someone ran in and grabbed hold of him, dragging him out of the room.

'No!' He tried to shout, but it was barely audible. 'Two more!'

'We've got them. Come on.'

He didn't know the voice. They were herding him down the corridor, through darkness, but he somehow kept his feet under him. Then he was climbing, up a metal ladder, up and away – and he was above ground once more.

Another pair of hands took hold of him and guided him to a sofa. An oxygen mask was placed over his face and he reached up to hold it, noticing his hands were blackened with soot. The person beside him stayed close and as he turned to see who was tending to him, he realised he knew her. Or, at least, he'd known a younger version of her who'd hated everything and everyone, like all teenagers did.

'Don't talk,' Cerys said, forcing a smile. 'Just breathe.'

Chapter 53: Smoked Out

When Lewis came out of the hatch without Jason, Amy could've murdered him.

She forced herself to stay by the computer, to not race towards the fire, towards Jason – because she would only make it worse. She wasn't strong enough, wasn't disciplined enough. *A little prone to panic.*

The next person hauled up by the agents was another prisoner – P3, one of the enhanced men. A personal friend of Lewis, from what she'd seen on the tapes. She wondered if Jason knew. She wondered what he would say. She wanted him to say it, so she could hear it, so she could tease him about his small town mind and his endless heart. She wanted him here.

Finally, Jason was handed up through the hatch – mostly unconscious, covered in blood, but alive. They needed an airlift, reinforcements. Would Frieda still not send anyone? Though right now the building was not secured, the area a potential minefield. She couldn't introduce civilians to this place without making it safe.

Civilians. She was turning into one of them. See how she hadn't run over to Jason as soon as she'd seen him. Instead, she sat at the computer, awaiting the all-clear. Doing her job. Keeping the mask in place.

'The fire door is closed,' Twofer said, a little out of breath. 'We didn't see any other hostiles.'

She ignored the word and merely nodded her acknowledgement, wincing as her headache intensified. She had restored power to limited systems, such as the video monitoring and processing, but now she needed to take one out again. Using her administrator privileges, Amy shut down the air supply to the Eye Room.

There was still plenty of oxygen to burn in there, but it was now finite. Eventually, the fire would burn itself out and the bunker would remain. She hoped the other prisoners had fled, but they might be safer down there. At least there weren't armed security trying to shoot them in the bunker.

Cerys and Catriona had filled her in, Owain silent throughout. He hadn't tried to take command or interfere with what she was doing, but she could sense his unhappiness. He was here to be the conquering hero, but she already had it under control. Or, at least, the illusion of control.

She flicked to another computer, where Twofer was logged in and she could see all the surveillance cameras in the bunker. The ones they had never known were there. It turned out the security agents did watch the watchers – not to keep detailed records, but to make sure they were behaving, reporting any funny business directly to Frieda. To his credit, Twofer had seemed genuinely surprised she knew nothing about it.

The agents who had taken out P3 had immediately decided to leave with their other colleagues and make straight for the farm-side of the woods. Travelling slowly and in a large group, they hoped the guards wouldn't mistake them for prisoners. Amy had been at the point of ordering them to stay, when the fire had been discovered.

There were two people in the dormitories, one in each, but one of them was Roshan's corpse. The other would likely need retrieval. The other prisoners were nowhere to be found on the bunker feeds, so Amy switched to the compound video.

Behind her, she heard Cerys making a fuss of Jason and telling him to keep his mask on. She still wasn't entirely clear on what Owain, Cerys, and Catriona were doing here, but here they were. They had been instrumental in rescuing and tending to the prisoners. *The prisoners.* So impersonal, so cold. Amy suddenly experienced a spike of fear – was the Frieda mask fusing with her face, changing her from the outside in? Would she still be able to take it off after this?

Checking the feeds from the last half hour, Amy saw that the agents had followed her advice and stayed outside the compound building. Cerys had said as much when they came in, but Amy wanted to be sure there were no stragglers.

Amy suddenly realised what she was looking at. This was a perfect night vision shot of the front of the compound and she could see agents moving at a distance from the building. On 5th March, this camera would've given a perfect view of Mole's murderer disposing of the body.

She looked over at Twofer. His eyes were bright with a mania she hadn't seen before, eager to get involved in the mess outside. And with her. She wasn't sure if the sickness she felt was from her concussion or from the man's creepy, manipulative attention.

'You know who killed Mole,' she said.

He looked uncomfortable, looked away.

'Is that really a priority, ma'am?'

'If you were involved in a cover-up…' His head shot up. 'Then, it is a priority, yes. Can I trust you, SN2?'

Every cell in her body screamed that she couldn't, but she wasn't talking about trusting him with her, with her body. She was trying to focus purely on the moment, on the night they had before them. She had to know if Twofer was running a different agenda.

'I swear it,' he said. 'And…uh, after all this, I'll name him. To you.'

It would have to do. Amy nodded her acceptance and started cycling through the main camera views using both computers. She couldn't afford to miss a single thing. The only person she could trust right now was herself.

About five minutes after the fire started, four men emerged out of the blind spot in the corridor and made their way to the mess. Their body language was tense, and she had caught them in the middle of an argument. She recognised Anchor and Pansy from their recent encounters, but the other two weren't big players in the compound drama. She wouldn't have picked these four men to be the last ones standing or thought any of them could be a twisted fire-starter.

Supposing that the unconscious man in the dormitory was Nikolai, that left two people unaccounted for. One was Dreadlock – and the other was Martin.

She tried not to think about him, but his presence was still there, itching at the inside of her skull. She could feel pressure on her neck when she tried not to think about him. Amy cleared her throat. He was nothing to be afraid of. She was the one with the power now.

Let's give those cowboys outside some work to do.

'Yes, ma'am.'

She only realised she'd spoken aloud when Twofer answered her.

'We need to evacuate the agents from inside the fence. Tell SD1 that the remaining active hostiles are inside the compound building and he should…hold a perimeter.'

The look Twofer gave her echoed her own thoughts. SD1 would not hold a perimeter, not when he knew his targets were fish in a barrel. He would charge in there and start shooting. Was she really okay with that?

'The evacuation is the priority,' she told Twofer, and herself.

The ends and the means and all that. So, why did it all feel like shit?

'Excuse me,' she said, and left her post to go to Jason.

Chapter 54: Short Circuit

Jason's head throbbed. His skin burned. He had never been this thirsty in his life. And Amy was…

Her hand slipped into his, and he closed his fingers over hers in relief, even though it stung.

'Where have you been?' he asked drowsily.

'I've been working. What happened to you?'

'Fire. Lots and lots of fire.'

'It looked like a Molotov cocktail,' Amy said, matter-of-factly. As if it was an everyday occurrence, a casually chucked bomb or two.

'Who the fuck is carrying those around?' Lewis chimed in, from somewhere to Jason's left

'More importantly, why are they throwing them at you?' Cerys asked, popping into his field of vision. The 'what have you done now?' was silent.

'This is an escalation,' Amy said, cool and efficient and detached. 'We need to find out who's responsible for the assaults. We need to assess the danger to the agents.'

'Mole and Bo and Roshan,' Lewis said, sounding like he was counting off on his fingers. 'You and me and Ben. Why them? Why us? Nothing ties us all together.'

'Do you think one person is responsible for all the attacks?' Amy asked.

One person.

All the attacks.

'Maybe not,' Jason said. 'We already know someone else pushed me off the roof.'

'Yes, and who was that?' Amy said, her tone acid and fire.

'Anyway,' Jason said, firmly, determined to keep going. 'What if they're not all related? These latest ones have all been very close together, all over one week. But Mole was two weeks ago. Joe said… well, he said he knows who killed Mole. But he said it definitely couldn't have been the person who killed Roshan.'

'I've still got Joe's watch, if that helps,' Lewis said.

Jason could've kissed him. If he were that way inclined. Which he wasn't.

'Here, let me,' Catriona said.

Jason saw the edge of her shoulder as she leaned over him to take the watch from Lewis. Within seconds, a quiet tinny voice started playing from the speakers. Jason didn't recognise the man, so he assumed it was Mole.

'Andy says he can do it. Told everyone, he did.'

'Do you think he can?' Martin's voice, quietly confident.

'I don't know. But a lot of the others are excited. Gareth and Bo, mainly, and Bo's never excited about nothing.'

'Thank you, Mole.'

'Welcome, guv.'

The sound of a door closing. The shuffling of papers.

'See to it, would you?' Martin, again. Sounding a little strained this time.

'Yes, sir.'

The speech was brief but the speaker was instantly recognisable: Dreadlock.

'If they're the only two people in the room—' Amy began.

'One of them is in charge of the recording,' Jason finished.

'There's no reason for Martin to record himself, not when he's the one doing…whatever he's doing.' Amy looked at the watch as if it would open out like a flower and give her answers.

'Planning a takedown,' Lewis said. 'I've heard of this Andy bloke. Gareth was saying he was the closest they'd come to escaping, but then Bo found out he was a racist, and he was voted out before he was torn to shreds.'

'Why would Martin want to stop everyone escaping? Isn't that the point of the experiment? Why exactly would Dreadlock want to record it?'

Amy was wearing her thinking face, which Jason now realised was unbearably sexy. He'd always thought it was professional admiration and pride that made him warm when she looked like this, but it was mostly good old-fashioned libido. This was going to make working together very interesting. And very unprofessional.

'He's the king, isn't he?'

Stoker's voice was slurred, sounding like he'd just woken up from a long hibernation. Jason could hear Lewis fussing over him and Stoker shrugging him off.

'He is that,' Jason said, distracting himself from the scene Lewis was making. 'What's he got on the outside? Nothing. Inside, he's got a kingdom to rule.'

'Dreadlock wanted them to get out then,' Cerys said. 'He wanted to escape.'

'He's an undercover,' Owain said, suddenly. 'He's there to make sure the experiment keeps running as it should.'

Suddenly, it all slid into place. The reason there was a communication shaft installed, the way Dreadlock had reacted to Anchor becoming elite, and the obsession with gathering evidence instead of settling matters with his fists. Dreadlock was an NCA agent.

'But Joe said that the watch and the killer were related,' Lewis said. 'Isn't that what you said, Jay?'

'It's not like NCA agents are good people,' Catriona said, bitterness evident in her voice.

'We draw the line at murder,' Owain said, harshly.

'Maybe some of us don't,' Amy said.

Some of us. She was still an NCA agent, like it or not. Still one of them, one of Frieda's minions. They were still working for Frieda now, clearing up her mess.

'Where is he now?' Amy asked. 'Why can't we find him?'

'Agent Lane,' Twofer called from the desk. 'Something's wrong with the monitors.'

Amy left Jason's field of vision. With great effort, Jason lurched upright and grabbed hold of the nearest object – his sister – to haul himself up onto the sofa. Amy was standing at the computer terminal, frowning at the screen.

'It's not the display – it's the application. I've never known it to run so slowly. I can't access anything. Even the folder system isn't retrieving all the files…'

She trailed off and stopped. After a long moment, she sprang to life, clicking impatiently with her mouse as she brought up a new screen.

'Twofer, who is this?'

'I don't know that login,' Twofer said, leaning a little too close to Amy for Jason's comfort. 'But you'd know better than me.'

'It should only be the two of us logged in right now. It's not that the folder system isn't fetching files – it's that the files are gone. He's deleting the evidence.'

'That doesn't explain why the application isn't working.'

'The fire,' Owain said. 'The server is literally melting down.'

'That's where he is,' Jason and Amy said together.

Then, the gunfire started.

Chapter 55: Ground Control to SD1

Cerys leapt to her feet, Catriona half a second behind her. Running into danger was her job now.

Owain was already heading for a metal locker in the corner, opening it out to reveal a truly terrifying number of guns.

'Arm yourselves. I am taking command.'

'I'm staying with the wounded,' Amy said.

Cerys didn't believe her and clearly neither did Owain, but they didn't have time to argue.

'Sit tight,' Owain said, knowing she wouldn't.

'Good luck out there,' Amy replied.

Cerys took a semi-automatic pistol from the locker. She wanted to be considered for the Armed Response Unit eventually, so she'd started practicing at a range. She was getting good. But that was shooting a stationary target in a well-lit gun range, not shooting rogue agents in the dark.

Catriona still had her shotgun. Owain had picked up an assault rifle, as had Twofer. Lewis wasn't going to be left out, so he picked up a semi-automatic pistol – even though Cerys knew his only experience with guns had been messing around with that old revolver of her father's.

Owain led them out, the gunfire intermittent, punctuated with cries of panic. The evacuation wasn't going to plan. Nothing was going to plan.

'Our objective is to neutralise SD1,' Owain said, a harsh bite of command in his tone. 'Cut off the head of the snake.'

'Description?' Catriona asked.

'Tall, blond buzzcut, red reflective armband on his right side.'

'We are so fucked,' Lewis muttered.

'Questions?' Owain said.

'What if the others don't stand down?' Catriona asked.

'Then we neutralise them too,' Owain said, as if he were talking about the weather.

Cerys found it hard to imagine that she had ever loved him, this cold unemotional killing machine. Did she really believe her Owain had been replaced with this? Or was it merely a front? Was he trying to convince himself as much as he was trying to convince them? She'd heard the same tone come out of Amy's mouth. Maybe this was just what Frieda did to people.

They advanced through the deep, dark wood, the moon still in hiding and the creatures of the night all gone quiet. Owain was at the front and Twofer at the back, with Cerys, Catriona, and Lewis huddling together in the middle. They weren't moving fast enough, everyone would be dead by the time they arrived – Cerys could see them in her mind's eye, like a horror movie finale, blood on contorted, screaming faces.

'The gates are open,' Owain said. 'No agents or prisoners sighted.'

Cerys could see a faint glimmer of light off the metal of the gates, the beam stretching from the torch mounted on Owain's gun. They were being lit up like a beacon, an obvious, shambling target for anyone who wanted to take a pop. She felt a tightening in her throat. Was it pressure on her neck wounds, or was she starting to panic? She had never panicked before.

Catriona stumbled slightly into Cerys. 'Stop.'

She leaned down and plucked something up from the ground. Lewis shined a light from his fancy watch on it.

'It's a spent cartridge,' Catriona said. 'They were shooting from here.'

'Let's continue,' Owain said.

They were close to the gates now. The whole place was silent as a snowy graveyard, the night swallowing all sound, the aftermath of the gunfire echoing in their ears. Now there was nothing. No crying, no shooting, no running. Just…nothing.

'Twofer, what is the protocol for the agents in an active shooter situation?'

'Unarmed agents to retreat to cover and remain concealed. Armed agents to form a perimeter around them.'

'If they didn't retreat into the building,' Lewis said, 'they would've gone round the back into the garden.'

'Why?' Catriona said.

'We took out the cameras and the lights. They'd know that, because they watched us – didn't they?'

The silence turned awkward. But that didn't deter Owain, who forged ahead – and through the gates. As soon as they crossed the threshold, Cerys felt the hairs on the back of her neck stand on end. Something was wrong here. Very, very wrong.

The moon came out from behind a cloud – and there they were. Six armed agents lying in a shallow pool of water in front of the main doors to the compound, bodies twitching, dead or dying. Waiting to be found, to be witnessed.

'We need to get them out!' Twofer shouted, lurching towards the victims.

'No!' Lewis grabbed the back of his shirt and yanked him back.

Twofer twisted in his grip, ready to punch him, but Lewis shook him hard.

'It's live!' he said. 'The water is fucking electric.'

Lewis pushed the torch on Twofer's gun towards the door, where a black length of wire was submerged in the puddle.

'How did you know?' Owain asked.

'I've seen this plan,' Lewis said tightly.

He yanked Twofer's gun away from his unresisting grip and jogged away around the back of the building. The rest of them stood in shock, like mourners at a funeral, awaiting the final words of the minister so they could run away from the spectacle of death.

It seemed like both a second and forever until Lewis returned. He shoved two long rakes into Cerys' arms and then, keeping his distance from the water, circled around to the door. He hooked the black snake with a wooden-handled hoe, lifting it clear of the water.

'Use the rakes!' he yelled to Cerys.

Cerys just stared at them in ignorance, but Catriona grabbed one from her and jabbed it towards the nearest person, jabbing the plastic tines over and under his torso and hauling him out of the water with brute strength. Owain grabbed the other rake and followed Catriona's method exactly.

'I'll get the defibrillator,' Twofer said, running back towards the gates.

'Cerys! This man is breathing – stay with him.'

She jerked to life then, stumbling towards Catriona and the downed man. She wasn't sure if she should touch him, if he would shock her. Only his legs had been submerged in the water, the rest of his body spared, but his breathing was coming too quickly. The smell of burnt flesh assaulted her nostrils.

'You're all right,' she mumbled. 'It'll be all right.'

The man's eyes flew open. It was SD1, the man who had been so cutting to them only a short time before. He looked scared now, terrified – and he reached out to grab her arm. She tensed, but she didn't die.

'They're inside,' he whispered, voice harsh and broken. 'They've taken hostages.'

Chapter 56: We See Each Other Plain

As soon as they had gone, Amy was on her feet and over by the computer monitors.

'Can you see them?' Jason asked.

'I'm not looking,' she said.

The application was shutting down, the computer entering hibernation. The server was about to fry. Even if Dreadlock didn't manage to delete the last files, the data storage would be all but destroyed by the intense heat. Either the fire suppression system was inadequate or the heat in the server was overpowering it. Not that it mattered, because Amy had just lost her access to it with the computers shutting down.

The evidence would soon be destroyed. Except there wasn't any evidence, was there? Why didn't Dreadlock know that? Someone in the bunker had covered up the murder he committed and he didn't even know.

Amy knew she should go after him, bring him to justice – or she could stay here, with Jason, and wait for the dust to settle. Amy knew which option she preferred, and it was the one where she huddled down behind the sofa and hid until it all went away. But this idea of leadership had infected her. She was responsible for this trash fire of a compound, this irredeemably failed experiment. She had come here to get Lewis out and find out who had murdered Mole, to bring him to justice. She was so close to achieving it all.

Was this cowardice or was this common sense? She didn't know anymore. She couldn't quite tell where Amy ended and Agent Lane began, which parts of her were a Frieda mask fused to her face, fused to her soul. She had watched Owain march into the night with a machine gun, the man who had left the police force because he didn't want to be endangered anymore. She didn't know who he was anymore.

She didn't know herself.

'The system is offline,' she told Jason, who made a sympathetic noise.

With the server gone, she had lost all access to the cameras. She didn't know what was happening in the compound, or outside the gates. Her communication with the outside world was cut off—

The signal jammer was still in here.

'I'll try to call for backup.'

Amy crossed to the metal box that housed Dodger, and found a screwdriver sitting on top of it. No doubt left behind by whoever had undone her previous work. She opened out the casing and, with no need to worry about deception, switched off the machine. The whirring of the fan died away and silence followed.

She took her phone out of her pocket and found only the barest signal. She called the NCA emergency line, but it cut out immediately. She tried again, walking around the room to find better reception. It rang twice and—

The phone was knocked from her hand and skittered across the room, shedding shards of plastic as it went. A broad arm yanked her up against a tall, muscular frame and something cold and metallic settled against the side of her head. Out of the corner of her eye, she could see long matted clumps of hair swinging into her peripheral vision.

'Me and the boss lady are leaving. Any questions?'

Amy watched Jason slowly stand up, raising his hands above his head.

'Dreadlock, what are you doing?'

'Making sure I get out of here alive.'

'Drop the act, agent – we know who you are.' Amy used her best Frieda voice, and was pleased when it didn't shake. The only thing she had to be pleased about right now.

However, that only lead to Dreadlock laughing, his whole body vibrating with it.

'Oh, I know. You think I can't sniff out a fellow undercover? I knew there was something odd about you, Jay Bird, but it was only when you had that little fight with Bo... Too early in the game. You should've waited.'

Jason was holding his nerve, but his eyes met hers, not Dreadlock's.

'Like you waited. Playing the long game, were you? Spying on the Governor.'

Amy felt the metal drop away from her head by a few inches. She darted her eyes right to see it – a thick metal rod. *Defector Dreadlock in The Hide with the Lead Piping…*

'You've been talking to Joe, have you?'

'I have Joe's watch,' Jason said.

Amy wanted to tell Jason not to be an idiot, not to provoke him, not to show their hand. Just let him walk out of here with her and he'd probably be on his way in ten minutes, leaving her behind. That made the most sense. She had to believe that he still had sense on his side.

'Give it to me.'

Dreadlock's breathing was harsh against her cheek. She could smell alcohol. Her brain threw up crime statistics about intoxication and violence, even though she tried to make it shut up. She had to think. Why couldn't she think?

'It's not here,' Jason said. 'It's out wandering around in the woods. Tough luck.'

Another laugh, this time shakier. 'It doesn't matter. The server's gone.'

'The evidence hasn't,' Jason said. 'We're all still here and we know what you did.'

'You don't know shit.'

'You murdered Mole.'

'He died of exposure.'

'He drowned in the kitchen sink.'

There was a dull *clunk* as the end of the pipe hit the floor. Dreadlock's arm was slack around her. If she wanted to, she could run. And he would run too, far away, never caught. She stayed still, quiet. *Wait for it.*

'You dragged his body outside and left it the garden.' Jason's voice was hard – but deathly calm. 'He knew too much, did he?'

'It was an accident.' Amy barely heard the words, and she was standing right next to him. 'I only meant to scare him a little. He panicked and I guess I panicked too. Then he was dead.'

'You think Agent Haas will forgive you?'

'I just want out. That's it. Everyone inside gets their records erased, right? Why not me?'

'You were there to protect them.' Amy spoke without thinking and then couldn't stop. 'The mistake you made was becoming one of them.'

'I was there to protect the experiment. There was never meant to be governors or guards. Martin wanted to play by his own rules. I had to stop him.'

The tone of his voice told her that he still believed that, perhaps even as far as believing he had good intentions on the road leading up to Mole's death. That the coverup was part of the same higher plan: the experiment above all else.

Amy stepped away from Dreadlock and faced him. He looked worn. He fiddled with his hair, which made him seem nervous and uncertain. More a young agent than a hardened criminal.

Then, suddenly, he returned to life. Lifting the pipe, he brandished it in front of him. Jason grabbed Amy's shoulder and yanked her back towards him. They circled slowly, until Dreadlock was close to the door. To his freedom.

'I did it,' he said, almost wonderingly. 'We finished the experiment.'

From nowhere, Stoker barrelled into his side, seizing and twisting Dreadlock's arm until he cried out and dropped the pipe.

Then, he wrapped his arm around his neck and snapped it.

The body fell to the floor, with Stoker looking calmly at both of them, making no move to run. He was barely even out of breath.

'I liked Mole,' he said.

Chapter 57: And Now, the End Is Near

Lewis peered through the blinds that concealed the broken window, spying for the cops on his fellow prisoners and the agents who had tormented them. He was having quite the day.

Of the agents Pansy had electrocuted, two were dead, three were unconscious, and one was crying in agony. Lewis was finding it very difficult to care. He wanted to feel something for these men, injured in the line of duty, but this wasn't an ordinary nine-to-five. They had chosen this life, this assignment. They had come here tonight to murder men he had called friends.

Pansy was a piece of work, he knew that. But Gareth and Joe? Anchor, it turned out, was one of Them, but he hadn't seemed all that bad on the face of it. Were they all going to have to die here tonight? Was he going to play a part in ending their lives, in this room where they'd played cards and shared drinks and lived? He didn't know if he could. He didn't know if it was right.

Once upon a time, he'd wanted to be in the military. When they were fifteen, he and Jason had seriously considered it, even going to one of those recruiting fairs. Then his uncle had sat him down and told him about Iraq, the first time round. About how many people he'd seen die for no good reason. How many people he had killed for nothing but sand. Lewis had known then that he couldn't kill a man. The closest he had come since was placing his hands around Jason's neck, but that felt like a very long time ago now. He had been a different man then.

'What can you see?' Cerys hissed at him.

The four prisoners were sitting around a table, using one of the torches for light. They had barricaded the doors with tables, expecting the assault to come from the front, over the bodies of the downed security agents. The agents they had captured were on the floor, in silence. Lewis counted six. They looked frightened. All of them, agents and prisoners, looked frightened.

283

If any one of them was a good shot, they could probably kill the prisoners before they could hurt an agent. There probably wouldn't be casualties on the agent side. It could all be nice and quick, job done, thank you very much.

'They're waiting,' he said, voice equally low.

'We can't,' Owain said, decisively. 'We have no time to waste here.'

The smell hit him. Lewis looked around for the source, and saw the bright red cylinder placed between the agents on the floor. Another special from Pansy, had to be. He'd always come up with the cruel and unusual plans.

'He's got an open cannister of gas in with the hostages,' he said. 'We can't use the guns.'

'That was the only advantage we had,' Catriona said, numbly.

'We have to move,' Owain said, urgently.

Lewis gritted his teeth, dropping his handgun into the dirt, and crawled over the windowsill. He had never been lightfooted and his drop to the floor would draw attention. He had to be up and running within a couple of seconds. How far away from the window were they? Who should he aim for? Would someone else take him out first? Should he grab hostages?

Too many questions. No answers. No time.

He braced himself to jump.

The lights suddenly came on, blinking awake and flooding the room with light. Lewis froze, hanging through the window, sure he was about to be seen. The curtain wafted in front of his face. He held his breath.

'The server must be online,' Pansy said, standing up from the table. 'They're toying with us. I need my computer.'

'Sit down,' Anchor growled. 'Your computer is out there. We're staying in here.'

'What is going on in there?' Owain whispered urgently.

Lewis waved a hand at him to keep quiet.

'What happened to the laptop?' Gareth asked.

Something heavy thudded against the floor. 'Bricked. I need my computer.'

The lights went off, and they all fell silent. Lewis breathed. He slipped down onto the floor of the room, lying flat on the floor like a snake on its belly. He commando crawled along the edge of the wall, heading for the shelter of the nearest table.

The lights flared to life, glaring down on them once more.

Lewis swung his legs behind the table, his torso concealed. He glanced back. Cerys was underneath the window, back arched like a cat.

Anchor was staring straight at her, open-mouthed. Then, he looked away.

The lights went out.

'What if they just decide to wait us out?' Joe said, sounding nervous. 'We didn't bring in any supplies and, with this fucking light show, we won't sleep. Three days and we'll all be dried out and drowsy.'

A hand touched Lewis' ankle. He flexed his foot in response, before moving on to the next table. Like baseball, except there were far better ways to get to third base.

'They wouldn't risk the hostages,' Anchor said, firmly.

'We killed their agents,' Pansy said. 'They'll want revenge.'

Lewis felt the tension increase. He peered between the legs of a chair and saw Anchor turn to Pansy with a look on his face that resembled Death itself.

'You what?'

'Pansy, what the fuck have you done?' Gareth said, wary, angry.

They didn't know.

Another touch on Lewis' leg. He moved. His destination was the table next to the prisoners', right next to the barricaded door. As long as the lights stayed off…

'This is a fucking war!' Pansy said, still on his feet. 'They set us up to die here, the first wave of the genocide. I'm not going to wait for them to take me out. "If the tanks succeed, then victory follows!"'

'They don't want to fucking kill us!' Gareth yelled. 'We're lab rats to them. They just want to see how the whole thing plays out.'

'Yes! It's all a test! I passed their fucking test!'

Pansy was still shouting, his face growing redder. Lewis saw he was moving towards the gas cannister – and something metal was glinting in his hand. He was on the other side of the room. He would never get near him in time.

'It's not personal, you idiot,' Joe said.

285

'Can't you see? They put us in with the blacks and the gays, to see what we'd do. To see who would win the war, who would become corrupted. That's the experiment. They want to know who'll win. Well, look at the last men standing. We fucking showed them.'

'It was you who did for Bo,' Anchor said, slowly. 'You killed Roshan.'

'What? It was the filth that took out Roshan.' Gareth sounded disbelieving, horrified.

Lewis tensed. It had been Pansy who had thrown the Molotov cocktails, who had marked Lewis, Ben, and Jason for death. He'd been the one to goad Ben into pushing Jason off the roof. They'd all almost died because of Pansy.

'He's a Nazi,' Anchor said.

'You'd know, wouldn't you?' Pansy said. 'You're one of Them.'

Joe and Gareth turned their attention to Anchor.

Pansy stood next to the hostages – and raised his lighter in the air.

'I don't want to die,' he said, his voice shaking. 'But I will if I have to. To show those fuckers who's in charge here. The Jews running this thing – they'll get the message.'

That's when Jason jumped down from the ceiling and all the lights went out.

Chapter 58: Murder in the Dark

Amy's plan had been to wait. Jason's was to dive straight in. In the end, they had compromised.

Jason had half a second to register the surprise on Pansy's face before the lights went out. He surged forward, throwing his body in the direction of Pansy and forcing him across the room. The lighter fell to the ground with a thud – but no spark.

He heard the *clang* of metal as someone kicked the gas cannister. The torch started moving towards the door, the rush of fleeing people registering with him at the same time as a rush of cold air – from an open window.

And Pansy slipped from his grasp.

'Fucker! Get off me!'

Joe's yell came from behind him and Jason turned. The lights were still out, a bubble of light around the doorway, where people were trying to haul aside the tables. Everywhere else in the room was black as night. Jason could feel people around him, but he couldn't see any of them.

Someone grabbed at his sleeve and he stopped himself striking out.

'Miss me?' He could hear Cerys' grin.

'How'd you find me?'

'Your head's a reflector.'

Suddenly, he was knocked aside, a heavy weight landing on him. He was a reflector and he was loud – a target.

'You're a fucking traitor too!' Gareth yelled in his face.

'Better than a fucking Nazi!' Jason yelled back.

Abruptly, the weight was gone from him, Gareth disappearing as if he'd never been there.

'Cat, get a zip-tie on him and put him with the other,' Owain said, and then he was gone.

'It's Catriona,' she growled, before hauling Jason to his feet. 'Stay out of trouble.'

Jason's eyes were adjusting to the dark. The crowd by the door were still moving the tables, while Catriona saw to Gareth. The rest of the room was inky black, with Anchor and Pansy unaccounted for. The darkness had outstayed its welcome.

'Lights on!' he yelled at the top of his lungs.

They obeyed his command, burning bright. He picked out Lewis guarding the agents at the door, armed with nothing but his fists. Cerys and Owain were standing apart, in the centre of the room, arms outstretched to grab at passing shadows.

No Anchor. No Pansy.

Jason ran for the door, as the tables were finally shifted away. It burst open – and Nikolai stood in the doorway, his head matted with old blood and his eyes burning with hatred.

'No fucking time for this.'

Jason punched him in the face and Nikolai listed to the side, clutching at his jaw. Jason barrelled on through and headed straight down the corridor to the front door of the building. A hand yanked his shoulder away from the door.

'You'll fry,' Lewis said, out of breath.

'What?'

'There's a loose cable and a large puddle. Agents are dead.'

A small figure appeared at the end of the corridor and Jason waved his arm.

'Shut down all the power,' he called to her.

Amy nodded and retreated again, back to manipulating the circuit board in the laundry room of the compound. The illusion of environmental control.

The lights went out again and they were slowly joined by a crowd of voices, before the all-clear came. Owain herded them into a group and told them to stay together. He was going to lead them to salvation.

'Look straight ahead,' he told them. 'Don't stop for anything.'

Outside, the moon was out and there were dead men on the ground. He heard the cries from the agents with them, the disbelief and the grief. Jason didn't have time to look, to care – he had to go after Pansy and Anchor.

He felt that tug at his sleeve again and knew his sister was at his side.

'Where now?' she asked.

'I don't know,' he admitted.

'Pansy won't run,' Lewis said. 'He's a runty little thing. He'll go to ground.'

'But where?'

'What about literally?' Amy asked.

Jason looked around the corner of the building. They had clearly gone out the window – why not stay in the garden? This place would soon be crawling with clean-up crew, but no one would notice one extra man. The ground had deep furrows ready for Stoker's next crop of vegetables – a small man could lie down in one, under a tarpaulin, and survive the night to slip out in the day.

Tacitly, they agreed to go look. Jason took the lead, with Amy at his right shoulder. Cerys and Lewis were behind them, all absolutely silent. They felt like hunters stalking prey, stalking a man who didn't kill in passion or from madness – but because he believed himself superior to every other being. It made Jason feel sick, listening to his 'confession' – his manifesto. If Jason had picked up on the signs earlier, Bo might still have his sight and Roshan his life.

The cold dark earth stretched before them, only a sliver of moon to illuminate the way. They fanned out without waiting to be told, each walking the length of the garden with a furrow either side of them. Amy had something dangling from her hand. Jason wished he'd brought a weapon.

The silence was oppressive, but it was the only thing they had. The noise from the front of the building, from inside, sounded very far away – like another world. Soil slipped beneath Jason's boots, the soft sound of tumbling earth breaking up the emptiness of the place. He remembered that Mole had been found here. Dreadlock had brought him out here to rest, in the place he had loved most.

Stoker had made sure Dreadlock had found his rest. Jason had no idea how to tell Lewis. How did you say, 'your boyfriend killed a man with his bare hands'? How did you—

His leg was pulled sharply to the right and he slid into the trench. He felt a crushing weight on his shoulders – and then he was sucking mud, his face buried in the earth. The soil was in his mouth, his nose, his eyes. He was drowning in it. He was dying in it.

He hadn't made a sound. They wouldn't realise he had stopped walking with them until it was too late. It took three minutes to suffocate, and he could feel the last seconds of his life ticking away. Wasting away.

The weight was gone. Two people dragged him upright and he coughed the dirt out of his mouth, spluttering as a bucket of stagnant water drenched his face. He blinked it away, saw his sister holding the bucket, and wondered if he should be grateful.

Kneeling in the ditch before him, Pansy was staring at him, gasping for his help. Amy stood behind him, a USB cord around his neck, pulling hard on the ends with a look of determined violence on her face.

'Amy,' he said, somehow finding his voice. 'That's enough.'

'No. It's not.'

He watched Pansy slump forward, unconscious – but she still held on. Jason couldn't see her eyes, just dark holes in her face beneath the night sky. In that moment, he believed she could kill Pansy. That this place had corrupted her like it had corrupted everyone else who set foot in it.

Then, she let go, dropping the cord and letting Pansy fall forward into the dirt. Cerys kicked him over onto his back and Jason watched his chest rise and fall, as he breathed, as they breathed.

As Amy stepped forward and her eyes returned to his sight, and she tried to smile. Perhaps it would be all right.

Perhaps.

Chapter 59: The Price of Silence

They'd found Anchor in the Hide, kneeling over Dreadlock's body while Stoker mutely looked on. He had failed to watch him, and now he was dead. The experiment was ruined. Amy had wanted it to fail, but not like this

Frieda had arrived two hours after it was all over. The agents who'd received electric shocks and lived had all been airlifted away. The remaining agents gathered together in a barn on their friendly farmer's land, with Owain as caretaker. The four bodies – Dreadlock, Roshan, and the two security agents – were laid out in the Hide, with Twofer keeping a vigil. The prisoners were all inside the compound, even the pretend ones, with Cerys, Catriona, and Amy watching over them. Everyone was accounted for.

Everyone except Martin, who had vanished without a trace. Amy and Jason had searched the bunker and compound. Nothing.

The Cardiff Ripper had disappeared into thin air.

'Agent Lane.'

'Agent Haas.'

Amy turned towards the voice, her expression matched in blankness to Frieda's. The agent left her escort by the door and came close, too close, voice lowered to speak confidentially

'Report please.'

'An escape attempt was made. There were four fatalities. Hostages were taken, so the monitoring team intervened.'

Frieda looked pointedly at Cerys and Catriona. 'You brought in external contractors.'

'They brought themselves.'

'The conditions of the experiment were violated.'

'Yes, they were.'

Amy saw Frieda hesitate. She hadn't been expecting agreement.

'Please explain why you did not maintain the integrity of the experiment.'

'It was already compromised when I arrived.'

Frieda's eyes narrowed. 'Go on.'

291

'The undercover agent was responsible for the death of a prisoner. A coverup was orchestrated by IN1, who then entered the compound as a second undercover. Despite the presence of two undercover agents in the compound, they allowed a neo-Nazi to go on a spree of violence and murder. The four fatalities and multiple injuries are all directly and indirectly the result of agent action and inaction.'

'So you decided to intervene.'

'I terminated the experiment before it incurred further loss of life.'

'Why didn't you contact me prior to making that unilateral decision?'

'Perhaps you should answer your phone.'

Frieda's usual calm expression had been replaced by a taut smile. She turned to address the room, drawing the attention of the nine gathered men.

'As per our agreement, you are all free to leave. Your criminal records have been erased. However, if you commit a further crime, you will find them reinstated. I hope I am clear.'

Stoker looked bewildered. Pansy laughed and crowed, looking around for someone to shake his hand, but no one was paying him any attention. Anchor stared at Frieda, betrayed.

She gestured towards the door, as if asking what they were waiting for, and most wasted no time in leaving. Stoker tried to catch Lewis' eye, but he was staring straight ahead, refusing to be tempted again. Jason lingered, but Frieda ignored him, turning her attention to Cerys and Catriona.

'Neither of you were here,' she told them. 'Your superior officers won't hear anything from me and I expect the same courtesy.'

Cerys shrugged one shoulder, a gesture eerily similar to Jason's. Catriona looked like she would say something, then thought better of it. They left together.

'Are you going to tell us what the fuck's going on?' Jason asked.

'I wouldn't waste my breath trying to make you understand.'

'Try us,' Amy said, coolly.

'I believe you know most of it – the prisoners had to escape the bunker, then they would receive their second set of orders. But Martin Marldon had other ideas, didn't he? He wanted to be the king of this insignificant castle. It was amusing, for a while, and then it was tedious. I directed my agent to intervene.'

'By murdering Mole?'

Frieda's lip curled. 'He exceeded his orders.'

'So, what happens now? You just let the Cardiff Ripper and a bunch of dangerous fuckers wander off!' Amy could feel Jason vibrating with fury beside her.

Frieda looked at him, amused. 'I said they were free to leave. I did not say they would go unwatched.'

Amy didn't know whether to laugh or cry. Frieda still thought she had control of them, of the experiment. She had no sense of the scale of the disaster she had overseen.

'You did not perform in the field as anticipated,' Frieda told Amy, unexpectedly.

'I was much better than anticipated.'

'You were.'

Amy tried not to feel the surprise, just rode it out. She felt Jason's body close to hers, felt his warmth. She held on to her one demand, fixing it in her mind's eye.

'I want to give you a promotion.'

'I want out.'

'You are serving a suspended sentence.'

'You just released at least two murderers.'

Frieda's eyes narrowed. 'This is not a negotiation.'

'This is the price of my silence. Take it or leave it.'

'Are you threatening me?'

'Are you refusing my offer?'

The mask fitted snugly now. She also felt disconnected from it, like it was a face she could let go at any time. It felt close, the moment of letting go. But nothing was certain until it was done.

'Fine. I accept your... proposal, on the same terms as the pardons I just granted. If you commit another crime—'

'You'll have to catch me first – and turn the bloody cameras off, would you? Come on, Jason.'

She left Frieda without waiting to be dismissed, nodding aside the minions at the door, feeling Jason strong at her shoulder. The door opened out onto the early light of dawn and she felt something warm and welcome bubble up inside her. It felt like hope.

Chapter 60: Fly Away Home

Amy opened the last of the boxes containing her newest computer – Lovelace. She patted all its pieces like a brood of guinea pigs, and Jason tried not to laugh at the shining expression on her face.

They had barely been home a day, but he already felt the feeling returning to his head and his heart. He hadn't realised how much he had shut himself off in the compound, falling into the prison mentality and buying into the cult of weirdness inside without question.

Amy was starting to come back to herself too. The stiff formality was fading, the echoes of Frieda leaving her face. Jason had found that whole experience creepy as fuck, watching the two of them face off with identical masks overlying their features.

Amy ate another biscuit from the packet on the kitchen counter and gulped down her coffee. 'Have you heard from the others?'

'Cerys is fine. She's moving out of our mam's house.'

Amy looked at him as if he'd grown a second head. 'Please tell me she's not moving in with *him*.'

'Catriona and her dad. Apparently, they're 'besties' or whatever.'

'You're so old,' Amy teased.

'I'm classic,' he said.

Amy folded a box and made an attempt to stuff it into a recycling bag. He came to her aid and they silently, steadily cleared their living room of its cardboard infestation. Their living room. The one without an agent perched at the counter. The one that contained the futon he no longer had to sleep on, if he was very lucky.

'What do we do now?' Jason asked.

She turned to him, looking up into his eyes, searching for something. He had only meant the constructing of her new computer or the grocery shopping, but he could tell that his question was loaded for her.

'What do you want?'

He had to think this answer through. He couldn't just blurt the first thing that came into his head and run with it. She deserved better than that.

'Well, uh, I was thinking of setting up a garage with Lewis. Maybe bringing in Dylan. It's what I'm good at…'

He could see the tension rising in her and resisted the urge to hug her, to kiss away that frown, to kiss away the entire day if it meant she would smile again. They had to talk about this without distractions.

Yet, if he were honest with himself, he was waiting on her, hesitating in committing to anything. His eyes met hers, silently begging her to give him a reason to stay, to say no to Lewis. To come home and to be with her in every possible way – in her work, in her life, in her bed.

'I'm setting up a private investigation agency,' she said. 'It will be a legal one this time. I want you to be my partner – my full partner, not an assistant. I want you to work with me.'

He hadn't expected that. He imagined he looked as stunned as he felt. A private investigation agency? They would be working independently again, and he would be her equal. Not the errand boy, not the cleaner. Her *partner*.

'It will be slow to start, of course,' she said, starting to ramble. 'I have some savings from our NCA salary to keep us going, and of course we don't have a mortgage to pay – thanks Grandma – but I don't want you to feel like I'm twisting your arm or anything, just because you live here. You have to want it, because—'

'All right then,' he said, and kissed her.

After one frozen moment, she returned the kiss, joyful and sure, crushing him to her. Any lingering doubts melted away and he knew that he was making the right decision for both of them. For their future.

He broke away, and saw her grin mirroring hers. Lewis would forgive him. He always did. They would always have the pub on Sundays, now that they were both free men. Lewis would set up his garage and find himself a partner, and Jason would co-run a detective agency with his number one hacker – and his girlfriend.

'What are you thinking?' she asked.

'I think we really need a cup of tea,' he said.

About the Author

Rosie Claverton grew up in Devon to a Sri Lankan father and a Norfolk mother. She studied medicine in Cardiff and quickly turned Wales into her home. When she is not writing or working in medicine, she blogs about psychiatry and psychology for writers in her Freudian Script series. Her aim is to help writers accurately portray individuals with mental health problems in fiction.

Other books in the Amy Lane Mysteries series:

Binary Witness
Code Runner
Captcha Thief
Terror 404

Dear Reader,

I hope you enjoyed *Hard Return*. Please let me know your thoughts by emailing rosie@rosieclaverton.com or finding me on Twitter – @rosieclaverton.

Minor spoilers ahead…

The idea for this novel came from a desire to tell a modern country house mystery – except this house is full of convicts and the basement's rammed with spooks. I wanted to create a claustrophobic atmosphere, one that pushed Amy particularly into a whole raft of new, dangerous experiences.

The time skip between *Terror 404* and *Hard Return* came about for a couple of reasons. One was to narrow the gap between when the books are set and when they are published, as the brief in-universe pause between *Captcha Thief* and *Terror 404* meant that our protagonists could end up stuck in an endless 2014. However, I'm not sure that dragging them to terrible 2016 was a kindness.

The second reason was to eke out the last of that unresolved sexual tension before I finally answered the 'will they, won't they' question. When *Binary Witness* was first published, a number of readers thought it was a romantic suspense novel. Instead, it took me five books to finally take the plunge.

The next offering in the series will be a short story released in time for Christmas, so look out for 'Blinking Lights'. Hunting for the perfect Christmas present turns into a disaster when all the lights go out in Cardiff on Christmas Eve, but Jason and Amy are on the case.

As for the next full-length novel, it all starts with a girl on a train… Except we actually care more about her laptop. Keep your eyes open for news about *Last Save*.

And don't go walking in the woods after dark.

Best wishes,
Rosie Claverton
amylanemysteries.com